48 28032088 13102042 12082013 23122067
1 24112022 16072023 01082064 21042066
09 7112034 16072072 04082032 22072024
48 28032088 13102042 12082013 23122067
1 3112022 16072023 01082064 21042066
09 7112034 16072072 04082032 22072024
1 24112022 16072023 01082064 21042066
09 7112034 16072072 04082032 22072024
48 28032088 13102042 12082013 23122067
48 28032088 13102042 12082013 23122067
1 24112022 16072023 01082064 21042066
09 24112034 16072072 04082032 22072024
48 28032088 13102042 12082013 23122067

RACHEL WARD 01082064 21042066

9 24112034 16072072 04082032 22072024
8 28032088 13102042 12082013 23122067
1 24112022 16072023 01082064 21042066
09 7112034 16072072 04082032 22072024
48 28032088 13102042 12082013 23122067
48 28032088 13102042 12082013 23122067
1 24112022 16072023 01082064 21042066
09 7112034 16072072 04082032 22072024
48 28032088 13102042 12082013 23122067
1 3112022 16072023 01082064 21042066

9 7112034 16072072 **NUMBERS** 22072024

48 28032088 13102042 12082013 23122067
1 24112022 16072023 01082064 21042066
09 7112034 16072072 04082032 22072024
48 28032088 13102042 12082013 23122067
1 24112022 16072023 01082064 21042066
09 24112034 16072072 04082032 22072024
48 28032088 13102042 12082013 23122067
1 24112022 16072023 01082064 21042066
9 24112034 16072072 04082032 22072024
8 28032088 13102042 12082013 23122067
1 24112022 16072023 01082064 21042066

D0438989

From the Chicken House

This is a startling book. It's the ultimate thriller – gripping and disturbing. Rachel Ward introduces something terrifying yet utterly real, which makes this novel important to every one of us. It's unforgettable.

Is your Number up?

Barry Cunningham

NUMBERS

RACHEL WARD

Chicken House 2 Palmer Street, Frome, Somerset BA11 1DS

Text © Rachel Ward 2009

First published in Great Britain in 2009
The Chicken House
2 Palmer Street
Frome, Somerset BA11 1DS
United Kingdom
www.doublecluck.com

Jacket design Steve Wells
Interior design Steve Wells
Typeset by Dorchester Typesetting Group Ltd
Printed and bound in Great Britain by CPI Bookmarque, Croydon, CR0 4TD

The paper used in this Chicken House book is made from wood grown in
sustainable forests.

5 7 9 10 8 6 4

British Library Cataloguing in Publication data available.

ISBN 978-1-905294-93-0

For Ozzy, Ali and Peter

082013 23122
82064 210420
82032 220720
3122
206

20720

420
0720
312
3122   23
04
2072
3122
6

22   07   2

5122
1420
072   0
312   2
312
1420
0720 2
312
420   6
7202   0
3122
              42
0   72   0

1420
2072
      2   1   131

      082032
      013 23122

Chapter 1

There are places where kids like me go. Sad kids, bad kids, bored kids and lonely kids, kids that are different. Any day of the week, if you know where to look, you'll find us: behind the shops, in back lanes, under bridges by canals and rivers, round garages, in sheds, on allotments. There are thousands of us. If you choose to find us, that is – most people don't. If they do see us, they look away, pretend we're not there. It's easier that way. Don't believe all that crap about giving everyone a chance – when they see us, they're glad we're not in school with their kids, disrupting their lessons, making their lives a misery. The teachers, too. Do you think they're disappointed when we don't turn up for registration? Do me a favour, they're laughing – they don't want kids like us in their classrooms, and we don't want to be there.

Most hang about in small groups, twos or threes, whiling away the hours. Me, I like to be on my own. I like to find the places where nobody is – where I don't have to look at

1

anyone, where I don't have to see their numbers.

That's why I was pissed off when I got to my favourite haunt down by the canal and found someone had got there before me. If it had just been a stranger, some old dosser or junkie, I'd have gone somewhere else, easy, but, just my luck, it was one of the other kids from Mr McNulty's 'special' class: the restless, gangly, mouthy one they call Spider.

He laughed when he saw me, came right up to me and wagged a finger in my face. 'Naughty, naughty! What you doing here, girl?'

I shrugged, looked down at the ground.

He carried on for me. 'Couldn't face another day of the Nutter? Don't blame you, Jem – he's a psycho. Shouldn't be allowed out, that one, should he?'

He's big, Spider, tall. One of those people who stand too close to you, doesn't know when to back off. Suppose that's why he gets into fights at school. He's in your face all the time, you can smell him. Even if you twist and turn away, he's still there – doesn't read the signs at all, never takes the hint. My view of him was blocked by the edge of my hood, but as he loomed up to me and I moved my head instinctively away from him, our eyes met for a moment and it was there. His number. 15122009. That was the other reason why he made me feel uncomfortable. Poor sod – he doesn't stand a chance, does he, with a number like that?

Everyone's got one, but I reckon I'm the only one that sees them. Well, I don't exactly 'see' them, like something hanging in the air; they kind of appear in my head. I feel them, somewhere behind my eyes. But they're real. I don't care if you don't believe me – please yourself, I know they're real. And I know what they mean. The penny dropped the day my mum went.

I'd always seen the numbers, for as long as I could remember. I thought everyone did. Walking down the street, if my eyes met someone else's there it would be, their number. I used to tell my mum people's numbers as she pushed me along in my buggy. I thought she'd be pleased. She'd think I was clever. Yeah, right.

We were making our way rapidly along the High Street, on the way to the DSS to pick up her weekly money. Thursday was normally a good day. Soon, very soon, she would be able to buy that stuff from the boarded-up house down our street, and she would be happy for a few hours. Every taut muscle in her body would relax, she'd talk to me, even read to me sometimes. I called out people's numbers cheerily as we hurtled along. 'Two, one, four, two, nothing, one, nine! Seven, two, two, nothing, four, six!'

Suddenly, Mum jerked the pushchair to a halt and swung it round to face her. She crouched down and held both sides of the frame with her hands, making a cage with her body, clutching so tightly I could see the cords in her arms standing out, the bruises and pinpricks more vivid than ever. She looked me straight in the eye, the fury clear on her face. 'Listen, Jem,' the words came spitting out of her face, 'I don't know what you're going on about, but I want you to stop. It's doing my head in. I don't need it today. Okay? I don't need it, so just . . . bloody . . . shut . . . up.' Syllables stinging like angry wasps, her venom fizzing all around me. And all the time, as we sat there eye-to-eye, her number was there, stamped on the inside of my skull: 10102001.

Four years later, I watched a man in a scruffy suit write it down on a piece of paper: *Date of Death: 10.10.2001.* I'd found her in the morning. I'd got up, like normal, put my school things on, helped myself to some cereal. No milk, because it stank when I got it out of the fridge. I left the carton on the side, put the kettle on and ate my Coco Pops while it boiled. Then I made Mum a black coffee and carried it carefully into her room. She was still in bed, kind of leaning over. Her eyes were open, and there was stuff, sick, down her front and on the covers. I put the coffee down on the floor, next to the needle.

'Mum?' I said, even though I knew she wouldn't reply. There was no-one there. She was gone. And her number was gone too. I could remember it, but I couldn't see it any more when I looked into her dull, empty eyes.

I stood there for a few minutes, a few hours – I don't know – then I went downstairs and told the lady in the flat below us. She went up to look. Made me wait outside the flat, like I hadn't already seen it, silly cow. She was only gone about thirty seconds, and then she rushed out past me and was sick in the hallway. When she'd done, she wiped her mouth on her hanky, took me back to her flat and rang for an ambulance. Then all these people came: people in uniform – police, ambulance men; people in suits – like that man with the clipboard and paper; and a lady, who spoke to me like I was simple and took me away from there, just like that, the only place I'd ever known.

In her car, on the way to God knows where, I kept going over and over it in my mind. Not numbers this time, words. Three words. *Date of Death. Date of Death.* If only I'd known that was what it was, I could have told her, stopped her, I don't know. Would it have made a difference? If she'd known that we only had seven years together? Would it hell – she would still have been a junkie. There was nothing on this earth that could have stopped her. She was hooked.

I didn't like being there under the bridge with Spider. I

4

know it was outside, but I felt closed in, trapped there with him. He filled the space with his gangly arms and legs, constantly moving – twitching, almost – and that smell. I ducked past him and out onto the towpath.

'Where you going?' he shouted behind me, his voice booming off the concrete walls.

'Just walking,' I mumbled.

'Right,' he said, catching up with me. 'Walk and talk,' he said, 'walk and talk.' Drawing level, too close to my shoulder, brushing against me. I carried on, head down, hood up, a blinkered patch of gravel and rubbish moving under my trainers. He loped along beside me. We must have looked so stupid, me being small for fifteen and him like a black giraffe on speed. He tried to chat a bit, and I just ignored him. Hoped he'd give up and go away. No chance. Reckon you'd have to tell him to piss off to get rid of him, and even then he probably wouldn't.

'So you're new around here, yeah?' I shrugged. 'Got kicked out your old school? Been a bad girl, have ya?'

Kicked out of school, kicked out of my last 'home', and the one before that and the one before that. People just don't seem to get me. Don't understand that I need a bit of space. Always telling me what to do. They think rules and routine and clean hands and minding your p's and q's will make everything all right. They haven't got a clue.

He reached into his pocket. 'D'you wanna fag? I've got some, look.'

I stopped, and watched as he extracted a crumpled packet. 'Go on, then.'

He handed me a cigarette, and flicked his lighter for me. I leaned forward and inhaled until it caught, drawing in some of his stink at the same time. I moved back quickly, and breathed out again. 'Ta,' I mumbled.

He drew on his fag, like it was the best thing on earth, then blew the smoke out theatrically and smiled. And I thought, *Less than three months to go, that's all. All this poor bugger's got is skiving off school and having a smoke by the canal. Not what you'd call a life, is it?*

I sat down on a heap of old railway sleepers. The nicotine made me feel less edgy, but nothing calmed Spider down. He was up and down, climbing on the sleepers, leaping off, balancing on the edge of the canal on the balls of his feet, jumping back again. I thought to myself, *That's how he'll go, the silly sod, jumping off something, breaking his bloody neck.*

'Don't you ever keep still?' I said.

'Nah, I'm not a statue. Not a waxwork like at Madame Tussauds. I've got all this energy, man.' He did a little dance there on the towpath. Made me smile, couldn't help it. Felt like the first time in years. He grinned back at me.

'You got a nice smile,' he said.

That did it. I don't like personal comments. 'Fuck off, Spider,' I said, 'just fuck off.'

'Relax, man. I didn't mean nothing by it.'

'Yeah, well . . . I don't like it.'

'You don't like looking at people neither, do you?' I shrugged. 'People think you're up yourself, the way you keep looking down, don't look no-one in the eye.'

'Well, that's personal too. I've got reasons.'

He turned and kicked a stone into the canal. 'Whatever. Listen, I'll never say nothing nice to you again, okay?'

'Okay,' I said. There were alarm bells going off inside my head. Part of me wanted this more than anything else in the world – to have someone to hang out with, be like everyone else for a while. The rest of me screamed to get the hell out of there, not to get sucked in. You get used to someone – start to like them, even – and they leave. In the end, everyone leaves. I looked at him jiggling restlessly from foot to foot, now scooping up some stones and chucking them into the water. *Don't go there, Jem*, I thought. *In a few months, he'll be gone.*

While his back was turned, I got up quietly from my perch on the sleepers and started running. No explanations, no goodbyes.

From behind me I could hear him calling, 'Hey, where you going?' I was willing him to stay there, not to follow. His voice faded away as I put some distance between us.

'Okay, be like that. See you tomorrow, man.'

Chapter 2

The Nutter was cracking the whip. Someone must have rattled his cage – whatever, he was definitely on our case. No messing about, no backchat, heads down, English comprehension test, thirty minutes. Trouble is, when someone tells me to do something, I have this problem. I just wanna tell them to piss off, I'll do it in my own time. Even if it's something I actually want to do. Which this wasn't. Don't get me wrong, I read, sort of, but I'm not very fast. My brain kind of needs time to sort out the words. If I try and read quickly, everything gets muddled up, the words don't mean nothing.

Anyway, I was trying my best, this time. I really was. Karen, my foster mum, had read me the riot act over bunking off school. You know how it goes, don't you? 'Time to knuckle down . . . important to get some qualifications . . . life's not a rehearsal. . .' She'd been talking to the school, to my social worker – all the usual suspects – and I reckoned I didn't need the hassle any more. I'd go along with it all, keep my head down for a bit, get me some breathing space.

Everyone else was quiet too, for a change. They'd picked up on the Nutter's evil mood and decided not to push it. There was a bit of shuffling about and sighing, but basically everyone was sitting still and working – or pretending to – when, without any warning, something exploded into the room. The door swung back on its hinges and crashed into the wall behind, and Spider burst in like he'd been fired out of a cannon, stumbling on his feet, almost falling over. Instantly the mood was broken. Kids started cheering and jeering, shouting out to him.

The Nutter wasn't impressed. 'What do you mean by bursting in here like that? Go outside into the corridor, and come back in like a civilised human being.'

Spider slumped forward with an exaggerated sigh and rolled his eyes to the ceiling. 'Ah, come on, Sir. I'm in now, aren't I? I'm here.'

McNulty spoke quietly, but with force, if you know what I mean, like he was just managing to keep a lid on things. 'Just do what I say, and we'll start again.'

'What you doing this for, Sir? I don't need to be here, but I'm here. I'm ready to learn, Sir.' An ironic look to the rest of us, met with an answering jeer. 'Why d'ya have to give me all this grief?'

The Nutter took a deep breath. 'I don't know why you've decided to join us today, but something has brought you here. Now if you want to join in, and I hope that you do, you need to go out, come in quietly like I've asked you, and we'll get on with the lesson.'

There was a long pause, while they eyeballed each other. The rest of us went quiet, waiting to see how it would play out. For once, Spider was almost keeping still, standing there, staring at the Nutter, with just one leg jiggling. Then he turned and went out, just like that. Every eye in that classroom watched him go and kept watching the empty doorway. Had he gone for good? There was a low murmur as he reappeared, drawn up to his full height, cool as anything. He paused on the threshold. 'Morning, Sir,' he said and nodded in the Nutter's direction.

'Good morning, Dawson.' There was a wary look in McNulty's eye, not sure how to take Spider's apparent backdown. Worried that victory had been too easy. He placed the comprehension sheet, some paper and a pen on Spider's desk. 'Sit down, lad, and do your best with this.' Spider sauntered over to his desk, while McNulty returned to the front and stood there, watching us. 'Okay, everyone, settle down. Twenty-five minutes to go. Let's see what you can do.'

But Spider's unexpected return had broken the mood. We were agitated now, a bit of a buzz going round. Everyone was fidgeting; there was backchat, chair legs scraping on the floor. McNulty kept picking away at people, trying to get back on top of things: 'Eyes on the page, please.' 'Keep your hands to yourself.' He was fighting a losing battle.

As for me, the words in front of me swam and danced. They were meaningless, a pattern, nothing more, like Chinese or Arabic. Because I couldn't stop myself wondering if I was the reason Spider was back. Down by the canal I thought I'd felt the start of a connection, and it had scared me. I'd avoided him since then, but I'd no reason to think that Spider had given me a second thought, until now. Because I could have sworn that as he'd sauntered over to his desk, he'd winked at me. Bloody nerve. Who did he think he was?

After lunch, the Nutter had had enough. Against a background of noise, laughter, general chat, he suddenly stopped.

'Right, books away, pens away, paper away. All of you. Now!' Now what was he up to? 'Come on, get on with it. All your stuff away. We need to talk.' Rolled eyes, yawns – yeah, we got it, here comes the pep talk. We put our things in our bags or stuffed them into pockets, and waited for the standard bollocking: '*Unacceptable behaviour . . . letting yourselves down . . . lack of respect. . .*' But it didn't happen.

Instead he walked up and down between the desks, stopping and saying something to each of us before going on to the next one. 'Unemployed.' 'Checkout girl.' 'Bin man.' When he got to me, he didn't even pause. 'Cleaner,' he said and carried on walking. He worked his way back to the front, turned and faced us. 'Okay, how did that make you feel?'

We stared at our desks or out the window. It had made us feel exactly how he wanted us to feel. Like shit. We all knew what sort of futures were waiting for us after school, didn't need a puffed-up little tit like him to remind us.

Then Spider blurted out, 'I feel fine, Sir. It's just your opinion, isn't it? It don't mean shit. I can do anything I want, can't I?'

'No, Dawson, that's the whole point, and I want you all to listen. At the moment, with the attitude you've all got now, that's where you're heading. However, if you apply yourselves a bit more, concentrate, make the best of your last year here, it could be different. If you get some GCSEs, get a good report from school, you can achieve so much more.'

'My mum works on the checkout.' That was Charmaine, two seats along from me.

'Yes, and there's nothing wrong with that, but, you, Charmaine, could be the shop manager if you wanted to. You all need to look a bit further, realise what you can achieve. What do you see yourselves doing? Come on, what are you going to be doing in a year, two years, five years? Laura, you start.'

He went round the room. Most of the kids hadn't got a clue. Or rather, they knew his first assessment had been pretty accurate. When he got to Spider, I held my breath. The boy with no future, what would he say?

Of course, he rose to the challenge. He sat on the back of his chair, like he was addressing a crowd. 'Five years' time, I'm gonna be cruising the streets in my black BMW, got some vibes on the sound system, got money in my pocket.' The other boys jeered.

McNulty looked at him witheringly. 'And how, Dawson, are you going to do that?'

'Bit of this, bit of that, Sir. Buying and selling.'

McNulty's face changed. 'Theft, Dawson? Drug dealing?' he said, coldly. He shook his head. 'I'm almost speechless, Dawson. Breaking the law, peddling in misery. Is that all you can aspire to?'

'It's the only way any of us are going to get any cash, man. What do you drive, Sir? That little red Astra in the car park? Teaching? Working for twenty years? I'm tellin' you, I ain't driving no Astra.'

'Sit down on your chair, Dawson, and shut up. Someone else, please. Jem, what about you?'

How could I possibly know what was going to happen to me? I didn't even know where I was going to be living in a year's time. Why was this man torturing us, making us squirm like this? I took a deep breath and said, as sweet as I could manage, 'Me, Sir? I know what I want.'

'Oh, good. Carry on.'

I made myself look him right in the eye. 25122023. How

old was he now? Forty-eight? Forty-nine? He'd go just around the time he retired then. On Christmas Day too. Life's cruel, isn't it? Christmas spoiled for his family for the rest of their lives. Serve him right, the cruel bastard.

'Sir,' I said, 'I want to be exactly . . . like . . . you.'

He brightened for a second, a half-smile forming, then realised I was taking the mick. His face shut down, and he shook his head. His mouth was a hard line, you could see the bones sticking out as he clenched his jaw.

'Get your maths books out,' he barked. 'Wasting my time,' he muttered under his breath. 'Wasting my time.'

On the way out of class, Spider high-fived me. I didn't do that stuff normally, but my hand went up to meet his like it had a mind of its own.

'Like your style, man,' he said, nodding his approval. 'You got him good. Result.'

'Thanks,' I said. 'Spider?'

'Yeah.'

'You don't do drugs, do ya?'

'Nah, nothing heavy, I was just winding him up. Too easy, innit, sometimes? You walking home?'

'No, got detention.' I needed to hang back for a couple of minutes, let the crowds of kids thin out. Karen would be waiting outside the gate. She was walking me to and from school at the moment, just until I'd 'earned her trust'. No way I was going to let any of this lot see me with her.

'See ya around then.'

'Yeah, see ya.' He drop-kicked his bag through the classroom door and swung out after it, and as I watched him I thought, *Stay away from drugs, Spider, for Christ's sake. They're dangerous.*

Chapter 3

It was one of those grey October days when it never really gets light. The rain wasn't exactly falling – it was just there, hanging in the air, in your face, blotting everything out. I could feel it soaking through my hoodie, starting to make my shoulders and the top of my back go cold. We were round the back of the shopping centre, where the concrete slabs of its walls met the dull green streak of the canal.

'We should go in the shops, at least it's dry,' I suggested. Spider shrugged and sniffed. Even his movements were subdued today, like the weather had sapped his energy.

'Got no money. Anyway, those security guys are on my case.'

'I'm not staying here. It's cold and rank and boring.'

Spider caught my eye. 'But apart from that?'

'It's crap.'

He snorted in appreciation, then spun round and started off down the path. 'Come on, let's go to mine. It's only my nan there, and she's okay.'

I hesitated. We'd kind of drifted into hanging out together, after school and at weekends, since Karen had loosened the reins a bit. Not all the time – Spider sometimes went round with a gang of lads from school instead. From what I could tell, he'd run with them until they had a row, or even a fight, then he'd keep clear for a bit. There's always something going on with boys. It's like animals, isn't it, monkeys or lions, sorting out the pecking order, who's the boss. Anyway, for whatever reason, he wasn't with them this Saturday, he was with me and we were bored as hell. There was nothing for us to do.

Going to someone's house was a big deal for me. I'd never been asked before. Even when I was little, I was never one of those girls who skipped out of the classroom in pairs, holding hands sometimes, giggling, excited. Having a friend for tea didn't fit in with Mum's lifestyle.

'I dunno,' I said, reluctantly. Like usual, I was worried about meeting anyone new, not knowing whether to look at them or not. People think I'm shifty because I don't like looking at them, but really I'm just trying to keep out of their lives – too much information.

'Please yourself,' he said, sticking his hands in his pockets and setting off on his own.

The rain was getting in my face, annoying me now. 'No, wait!' I shouted, and ran to catch him up, and we walked along together, hoods up, heads down, in the filthy London drizzle.

It took about five minutes to get to his place, one of those maisonettes at the front of the Park Estate. It was in the middle of a row, on the ground floor, with a little square of garden at the front. The garden was something else, some grass and a few flowers and that, but the great thing was all these little statues and things: gnomes, animals. It was hilarious.

'Cool garden,' I said, half taking the piss, half meaning it. Spider pulled a face.

'It's my nan,' he said. 'She's mad.' He vaulted over the low wall and picked his way through the concrete crowd. He swung his leg at the head of a particularly ugly gnome.

'No, don't,' I called out. He stopped mid-kick. 'They're nice. Don't hurt them.'

'Oh God. Not you as well.' He shook his head, and waited while I opened the peeling tubular metal gate and walked up the path. Then he pushed the front door open – it must have been on the latch – and shouted out, 'Only me, Nan. I've brought a mate.'

Nervous as I was, I clocked that, him using the word *mate*. And I liked it.

There was a narrow hallway and then straight into the front room. Every shelf, every surface was covered with stuff: little china animals, plates, vases. Think of every car boot sale you've ever been to, all the stuff left over at the end that no-one wants, and you'll get the picture. The overpowering smell of fag smoke made the air thick. No windows open, obviously. A plume of it wafted through from the next room, and I followed Spider through there. His nan was perched on a stool at a breakfast bar, newspaper in front of her, cup of tea at hand, fag on. She didn't look nothing like her grandson. She was small, white, like me, with short spiky hair dyed a dark shade of purple. Her faced was lined, hard-looking. I watched as he stooped to peck her cheek, and thought that if you saw them in the street you'd never know they were family. But that's the way now, isn't it? The days of family photographs – Mum, Dad, two kids, all dressed up, all looking the same – did that ever happen? Is there anywhere that still happens? Not here, anyway. Families round here are what they are – just your nan, like Spider, or no-one, like me – black, white, brown, yellow, whatever. That's how it is.

As Spider stood back up, his nan looked at me. 'Hi,' she said. 'I'm Val.'

I tried to keep my eyes down, but for some reason I looked up briefly and, instantly, she held my gaze. I couldn't look away. Her eyes were amazing – hazel irises set in clear whites, despite the fag smoke. And it wasn't like she was just looking, like anyone else. No, she was taking me in, she was really seeing me. I clocked her number, 2022054: forty-five years to go with a heavy fag habit. Respect.

'Who are you, then?' she asked, the words sounding harsh, although I don't think she meant them to.

I couldn't think straight, couldn't even remember my name. I was like a rabbit trapped in the headlights of those eyes.

Spider came to my rescue. 'She's called Jem. We're gonna watch the telly.'

'In a minute. Don't rush off. Sit here a minute, Jem.' She indicated the stool next to her with a nod of her head.

'Na-an, leave her alone. Don't go off on one.'

'You mind your attitude, Terry. Don't listen to him, sit here.' She patted the stool, her hands small and lined with massive curled yellow nails, and I clambered up meekly. Spider's nan wasn't the sort of person you argued with, and on top of that there was something else going on. I could feel it in the air, like electricity sparking between us. It was frightening and exciting at the same time. I still hadn't stopped looking at her, and as I shifted on the stool to get my balance, she put her fag down and took one of my hands. You know that I don't like contact, but I didn't draw away. I couldn't, and we both felt it, a crackle, a buzz, as her skin touched mine.

The reek of stale smoke from her mouth was filling my nostrils. Made me feel a bit queasy. I like a fag as much as anyone, but someone else's, second hand? Nah.

'I have never met anyone like you,' she said, and I thought, *No, that's right, you haven't, but how do you know?* 'Do you know about auras?' she asked. The question was met by a snort of derision from Spider, who'd wandered into the front room.

'Leave it out, Nan. Leave her alone, you old witch.'

'Shut up, you!' She turned back to me, and her words, slow and carefully spoken, went deep into me, like I was listening with my whole body, not just my ears. 'You have the most amazing aura I've ever seen. Purple and white. All around you. The purple shows your spiritual energy, and the white that you're able to concentrate that energy. It's quite remarkable – I've never seen anyone with an aura as strong as yours.'

I hadn't a clue what she was talking about, but I wanted to know.

'Your aura, Jem, is the energy you carry with you. It radiates round you, all different colours. And the aura tells you more about that person than anything else. Everyone's got one, but not everyone can see them. Just us lucky ones.' She narrowed her eyes. 'You see them too, don't you?'

'No,' I said truthfully. 'I don't know what you're talking about.'

'She's talking bollocks, that's what,' shouted Spider.

'I've nearly had enough of you, son! You shut your

18

mouth!' She leaned in closer to me, and lowered her voice. 'You can tell me, Jem. I understand. It's a gift, but it's a curse too. Tells you more than you want to know sometimes.'

The pit of my stomach lurched. She knew what it was like. The first time I'd ever met someone who understood. God, I wanted to tell her, course I did, but fifteen years is a long time to keep a secret. Not telling becomes part of you. And I knew deep inside that once I started talking about it, even to someone like Spider's nan, everything would change. And I wasn't quite ready for that. Not yet.

'No. There's nothing,' I mumbled. I managed to wrench my eyes away from her piercing, seeing gaze.

She leaned back and sighed – I could almost see her breath, it was that thick. 'Suit yourself,' she said, lighting up another fag. 'You know where I am now. I'll be here. I'm always here.'

As I slipped off the stool, and went to find Spider, I could feel her eyes drilling into my back.

Spider was sprawled across an armchair, his long legs dangling over one side, feet twitching at the ankle. 'Don't take any notice of her. She lost the plot years ago. Didn't you?' he shouted out. 'Sport or something else?' he said as he flicked through the channels.

I shrugged, then spotted a black box on the floor. 'PlayStation?'

He untangled himself from the chair and flopped down on the carpet, sorting through the heap of games. 'Yeah, Grand Theft Auto?' I nodded. 'You've got no chance,' he said, 'Had a bit of practice. I'm so hot at this, I'm smoking.'

He was too. I should have known. Boys like him all seem to know how to drive and shoot. It's bred into them, isn't it? I wasn't going to let him psyche me out or anything, but he had the knack – that quickness and aggression. He put everything into it, concentrating like his life depended on it, playing with his whole body. I put up a fight, but he beat me every time.

'Not bad for a girl,' he teased.

I showed him the finger. He smiled, and I felt like I was fitting in at 32 Carlton Villas just fine.

We watched the telly for a bit, but there was only rubbish on. Bloody X Factor or something. Thousands of no-hopers queuing up for hours like cattle, thinking they're going to make it big. Retards. Even the ones who could sing. Do they really think the world is going to take them to its heart – fame, money, the whole lot? The Simon Cowells of this world just get as much money as they can out of them, and then spit them out, back to where they came from. It's not a future, is it? It's just an ego trip. Suckers. Still, we had a good time, laughing at them, Spider and me. Turned out we found the same things funny. Felt good sitting there – despite the smoke and that stale smell that Spider brought with him everywhere – although I was aware of his nan perched in the kitchen all the time, like one of those birds, hawks or buzzards or something. Vultures. Listening to us. Waiting.

'I'd better get back,' I said a bit later.

Spider unfolded himself from the chair. 'I'll go with ya.'

'Nah, s'all right. Won't take long.'

'I could drive ya, if I had some wheels.' He paused. 'I could get some wheels.'

I looked at him. He was dead serious, trying to impress me, I reckon. I made for the door. I didn't need to get involved in nothing like that. Didn't need the hassle. I could hear his nan shuffling around in the kitchen, the microwave door slamming, buttons beeping as she set the timer.

'Your dinner's nearly ready,' I said. 'I'll see you around. See ya!' I called out from the front door to his nan, not wanting to go in there and talk to her again. Her face appeared around the kitchen doorway. Lightning breached the gap between us, as her eyes met mine again. What was it about that woman?

'Bye, love,' she said. 'I'll see you again.' And she meant it.

Chapter 4

'I want you to write about your best day ever. Don't worry too much about spelling and punctuation. Just quickly. Write it from the heart.'

Another example of the Nutter's cruelty, to make us think about our sad and pointless lives. What was he expecting? *The day Daddy bought me my new pony? Our holiday in the Bahamas?* Me, I didn't like to look backwards. What was the point? The past was gone, nothing you could do about it now. Impossible to pick one day out and say that was the best one. Easier to pick the worst one, several candidates there – not that I'd tell the Nutter about any of them. None of his business. I thought about sitting there and refusing to write anything. There was nothing he could do. But then something flipped inside me and I thought, *No, I'll tell him how it is, if that's what he wants.* I picked up my pen and started to write.

'Time's up!' Howls of protest. 'Stop writing, please. Doesn't matter if you haven't finished. Now, instead of handing them in to me, I'm going to ask you to read them out.'

Outright rebellion – cries of 'no way' and 'get lost'. I felt cold inside, knew I'd made a mistake.

'I want you to stand up and speak the words you've written. No-one's going to be laughing at you. You're all in the same boat. Give it a try.' The barracking subsided.

'Amber, you start. Come up to the front. No? All right, stand where you are, and read it out in a nice, clear voice so we can all hear.'

And so he went round the class. Holidays, birthdays, days out. Kind of what you'd expect. Then one kid, Joel, described his little brother being born, and the room took on a different feeling. Suddenly, everyone was listening, as he told us about helping his mum in their bathroom at home, wrapping the baby up in an old towel. A couple of the girls said, 'Aah' when he'd finished, his friends high-fived him as he made his way back to his seat. Fair play to him, he'd done a good thing, but I felt sick inside – the thought of that vulnerability, the innocence, the knowledge that the end is written for them even on their first day, it's too much. I don't do little kids.

Spider was next. He shuffled to the front of the class, stood shifting his weight from foot to foot, eyes on the page in front of him. You could tell he wanted to be anywhere but there. 'Ah, man, do I have to do this?' he said, flapping the page down to his side, stretching his neck back to look up at the ceiling.

'You do,' McNulty said, firmly. 'Come on, we're listening.' And he was right. The class was quiet, everyone was getting into this.

'Okay.' Spider drew the paper up in front of his face, so he couldn't see us and we couldn't see him. 'My best day was when my nan took me to the seaside. It had a great name, like Weston-Super-Something. We went on the coach for hours, and I went to sleep. When we got there I'd never seen so much space in my life. The sea was miles away and there was this huge beach. We had chips and ice cream, and there was donkeys. I had a ride on a donkey, weirdest thing ever, but great. We stayed somewhere, had a couple of days there, just me and my nan. Bloody brilliant.'

A couple of kids started braying in the back row, but in a good-humoured way. Spider's shoulders dropped a bit as he relaxed. Job done, he went back to his seat.

And before long, it was my turn. My skin was tingling, I could feel every nerve-ending in my body, as I waited for McNulty to say my name. Finally . . . 'Jem, I think it's your turn next.'

Inside my clothes I felt naked as I walked up to the front. I turned around, kept my eyes down, didn't want to see everyone looking at me. Perhaps I should have made something up there and then, just pretended I was like everyone else, spun a cosy little tale about the perfect Christmas, presents round the tree, that sort of thing. But I don't think that quick, not when I'm the centre of attention. Are you the same? Is it only afterwards that you think of what you should have said, the killer response, the put-down that would make them stay put down? Standing up there, scared, panicking, I didn't have any choice but to read my words out. I took a deep breath and started to speak.

'My best day ever. Got up. Had breakfast. Came to school. Bored, like usual. Wishing I wasn't here, like usual. Kids ignoring me, suits me fine. Sitting with the other retards – we're so special. Wasting my time. Yesterday was the same, and it's gone anyway. Tomorrow may never come. There is only today. This is the best day and the worst day. Actually, it's crap.'

There was a pause when I stopped speaking. I didn't look up, just leaned against the whiteboard, aching with embarrassment. The silence was filling my ears, deafening me. Then, someone shouted out, 'Cheer up, love. It might never happen!' and the familiar jeering and barracking started up.

A crashing sound made me look up. Spider was vaulting over the rows of tables and chairs. When he got to the joker at the back, kid called Jordan, he drew his arm back and slammed his fist into the guy's face. The room erupted, as Jordan fought back and the rest of the kids turned into a baying pack, gathering round in a tight, over-excited little knot. McNulty sprinted to the back of the classroom and barged his way through the crowd, wrenching shoulders apart and squeezing between bodies.

I screwed up the piece of paper and let it fall to the floor, then slipped out of the door and along the corridor. I had just one thought in my mind – to disappear, find somewhere I could be on my own. I never wanted to go back to that torture chamber again. I stayed out for hours, nowhere in particular, all those places where nobody sees you and nobody cares, until I got tired of walking in the dark.

Back at Karen's, I went round to the kitchen door. I'd expected her to be in bed by the time I got home – it was gone midnight, after all – but she was sitting at the kitchen table, cradling a cup of tea, her face a washed-out grey. She'd had the lot, Karen: babies, little kids, 'problem' teenagers like me. Twenty-two foster kids. Worn her out. I clocked her number again. 1472012. She only had three years to go.

'Jem!' she said. 'Are you all right? Where've you been?'

'Out,' I said. I didn't have it in me to explain everything. Where would I start?

'Come in, Jem. Sit down.' She didn't seem angry just then, only tired.

'I just wanna go to bed.'

She opened her mouth, like she was going to start on at me, then thought better of it, just let out a big sigh and nodded.

'Okay, we'll talk about this in the morning. We will talk about it.' A threat, not a promise. 'I'd better ring the police – I reported you missing. Here, take this with you.' She handed me her cup, still three-quarters full.

I went upstairs, put the cup down on the table next to my bed, and climbed under my duvet without getting undressed. I propped the pillows up and reached for my tea. It was only when the warm, sweet liquid hit my bloodstream that I realised how cold and empty I was.

I was dog-tired, but couldn't close my eyes. So I sat there through the night, duvet pulled up to my neck, until the light seeped round the curtains, and somewhere between being asleep and being awake, I registered the start of another grim day.

Chapter 5

McNulty's class was still buzzing with it all. I had to face them on my own, as Spider had been excluded for three weeks. As it turned out, he never went back to school again. I reckon if he'd known that, he'd have done more than give Jordan a black eye and a split lip. There were rumours flying around about him being interviewed by the police, all sorts, and what Jordan was going to do to him when they were both back in circulation. But for the time being, they enjoyed sticking the boot into me.

'What you gonna do without your boyfriend here? No-one to defend your honour.'

'Jem and Spider sitting in a tree, K-I-S-S-I-N-G.'

Obviously, I told them where to go, but it didn't make any difference. They were like a pack of dogs with a bone.

I took it for a couple of days and then I couldn't stomach it any more. I'd set off for school like normal, then cut off round the back of the shops, make my way across to the park, or down to the canal and hang about on my own.

Don't feel sorry for me, it was just what I was used to. Been the same everywhere I'd lived, every school I'd been to. You can put up with a certain amount, but it gets to a point when you can't stick it any longer, you just need to be away from it. Lots of kids feel like that, but especially me. School lumps you in with so many people, like so many battery hens, and, as you know, I don't really do other people. Everything's easier if I keep myself to myself.

Those few days I did a good job of keeping out of Spider's way too. I saw him a couple of times, but I made sure he didn't see me. That whole thing at school had been well embarrassing. What did he think he was doing, wading in like that, making a show of us both? Made me feel a bit sad when I thought about it. For a few weeks there, I'd had a mate, sort of. But like everything else, it'd got too complicated, it had to stop. If the Jordan incident had shown me anything, it had shown me what I already knew: Spider was trouble, the sort of trouble I didn't need. Kind of missed him, though.

And, what do you know? I couldn't keep him out of my life anyway. Like a bad smell that follows you around, or a bit of chewing gum stuck on your shoe, Spider turned up again soon enough. You might say I couldn't shake him off. You might say we were meant to be together.

Anyway, that Wednesday I'd taken my eye off the ball for a minute. I was watching someone, an old dosser. He'd bumped into me ten minutes before, asked me for some money, and I'd followed him along the High Street. Now he was digging about in a bin on the other side of the road, and I was leaning against a wall, watching, when a familiar sourness drifted into my nostrils and someone said in my ear, 'Whatcha doing?'

My attention was all on the old bloke, so I didn't look round or nothing, just said to him, like we'd only seen each other five minutes ago, 'Spider, what's the date today?'

'Dunno, twenty-fifth?'

The old bloke had pulled something out of the bin, half a burger in its wrapper. He looked around quickly, seeing if anyone else was after it, and our eyes met for a second. There it was again, his number: 25112009.

He tucked the burger under his armpit and crossed his arms, then started scuttling off down the road. I set off after him.

'Where you going?' Spider called out, puzzled.

'I wanna go this way.'

He caught up with me. 'What for?'

I stopped, keeping an eye on Grandad as he weaved his way through the crowds, and lowered my voice. 'I wanna follow that guy, the old one with the jumper.'

'What you up to? We don't need to rob no-one, Jem. I got money.' He patted his pocket. 'If you want something, just ask.'

'No, I don't wanna rob him, just follow him. Like we were spies,' I said quickly, trying to make it into a game.

His face said, *You've lost your marbles*, but he just shrugged and said, 'Okay.' And we carried on walking, stepping up the pace as Grandad turned a corner ahead of us. He'd gone down a side street, not so many people there. We got within about ten metres of him when he turned round and clocked us. He knew I'd seen him get that burger out of the bin. Looking startled and shifty, he turned round again and started half-running, half-walking.

'We've been rumbled, man,' Spider said. 'Whatcha wanna do now?'

I wanted to see what would happen to him, but I didn't want to frighten the old guy, not on his last day.

'Let's hang back a bit. He's heading for the park, yeah? Let's let him get in there and then go in. Wanna fag?'

We lit up and then started walking slowly towards the park. At the far end of the street, Grandad was hurrying along. He got to the end, where the main road is, with the park the other side. He checked under his arm – yeah, the burger was still there – then looked back over his shoulder. Although we were way back, I knew that he could see us, that he was getting agitated. I was about to say to Spider to call it quits when, still looking back, Grandad stepped out into the road.

The car hit him straight on with a sickening thud. He went halfway up onto the bonnet, and then flew through the air. It was like one of those road safety adverts on the telly, but they use dummies for that, don't they? This was real – a real body, limbs waving crazily, head jerking forward and then back, finally lying on the ground.

We stood still for a few seconds, taking it in. People were screaming, starting to gather round. Spider started to run towards them. 'Come on, let's see if he's all right.' I hung back. I didn't want to see any more. If he wasn't dead now, he would be soon, before midnight anyway. Today was his day. Nothing you could do.

Spider was at the end of the street now, craning over the throng. I went up behind him. Someone near me was screaming, high-pitched, on and on. Her friend led her away. I could see through the gaps to the body. A heap of mis-matched old clothes with something inside. Not someone, not any more. Whoever he was had gone now. Gone to wherever people go, where my mum was. Heaven? More like hell for my mum, I should think. Or nowhere. Just gone.

I touched Spider's arm. 'Let's go.' He peeled himself away from the crowd and we headed off towards his house.

Spider was subdued, shaking his head. 'We freaked him out, man. He was scared.'

'I know,' I said, quietly. He had echoed the thought that was haunting me: *we'd caused it.* I'd chased him into that road. If it wasn't for me, he'd have been sat in that park, eating his manky old burger. Perhaps that's what would have taken him, choking on a gobful of meat and bun. Perhaps he was heading for a heart attack. And the thought that I tried to keep down, but which kept coming back up – perhaps it hadn't been his last day today after all. Maybe meeting me had made it his last day.

Before I knew it, we were at Spider's. I stopped at the gate. 'I think I'll just head back to Karen's,' I said. I needed a bit of space to get my head round all this.

'No, man, come inside for a bit. You don't wanna be alone after something like that.'

I had another reason to hesitate. Those hazel eyes that saw my secrets.

Right enough, Val was sitting on her perch in the kitchen. Spider bent to kiss her.

'Got off early, did you?' she asked, glancing at the kitchen clock.

'What?' Half-one. 'You know I'm excluded, Nan. What's wrong with you – losing your marbles? And Jem's got . . . private study.' He grinned, and Val smiled with him. She knew the score.

'You two going to settle down and read some books now, then?' Her gaze switched to me – direct, seeing, nowhere to hide.

'Actually we need to chill a bit. Just saw an old bloke get run over.'

She put down her fag.

'He all right, was he?'

'No, killed him. Died right there, on that road near the park. We saw it all.' There was a little quiver in his voice. Not such a tough guy after all.

Val heaved herself down from her perch and shuffled over to the kettle.

'That right? Here, sit down. I'll make you both some tea. Nice sweet tea, that's what you need. Bloody traffic, eh? Can't even cross the bloody road now, can you?'

She pottered about making a pot of tea while we crashed in the lounge, then came in to join us with three mugs and a packet of biscuits on a tray. She put the tray on the pouffe in the middle and eased herself into an armchair, puffing out as she did. 'No good for me back, these chairs. Go on, drink up.'

I sipped the hot tea, while Spider and his nan both sat dunking their biscuits and slurping down soggy crumby mouthfuls.

'So, you were just walking along and saw it all, did you?'

I caught Spider's eye. No need to worry, though, neither of us wanted her to know that this old guy spent his last minutes terrified we were going to mug him.

'Yeah, that's right.'

'Shocking, isn't it? You never know what's round the next corner, do you?'

Spider went off to the bog, leaving me trapped there with her. She shifted forward in her chair. 'You all right, Jem? Shakes you up, that sort of thing, doesn't it?'

I nodded. 'Yeah.'

'Seen a dead body before? Or was this your first time?' Christ, she didn't mess about, did she?

I should have just told her I didn't want to talk about it. But, like I said, there was something about her – resistance was useless.

'Me mum,' I said, quietly. Her mouth formed an O, and she nodded like she'd known it all along. I liked that – I liked the fact that she didn't get embarrassed or start gushing about how terrible it was. She just nodded. I kept going. 'I found her, like. She died in bed. Overdose. She didn't mean to. I mean, I don't think so. Just unlucky.'

She nodded again. 'Unlucky. Like my Cyril. Dropped dead at forty-one. Heart attack, bless him. No-one knew there was anything wrong. No warnings or nothing. He's over there, look, on the mantelpiece.'

I looked across to the wooden shelf above the fire. Right enough, among the china dogs and brass candlesticks, there was a framed photo, one of those posh ones done in a studio. Black and white, just his head and shoulders. A handsome man, with a bit of a twinkle in his eye. Just a bit of paper in a frame, but it had the power to reach you, make you want to smile back at it.

'Fetch it over, love, go on.' Reluctantly, self-consciously, I went over to the fireplace. 'Go on, pick him up.' I reached up to the frame. 'No, not the photo, Jem,' she said sharply, 'the ashes, in that box, look.'

What the . . . ?

Sure enough, the photo was standing next to a sturdy wooden box. I hesitated. 'Go on. He won't bite you.'

I moved a couple of ornaments further to the side, and took hold of the box. It was surprisingly heavy – thick, smooth wood with a little metal plaque on the top: *Cyril*

Dawson, died 12th January 1992, aged 41 years. I carried it carefully and put it on the pouffe, next to the tray. Val leaned right over and smoothed her hand across the top of it.

'Everyone says it's a terrible thing to go young, but he had a great life, a young man's life. None of this,' she rested her hand on her back, 'aches and pains, slowing down, everything heading south. No, he lived life to the full, lived like a lion, and went out like a light. Just like that.' She clicked her fingers. 'It's not a bad thing.' She put her hand back on the box, thumb stroking the brass plate. 'Just that you miss them so much. The ones that go. You miss them.'

Spider moved from the doorway, where he'd been leaning, and put his arms round his nan. 'This your way of cheering Jem up? Daft old cow.'

'Here, you, less of that.' Her hand shot up to give him a smack. He grabbed it before it made contact and gave her a kiss on the cheek. When he let go of her hand, it rested affectionately on his face for a second. 'He's not a bad lad, Jem. Not a bad lad. Put your grandad back then, son.'

'Val,' I said, speaking before I'd really thought about it, 'what sort of aura did he – Cyril – have?'

Her face registered surprise, and then she smiled, displaying a fine set of crooked, orange teeth. 'You know, I'd love to know that myself. But I only started seeing them after he'd gone, love. The grief and that, I suppose it opened up my spiritual side. Never saw them before.'

Then, quick as a flash, her voice low and intimate, 'What do you see, Jem?' I recoiled back into the sofa. 'What do you see? I know you do. We're the same, Jem. We know what it's like to lose someone.'

She'd caught me with my guard down. I wanted so much to tell her. I had an urge to hold her bony hands in mine, feel

34

her power. I knew that she would believe me. I could share this thing, unburden some of the loneliness it had brought me. I was teetering on the brink – she was drawing me to her. It was going to happen . . .

'Nan, if you do this to people I bring here, I'll never have any mates. For God's sake leave her alone.' Spider's voice cut through the energy lines between us like a sword. Released, I jumped up. 'I wanna show you my new sound system, man. Come on, it'll blow you away.' He led me up to his bedroom.

I glanced behind me as I went out of the lounge into the hallway. Val was still looking at me, eyes focused on me even as she scrabbled in the packet and then lit another fag.

Chapter 6

The music was throbbing through the stairwell. I picked my way over legs and bodies. People hardly noticed me threading my way through: they were getting loaded, getting into the beat, getting into each other.

I was on the lookout for Spider. 'Baz is having a party, Saturday night,' he'd said, the day after the tramp died. We were down by the canal again, chucking stones at a can. 'I'm in. Naturally. Come along, any time from ten. Third floor, Nightingale House.'

I didn't know what to say. He said it so casually, but a party on a Saturday night sounded suspiciously like a date, and there was no way I was getting into all that boy-girl stuff. I'd just about got my head around having a mate to hang out with, but it was a big step to anything more. Anyway, not that I'd ever say it, but it would have to be someone decent. If I'd ever thought about it, which I rarely did, I pictured someone good-looking, not ten out of ten, maybe, but at least an eight. Not someone like Spider – long, lanky, twitchy, with a major personal cleanliness problem. And a couple of weeks to live.

I needed to suss him out, find out whether those retards at school were on the right track after all. I wanted to be careful, though, not make either of us look stupid. I'm not a complete bitch.

'Spider?' I'd said, with a question mark in my voice.

'Yeah.'

'You know at school . . . what did you do that for? Wade in like that?'

Spider frowned. 'He was disrespectful, Jem. What you said – I could tell it was real. It was what you were really feeling. He had no right to make a joke of it.'

'Yeah, I know, he's a tosser, but it's nothing to do with you. You made a right show of yourself. You made a show of me.'

'I didn't want him to get away with it.'

'Yeah, but I don't need a knight in shining armour. I can look after myself.' He was smiling a bit now. I paused. 'It's not funny, man. It's made everything worse,' I said quietly. 'I've got comments all the time now, 'bout you and me. Sly comments.'

He looked away, studied his hands. The knuckles on the right one were nearly healed up now.

My mouth had gone dry, but I had to get this clear with him. 'You do know that there's no "you and me", don't you Spider?'

He looked up. 'What?'

'We're not, like . . . together. Just mates.'

There was something about his sullenness when he said, 'Yeah, course. Just mates. Mates is good,' that made me think he felt the exact opposite. I was churning inside, cursing that day under the bridge. People were so bloody difficult. Why had I ever got involved?

He stood up, came towards me, putting an arm out. I thought, *Shit, he's going to hug me, hasn't he listened to anything?* But his hand formed a fist and he lightly punched my arm. 'Listen, man, I know what you're like. I've told you I'll never say nothing nice to you. And now you've put me straight, I'll never do nothing nice for you either. Okay? If someone disrespects you, I'll let them. If you're being mugged on the street, I'll walk on by. If I see you on fire, I won't even piss on you. Okay?'

I grinned, relaxed a bit. That was better, bit of humour, bit of distance. And he was right, he was starting to know me. No-one else had ever been able to tease me like that, make me smile. After all that, me pushing him away, I almost felt like reaching out, putting my arms round him. Almost. But of course I didn't. Instead our hands met, fists together, knuckles touching.

'Safe, man.'

'Yeah, Spider,' I said. 'Safe.'

'So are you coming on Saturday? Not a date, retard, just a night out. Mates.'

'Dunno. I'll see.'

I'd thought about it for a long time. More or less every minute between him asking me and me going up those stairs a couple of days later. I'd decided not to go hundreds of times. For so many reasons, it was a bad idea: first, I didn't like people, they didn't like me; second, Baz was a well-known psycho, a dangerous guy to be around; and, finally, Karen wouldn't let me out that late. On the other hand, I'd never been asked to a party before, and part of me wanted to be out there, being normal. I told myself I would just go for a bit, see what it was like. I wouldn't have to stay if I didn't like it. As for Karen, what she didn't know wouldn't hurt her.

I slipped out through the kitchen while she was watching the telly in the lounge, carrying my shoes so I wouldn't make a noise on the stairs. I walked quickly, cocooned in the protection of my hood. Deep in my pocket, my hand felt the smoothness of the knife's plastic handle. I'd picked it up on my way through the kitchen, just something to boost my confidence – I'd never use it, you know I'm not aggressive or anything, but if trouble came looking for me, I reckoned the threat of a blade would make people back off long enough for me to leg it. Anyway, just knowing it was there was enough to get me over the doorstep and out into the dark. Another little secret to help me through.

It was easy enough to find Baz's place: the music got louder and louder as I made my way up the stairs and along the hallway, and the concentration of spaced-out kids got denser. I'd hoped to see Spider out on the landing, but no such luck. I'd have to go inside. Given all the people hanging about, I wasn't going to be able to just walk into the flat, though, I was going to have to push my way through. Considering I didn't know anyone, and didn't like being physically close to people, this was a bit of a tall order, but I was determined to go through with it now. Anyway, being small for my age, it was pretty easy to worm my way through – people didn't seem to take offence.

Inside, it was so much worse that what I'd imagined: boiling hot, music so loud you couldn't think, people crammed in, rancid armpits shoved in your face, overwhelming smell of fags, dope and sweat. And all the time, people's numbers right in front of me, close up, no escape.

They say life expectancy's going up, don't they, but I reckon that doesn't apply to kids on our estate. Most of them were only going to make their forties or fifties; quite a few were going way before that. Casualties of how we all live now, I reckoned – cars, booze, drugs, despair. I'd rather not have known, but it wasn't something I could switch on and off.

I'd got about three metres in when I started to panic, wedged between a guy with his T-shirt completely soaked in his own sweat, and his girlfriend, all hairspray and perfume. I didn't see how I could get much further forward, and the gap behind me had closed up. There was no air and the noise was so loud it was like it was actually inside my head, trying to burst out through my ears and eyes and nose. I was feeling light-headed, and as the strength started to go from my legs, I realised I didn't actually need them; my body was held up by all those around me.

Through the smallest of gaps I saw a familiar logo on the back of a yellow T-shirt, bobbing up and down as its occupant moved in time to the beat. Spider! I took a deep breath and dropped to the floor, ducking down to squeeze through the sea of legs. I resurfaced by Spider, and tapped him on the shoulder.

He half-turned, smiled and put his long arm across my back, holding me at my waist. Despite our little chat, I didn't object. Drawn into his side, the familiar smell of his BO was almost welcome, and his arm supported me, giving me a chance to relax and breathe again.

He was saying something to me, but I couldn't hear a thing. He bent down and yelled, 'Good vibes, man! Here . . .' From his other hand he offered me a big roll-up. Battered and dazed just by having made it there, I took it without thinking. 'Go on,' he shouted in my ear. 'It's good stuff.'

I looked at the roach, held between my fingers, blue

smoke spiralling out of the end. It was just dope, nothing heavy. Then I thought of my mum, the funny angle she was lying at when I found her. Was this how she started? A harmless smoke? There was no way I was going down that road. I handed it back to Spider.

'What's up?' he asked.

'Nothing. It's a bit hot in here – I think I need a drink.'

'You need to take your hoodie off, Jem, or you'll melt.'

He was right. I could feel the sweat running down my front. I wriggled out of it, trying not to elbow anyone as I drew it up and over my head. Of course, I'd forgotten the knife. It fell out onto the floor. I held my breath, wondering what the reaction would be. Quite a few people had noticed – they just laughed.

'Hey, there's no need for that here, honour among thieves, eh?' Someone ducked down, picked it up off the floor and handed it back to me.

'Spider, who's this you've got with you? She's hardcore.' A wink of the eye told me they were laughing at me. I was fifteen and five foot nothing, no threat to them.

Spider grinned. 'Yeah, this is Jem. You don't want to mess with her. She's little, but she's mean.'

I wouldn't normally like people talking about me, but squashed in there, it seemed like it was someone else they were talking about. It didn't matter.

After a while, a big bloke came over to us and had a word with Spider. He was covered in tattoos, and I mean covered. Arms, neck, face, the lot. It was the ones on his face that freaked me out, never seen nothing that extreme before. Spider leaned down to me and yelled, 'I've got to do a bit of business. I'll be back in a minute.'

I watched them disappear together into a room at the back

for a few minutes, while my mind tried to make sense of something. The tattooed guy had looked me up and down when he'd come over to Spider. Now his number was drifting round my mind and I was trying to make sense of it – I may not have taken a draw on Spider's roll-up, but I reckon I was breathing it in anyway. My mind wasn't quite working the way it should do – I hadn't exactly stopped thinking, but it was just all taking a bit longer than usual. 11122009. What the hell did that mean? Then it all kind of came into focus again. The eleventh of December this year. That was when Tattoo Face was going to die. Four days before Spider. Christ, what was going on around here?

Without Spider next to me, and with the numbers thing burning a hole in my head, I was definitely feeling edgy now. I hung around with Spider's new mates, but I didn't know them and they didn't know me. I shut my eyes and pretended to be getting into the music, wondering how long I could stick it out there, whether Spider would notice – or mind – if I wasn't there when he got back.

Something made me open my eyes again – something different about the noise, someone pushing against me, I don't know. Across the room, things were heating up. A group of guys, including the one with the tattoos, were shoving somebody around. Hands, shoulders, elbows all going in. In the middle of it all, towering above them, was Spider. Big as he was, there was no doubt what was going on. They were bullying him, intimidating him. He was holding his hands up, as if to say *hold on, guys*, while they ranged round him like hyenas. He's tall, Spider, but there's no meat on him, and my stomach flipped over to see him like that. So vulnerable.

After a couple of minutes, someone else came out of the back room, baseball cap and shades on. Nothing special to look at, but there was something about him, the way he carried himself. I didn't need an introduction: this was Baz, he was The Man around here. He said something and they all laid off Spider. Spider thanked the guy, and you could tell he was going over the top, head going like a nodding dog, and then he was back with me.

'Come on, Jem, it's time to go.'

He grabbed my arm, and instead of shrugging him off, I let him steer me towards the front door, glad to be getting out of there, sorry I'd come in the first place.

'Are you all right?' I asked.

'Yeah, course. Everything's cool. Everything's cool. Let's get out of here.' He was still nodding and mumbling to himself as we made our way through the crowd. No need to barge this time: people were making a path through. The bit of aggro in the corner hadn't escaped anyone's notice, and Spider was tainted with it.

The night air was shockingly cold after the sweatbox of Baz's flat. We walked down the stairs in silence. He didn't show any signs of telling me about it, so in the end I asked him straight out.

'What the fuck is going on?'

'Nothing.'

'I'm not stupid, Spider. Suddenly – out of nowhere – you've got a new sound system, you've got money to spend, and you get invited to Baz's party – a bloke who three weeks ago wouldn't have spat on you to save your life. I saw all those guys round you just now. What have you got yourself into? Are you in some sort of trouble?'

'No, Jem, not trouble. Nothing I can't handle anyway. They just . . . they just wanted to make sure I didn't screw up. And I'm not gonna. It's all gonna be cool. I've just got to

43

take a little package somewhere and then bring another one back.'

'Package?' My heart sank. 'Oh Jesus, Spider, what have they got you doing?'

'It's just helping out, that's all.' We were cutting through the High Road now. He looked quickly behind me, then darted into a shop doorway and beckoned to me. He looked so bloody shifty, it was hilarious. If I'd asked you to pick out someone from the whole street who was up to no good, you'd have picked him, no problem.

I squeezed in next to him. He opened his jacket, wafting his familiar stink out into the night air.

'What are you doing?'

He smiled the smile of a man with a secret he was just bursting to tell, reached into his inside pocket, and drew out an envelope. Then he leaned down towards me and almost whispered, 'I've got two thousand quid in here.'

I looked out of our alcove. There was no-one near enough to have heard. 'Shut up,' I said.

Spider snorted. 'No, really. Two thousand. They trust me, Jem, you see. They trust me with it.'

'What if you get mugged or something, carrying all that lot?'

Even in the dark, I could see his big grin. 'I'll be all right. I've got you and your blade to protect me. You can be my minder.'

'Sod off,' I said. I felt stupid now, bringing it with me. 'It's just being out at night. I didn't feel safe.'

'I'm not criticising, man. It's cool. Got one myself.'

'Put the bloody envelope away before someone sees and let's get out of here.'

He stuffed it back in his pocket and we set off again. He

was strutting now, like the cat that got the cream. I didn't want to spoil it for him, but I did want him to think about it before he got in too deep.

'Spider, he's using you. If it wasn't risky, he'd do it himself, whatever it is you're doing. You're the one who'll get picked up. Fancy a spell inside, do you?'

'Nah, I'll be fine. I'm careful. I'll just do it for a few months, couple of years and I'll be out of here. You can go a long, long way with a bit of money in your pocket.'

And I thought, with a chill, *You're not going anywhere, mate. Another couple of weeks in this hole, that's all.* And it made me feel sad, so sad. The thing was, with Spider and me, something weird was happening. For the first time in my life, I wasn't just observing. I'd got involved. I was starting to hope that his number was wrong, that it was all just in my head, not real. But I knew that it was real. One way or another he was going out in two weeks, and God help me, I wanted to protect him. More than that, I wanted to save him.

Chapter 7

Of course, Karen was waiting for me when I got in, and I got the usual grief from her. To try and calm her down, I went back to school, but a week later it all blew up again, big style. To be honest, most of the kids that had tormented me before left me alone. Someone had seen me at the party, and the association with Baz was keeping them quiet. Friends in high places. There were still a few comments about me and Spider, and the company we were keeping, but they were having a laugh, it wasn't so sly and there was a bit of respect now.

'Don't upset Jem. She's a gangsta now! Gangsta babe!'

I was starting to see why Spider was walking taller. It felt good not to be at the bottom of the heap.

But on the edge of this, all the time, were Jordan and his mates. He'd reappeared at school on the Monday after Baz's party, and kept his distance from me, but I knew he was watching. He was biding his time. Three rows behind me in the classroom, the thought of his eyes on the back of my head made my scalp itch.

He broke cover one day during morning break. I was walking round by the science block when I realised there were people closing in behind me. I looked round, and saw two of Jordan's mates following. I thought, *Sod it, I'm not going to run*, and carried on walking, round the corner and right into Jordan himself. His hand shot out, and he pushed me in the middle of my chest.

'Where you going, gangsta?'

'None of your fucking business. Just let me get past.'

'No, I want to talk to you.'

'I've got nothing to say to you.' I was talking tough, but feeling trapped, my heart pounding away like crazy. They'd got me in a quiet corner; there were five of them altogether. I didn't stand a chance unless I called on my secret friend. My hand tightened around the handle of the knife in my pocket.

'I don't like you, Jem, and I don't like your boyfriend.'

'He's not my—'

'Shut up! I'm talking.' He liked it, that feeling of power. It irritated me, how a prick like him had to have all his mates there to intimidate me. I know I should have kept my eyes down, said nothing, perhaps taken a punch or two, let it all blow over. But he'd got under my skin, and I wasn't thinking straight.

I pulled the knife out and held it in front of me. 'No, you shut up. I don't want to hear it. I just want you to let me get past and leave me alone.'

They'd all frozen. Every one of them was looking at the blade. Taking the advantage, I shoved past Jordan, who gave no resistance. I had a split second of feeling relieved before I ran straight into McNulty. Instantly, he grabbed my wrist and squeezed so hard that the knife fell to the ground. Still holding me, he took a hanky from his pocket, bent down and picked up the knife in it, like a copper on the telly retrieving his evidence. There was no mistaking his air of triumph. He'd got me now. He'd got the evidence. Tosser.

'It's all over, bell's about to ring. Get on to your classrooms,' he boomed. 'You,' he said to me, with grim satisfaction, 'are coming with me.'

With my wrist still clamped in his grip, he led me to the headmaster's office. We didn't wait outside like usual. Still holding on to me, McNulty walked straight past the school secretary in her office and knocked on the head's door, walking in there and then, full of self-importance. 'Headmaster, we've got a serious issue to deal with here. I caught Jem Marsh in the school grounds threatening another pupil with a knife.' He placed the knife on the head's desk.

The head, who'd been signing some papers, visibly recoiled, like McNulty had lobbed a ticking bomb in front of him. 'Right, I see,' he said, looking rapidly from me to the Nutter and back again. Then he picked up the phone. 'Miss Lester, ring the police and ask them to come in, please. We've got a pupil with a knife. Yes. Thank you. And ring the home contact for Miss Marsh. They'd better get down here too.'

And then it started: the questions, the lectures, the accusations, the disappointment. Not just the head and the police, they got Karen and my social worker, Sue, in too. The office was bulging at the seams by the time they were all there. 'I don't think you realise what trouble you're in – carrying an offensive weapon, threatening behaviour, and this on top of disruptive behaviour in the classroom, insolence, bullying . . .'

And on and on and on. I blanked them all, just sat there

while they talked at me. I wanted to believe that if I just kept quiet, eventually they would run out of steam, and it would all go away, but even I couldn't kid myself this time. The knife sat on the desk in front of me – a silent witness. Big mistake bringing that to school, I kept thinking, big mistake. This was serious business now. I was well and truly in the shit.

Eventually, it was agreed that I would be interviewed further at the police station. You could feel the ripple of excitement passing through the school as I was carted away in the cop car. There were kids hanging out of the windows, others gathered in doorways. As they led me out, I thought, *This is probably the last time I'll be here.* But I didn't care about the school or the kids there. It was only when I thought about Spider that I felt a sharp twinge in my stomach. If they locked me up now, would I ever see him again?

They did it all formally – booked me in, searched me, took my fingerprints. I think they were doing it to frighten me, but I wasn't that bothered. I'd kind of withdrawn from everything. I was there, but I was keeping myself to myself – watching what was going on, but not feeling it.

I went along with everything, didn't cause no trouble, but didn't tell them one thing. They tried being nice: 'You've got to understand that it's very dangerous to carry a knife. It's just as likely to be used back on you. Let's have a cup of tea and talk about it.' They tried threatening me: 'You're looking at custody if this gets to court. They're cracking down on little thugs like you.'

They got nothing.

Karen and Sue took turns sitting in with me. They tried to get me to talk too. Karen was desperate to coax something out of me – her chance of being the one to reform me was slipping away. She wasn't used to failure.

'Jem, it's important that you tell us everything you can. I don't believe that you're a violent person. You've not shown that at home. Something happened, didn't it? If you tell us, it will help us to understand.'

Her words started to break through my brick wall, worming their way into my head. She was getting to me, making me think that I could be listened to, but where would I start? With Jordan, with McNulty, with Spider and the party, with Mum, with knowing that you're never really safe anywhere and that it was all going to end sometime, today, tomorrow, the next day? I couldn't do it – it would be like scooping out the soft flesh from a snail's shell. Once it was all out there, there would be nothing to protect me. I fixed my eyes on the floor, tried to block out her voice, stay strong.

A long five hours later, I was released back into Karen's care, with an appointment to go back to the police station in three days' time to hear whether I was going to be charged or not. On top of that I had a month-long exclusion from school. I was grounded at Karen's while Social Services decided what to do with me. All I could do was sit and wait, knowing another move was coming up, another 'fresh start', somewhere away from the estate, away from Spider, the only friend I'd ever had.

I sat in my room, boiling at the injustice. Why hadn't they nicked Jordan for bullying? Why pick on me, when I was just defending myself? Why did they think things would be any better for me anywhere else? Moving you on doesn't solve the problem – it just gets you out of one person's hair and into someone else's.

I brought my fist down on the bed. It hardly made a noise, just bounced up again – a pathetic gesture. I got up and swept my arm across the top of the chest of drawers. My hairbrush and earrings and a couple of books flew across the room. It wasn't enough. I ripped up a T-shirt. That was better. I shredded what I could, threw the rest about wildly. My CD player was blasting out the Chili Peppers. I grabbed it and wrenched it away from the wall. The plug came out and I hurled it with all my strength towards the mirror. The mirror was shattered but the CD player was still in one piece. I picked it up again and flung it against the wall. Bits of plastic flew off, but the main set was still recognisable. It wasn't once I'd opened the window and lobbed it as far as I could, though. Like a dropped milk bottle, it shattered on impact as it hit the front path.

Karen rocketed through my door. Instead of the hot blast of rage, there was cold fury as she took in the state of my room.

'You silly girl,' she said. 'What have you got left now?' And she walked away. I listened to her footsteps going heavily down the stairs, as I slid down one wall, and clutched my knees to me. I hadn't had a lot of stuff to start with, and now I'd trashed it, leaving more or less the clothes I had on – that was all. It didn't add up to much.

I was tired of being me. All the shit I'd put up with over the years, being apart from people, on my own. And just when things were starting to get better, everything had gone wrong again. I huddled there, a tight ball of blackness. And then, a strangely comforting thought trickled through me – I had nothing, so I could do anything now. Anything I wanted. I had nothing left to lose.

Chapter 8

I woke up on the floor, surrounded by broken stuff, my stuff. The last thought that I'd had before I went to sleep was still in my head. I had nothing left to lose. What more could they do to me than they were already planning?

I checked my watch, still working despite a cracked face, twenty to seven. I unpeeled my stiff legs, got to my feet and picked my way across the floor. Then out onto the landing and carefully downstairs. I swigged some orange juice from the carton and stuck some bread in the toaster, then, when it popped up, slathered on some peanut butter and walked out, eating as I went.

Not many people about, although that background buzz was there. It's always there in London. I nipped up someone's front path and grabbed a pint of milk, something to wash down the toast.

I felt better than I had in a long time. I knew that sometime they'd catch up with me – lecture me, confine me, move me – but for now, for this moment, I was free.

I took my pint of milk down to the canal and drank it, perching on the sleepers where I'd had my first conversation with Spider. Light started seeping into the edge of the sky. As it started to spread, everything was grey: the buildings, the walls, the water, the sky. You could take a colour photo and it would be the same as a black and white one. It matched my mood – I was calm, muted, living in the moment, just hanging.

When I'd finished the milk, or nearly, I put the bottle on the edge of the canal bank and scooped up a handful of stones. One by one, I aimed them at the bottle. Some went past, you could hear them enter the water – *plip!* When they hit the target, it wobbled, threatened to fall over the edge, but didn't quite do it. I scuffed the ground with my trainer, looking for bigger stones. I found a couple and concentrated hard. The first one missed, plopped into the canal. The second one got it right on the neck, took it over the edge, just like that, hitting the water with a smack. I got up and peered over. It was bobbing about on its side, the dregs of the milk still slopping around, moving slowly to the left, heading for the Thames. I thought, *I should have put a message in it.* For some reason, that tickled me, the thought of some kid in France or Holland wading out into the sea to get my bottle and pulling out a bit of paper to find my message: *Up Yours.* Greetings from England.

The bottle was twenty metres away from me now. I had half a mind to follow it, see where we both ended up, but that wasn't how I wanted to spend my last few hours of freedom, before they picked me up. I wanted to say goodbye to my mate, so instead I turned back up the path to the shops and headed round to Spider's house. It was still only half past seven and there were no signs of life. I went up to the front door and my hand hovered over the doorbell. I felt unsure, like I'd look a bit desperate, needy, just turning up like that, so early. I gently tried the door, just in case. It moved beneath my fingers, and a wisp of smoke came floating out through the gap.

I pushed the door open and went in and there she was in the kitchen, Val, on her perch, with a cup of tea in one hand and a fag in the other. Christ, did that woman sleep there?

'All right, love?' she said, like she'd been expecting me. 'Come in.' I went further into the room. 'You're an early bird. You in trouble?' I nodded. 'There's some tea in that pot. Get yourself a cup from the sink, love, and come and sit down.'

And that's how Spider found us when he emerged at about nine: me and Val side by side at the breakfast bar, second pot of tea on the go, mound of fag ash on the saucer between us. He shambled into the kitchen with some jogging bottoms and an old, stained T-shirt on, eyes sort of small and puckered, like he'd been asleep for a hundred years. He looked a mess at the best of times, but this was something else, like someone had crumpled him up and thrown him away.

'What's all this?' he asked, once the shock of seeing someone other than his nan there had sunk in.

'Jem's come round to see you. She's in a bit of trouble, aren't you?'

He looked at me, and I said, 'I'm in the shit, Spider. They're going to move me again.' And for some reason, I could feel a little tremble in my chin when I looked at him. I turned away quickly, feeling stupid. And then, bless him, he said exactly the right thing.

'Stuff 'em, Jem. Let's have a day out. I've got some spends.' Val's eyes flicked up to search his face at that. 'They'll be looking for you round here, let's go into town.' He was starting to dance about on his toes again, the familiar energy fizzing through him. He clapped his hands together. 'Okay, let's go! Pour me a cuppa, Nan, and I'll get me trainers on.'

'I think you've got time to have a wash and find some clean clothes, Terry. There's a load of clean stuff in the hall.'

Spider's face registered agony and disgust.

'I'm fine, Nan. Don't nag.'

'You're not fine, you could cut the air with a knife around you, you smelly article!' she said, lighting another fag.

She turned to me. 'Boys! What can you do?' Despite his protest, I noticed Spider sloping out of the room, and when he came back he was in jeans and a clean T-shirt. There's no way he'd had a wash though, not that quickly. He slurped down his tea and bent to kiss Val.

'I suppose I should tell you to go to school, you naughty kids, but seeing as you're both suspended,' she winked one of those piercing hazel eyes, 'you go and have a good day out. I won't say nothing if anyone comes round here.'

She looked at me, not smiling, but there was a warmth underneath, you could tell, and I thought, *You lucky sod, Spider, having a nan like this*. If I'd had someone like her in my life, things could have been completely different.

He grabbed his hoodie on our way out through the front room, called out, 'Bye, Nan, see you later,' and we were gone.

Everything was up and running now, the traffic in full swing, people out and about. Earlier, it had felt like the city was mine, I'd owned the peace and quiet, just me. But now me and Spider were two ants in a city of millions, nothing more than that. The sun was out now, too. It was turning into one of those bright, crisp winter days.

'Don't have to walk today, we can get the tube. Could get a taxi, if you wanted – just about.'

'How much have you got, Spider?'

'Sixty quid – all mine.' He grinned. 'Got to be back this evening, though. Bit more business to do. But the whole of the day's ours,' he said, spreading his arms and twirling about. 'Where do you wanna go?'

'I dunno, Oxford Street?'

'Okay.' He drew himself up to his full height, then spread one arm in front of me, as if showing me the way, and in the loudest, most stupid toff's voice said, 'A little light shopping, madam. Is that to your liking?'

People were starting to look.

'Shut up, Spider!' He looked a bit crestfallen. 'Come on, you soft git, that sounds cool. Let's get on with it.' And I started running towards the tube, and then he was there next to me, long legs easily beating me in our race to the ticket hall.

'It's a fucking rip-off, man, that's what it is. Sixteen quid to go up in that thing.' He flipped his arm towards the London Eye, anger fizzing through his body right down to his fingertips. We'd spent most of our money in Oxford Street on stupid sunglasses and hats and Big Macs. Sixty quid doesn't go very far in London.

People were starting to stare at him. I suppose when you weren't used to him, he was something to stare at: a six-foot-four black guy, ranting in the street. The queue was gawping at him, like he was the cabaret – just there for their entertainment. I thought, *they'll start chucking coins at him in a minute*. Some of them were elbowing each other, saying things out of the corners of their mouths, laughing. Disrespectful, like Jordan had been to me.

'Leave it,' I said, trying to defuse the situation. 'I don't want to go on the poxy thing anyway. Let's go somewhere else.'

But he was off on one now. 'Everything's for sodding tourists in this town. What about us? What about normal people, ain't got sixteen quid for a poncey fairground ride?' Some of his audience were starting to look uneasy, shifting slowly a bit further away from him, exchanging worried glances. I was enjoying their reaction now. He was shaking them up a bit.

My eyes ran along the line – yeah, they were getting pretty uncomfortable. A couple of Japanese tourists, wearing matching blue anoraks, woolly hats and gloves, glanced in our direction. In that split second it took for them to look across and look away, I clocked their numbers, and got a jolt like an electric shock. They were the same. Weird, I thought, matching death dates – what were the odds? Then the actual numbers registered, like a punch to my head. 8122009. That was today. What the hell . . . ?

I looked back across at them, but Spider's antics had got too much: they'd turned their backs on us, probably hoping that we'd go away. I must have made a mistake, I thought. I needed to check this out. I started walking towards the queue, thinking I'd go round to the other side, have a look at them again. Spider didn't even notice I'd gone – I could hear him cursing away to himself, cocooned in his outrage.

The line was pretty dense. I made for a slight gap between a young guy in a tracksuit, with a rucksack on his back, and an old lady with a thick tweed coat on, carrying a straw bag.

''Scuse me,' I said as I walked towards the lady. I needn't have said anything, she was backing away anyway. 'Ta,' I said, as I squeezed through. She smiled thinly, clutching her bag to her body, and I caught the worry in her face as our eyes briefly met. I caught her number, too, and stopped in my tracks. I stared at her, I couldn't help it. 8122009.

This was unreal. What did it mean? Sweat came pricking out through my skin, all over me. I stood there, rooted to the spot, staring at her.

The old lady took a deep breath. Her pupils were wide with fear.

'I haven't got much money,' she said, quietly, voice wavering ever so slightly. Her hands were holding her bag so tightly the knuckles were white.

'What?' I said.

'I haven't got much money. This is a treat for me – I've been saving my pension . . . '

The penny dropped: the old dear thought I was going to rob her. 'No,' I said, taking a step backwards. 'No, I don't want your money. No, that's not it. Sorry.'

I'd bumped into the guy in front of us, and he swung round, the corner of his bloody bag catching my back. Christ, I'm going to get thumped, I thought. I started backing away in Spider's direction.

'Sorry, mate,' I said, head down, hands in pockets. 'I didn't mean nothing.'

'It's okay. This is not a problem.' His stilted English caught my attention. I peered out from under my hood. Weirdly, he looked as spooked as I was, sweat beading on his forehead, hair dark and damp around his scalp. 'Everything is okay,' he said, and nodded, willing me to agree with him.

'Sure, everything's okay,' I echoed, amazed that I could still speak like a normal human being. Inside me, my real voice was screaming now – a piercing shriek of terror tearing through me. He had it too, you see. 8122009. His number.

Something was going to happen to these people.

Today.

Here.

I turned round and stumbled back to Spider, who was still cussing like a good 'un.

'Spider, we've got to go now.' He ignored me, wrapped up in his own little world. I grabbed his sleeve. 'Please, mate, listen to me. We've got to get out of here.' Couldn't he hear the fear in my voice? Couldn't he feel my hand shaking on his arm?

'I ain't going nowhere, man. I ain't finished with this place.'

'Yes, Spider, you are. It doesn't matter. We just need to get away.'

Every second stood there talking was a second closer to whatever was going to wipe these people out. My heart was hammering away in my chest, like it was going to burst through my ribcage.

'I'm going to talk to the main man, whoever's in charge here. Someone needs to tell them, put them straight. It's disgusting, ripping people off like this. We shouldn't put up with it no more. We . . .'

He just wasn't listening. There was no way to make him listen.

'. . . take too much of this shit in this country. We're all treated like second-class citizens. We—'

Without even thinking about it, I lifted my hand up and slapped him hard in the face. And I do mean hard. *Smack!* He stopped mid-flow, frozen in total shock. Then he put his hand up to his cheek.

'What the fuck did you do that for?'

'I need you to listen. We've got to get out of here. Please,

please get me out of here, Spider. Come on.' I grabbed his other hand and pulled until, finally, he started to move. I broke into a run, kind of dragging him along, and then, at last, he was running too. Getting into it, he let go of my hand and sprinted ahead of me, long legs striding out, arms pumping. Fifty metres on, he stopped to wait for me, and then we jogged together, along the Embankment and over Hungerford Bridge. We slowed to a walk halfway along the bridge, then stopped and looked back where we'd come from. Everything was just as it had been, no problems.

'What's going on, Jem? What was that all about?'

'Nothing. You were just upsetting people, that's all. The next thing someone would've called the police.' It could have been true, couldn't it? But even as I said it, I knew it sounded lame, and it didn't fool Spider.

'Nah, that's not it. Look at you, there's something wrong. You look like a ghost, man. Even whiter than normal. What's wrong with you?'

Standing there, looking over the Thames and at the city just getting on with a normal day, I suddenly felt that I'd made a fool of myself. The words running through my head didn't sound real, even to me – *Numbers, death dates, disaster* . . . It sounded ridiculous, a stupid fantasy. And perhaps that was all it was, some twisted game my mind was playing on me.

'It's nothing, Spider. I had a bad feeling there, a panic attack. I'm okay now – well, not okay, but better.' I tried to turn the conversation back to him. 'I'm sorry I hit you.' I put my hand up to his face and held it there for a couple of seconds. 'Is it sore?'

He smiled ruefully. 'Still stinging a bit. I'd never have thought you could batter me like that.' He snorted and shook his head. 'Bloody Mike Tyson'd have trouble with you.'

'Sorry,' I said again.

'Don't worry about it,' he said, still smiling. And that's where we were, leaning on the bridge, looking along the river, when we heard the bang and saw the London Eye blown to bits in front of us.

Chapter 9

You'll have seen it on telly a hundred times, so you know what we saw that day: a sudden explosion, debris flying everywhere, a plume of smoke going up, one pod completely destroyed, others damaged and distorted in the blast. All around us people had stopped in their tracks and turned to face the Eye. We could hear screaming carrying across the water.

Spider and I said the same thing, 'Oh, my God!', and it was echoed from every mouth along the bridge – maybe a prayer from some people, just the words you say when you're in shock for most of us. We stood watching for a minute or two, as the dust settled and the sirens started wailing. I felt numb. I'd started to doubt the numbers, hoping they weren't real, that it was all some silly game in my head. Now I knew it was no game. The numbers were real – I was the girl who knew people's futures, and I always would be. I shivered.

'Let's get out of here, Spider,' I said. 'Let's go home.' Whatever was waiting for me at Karen's, it had to be better than watching London clear up its dead. I turned to carry on across the bridge, but Spider didn't follow. 'Come on,' I said, 'let's go.'

Still leaning on the bridge, he looked round at me, frowning. There was confusion there, but also accusation. I knew what was coming next. I couldn't avoid it. Still holding my eyes, he spat out the words.

'You knew. You knew about that.' We were perhaps five metres apart. His words were loud enough to reach me, and several other people nearby. A couple of them quickly turned their heads to look at us.

'Shut up, Spider,' I hissed.

He shook his head. 'No, I won't shut up. You knew about this. What the fuck's going on, Jem?' He straightened up and started walking towards me.

'Nothing. Shut up!'

He was close now, and made to grab me. I ducked away and started running. There were a lot of people on the bridge and I had to weave my way between them. Spider was way faster than me, but he was big and awkward and I could hear people shouting as he blundered through the crowd behind me. I made it to the other side and ran blindly through the streets. It didn't take Spider long to catch me, and he got hold of my arm and spun me round to face him.

'How did you know that was going to happen, Jem?' We were both breathing hard.

'I didn't. I didn't know nothing.'

'No, Jem, you knew about that. You knew about that. What's going on?' I tried to wrestle away from him, but he was gripping hard. With his height and his strength and his smell he seemed to be all around me, I couldn't get away. I tried to hit him but he had both my arms now. I rammed my head forward, but he'd seen me coming and just held me further away, still gripped in his vice. I couldn't stand it. I kicked out and my foot slammed into his leg. He winced, but didn't let go. 'Nah, man, you're gonna tell me what's going on.'

People were staring at us. I stopped struggling and went limp in his arms. *I don't want to do this on my own any more*, I thought. *I can't do it on my own.*

'Okay,' I said, 'but not here. Can we cut down to the canal?'

We walked up to the Edgware Road, and soon found a way through to the back of the shops that led down to the canal. At last we were away from people. All the strength had gone from me, my legs were starting to go.

'I've gotta sit down,' I said weakly, and slumped onto a broken bench. One of the wooden slats was missing, felt like you were going to fall through it. Spider sat next to me.

'You've gone a funny colour, man. Put your head between your knees or something.'

I leaned forward as a whooshing sound filled my ears. The space inside my head turned red, and then black.

'Whoa, steady, mate.' I could hear Spider's voice from a long way away, the other end of a tunnel. When I opened my eyes everything was the wrong way round. Took me a while to realise I was lying down. The bench dug into me where I was nearly falling through the gap, but my head was on a pillow, rank-smelling, but soft: Spider's hoodie. He was pacing up and down on the towpath, rocking his head, flipping his fingers, muttering under his breath.

'Hey,' I said, with hardly any sound at all. He stopped pacing and crouched down by me.

'You all right, man?' he said.

'Think so.'

He helped me to sit up slowly, then sat next to me. I was shivering. He grabbed his hoodie and held it out. 'Here. Put this on.'

'Nah, I'm all right.' Didn't want that foul-smelling thing on my clothes, my skin. I shivered again and he reached round behind me. I didn't know what he was up to, was about to tell him where to go, when I realised he'd draped the hoodie over my shoulders. Kind of wrapped me up. Made me think of my mum putting a blanket round us both on the sofa when the flat was so cold, cuddling up underneath it, one of her good days. Something was stabbing me in my eyes: pricking, stinging, hot. It spilled out and ran down my right cheek. Shit, I was crying. I don't cry. I just don't do that. I sniffed hard, wiped my face with the back of my hand.

'You gonna tell me now?' I looked hard at the ground in front of me. Spider was the closest thing I'd ever had to a friend. Could I trust him? I took a deep breath.

'Yeah,' I said. And I told him.

Chapter 10

There was silence between us – not an empty thing, a space full of thoughts and feelings, unspoken words and emotions. We sat there while the sounds of London in chaos played out half a mile away, sirens wailing, car horns going, helicopters circling. I felt stunned – still reeling from what had happened, and shocked that I'd finally told someone. My body and my head were all over the place. I hadn't looked at Spider all this time – I'd kept my eyes on the ground as the words came out of me. It was so unreal, like someone else was talking.

He'd been sitting bent forward, leaning his elbows on his knees, listening. It was probably the stillest he'd been since I'd met him. Finally, he breathed out, a long breath through pursed lips.

'No way, man, no way.' He sounded confused, scared almost.

'It's true, Spider. It's all true. I knew something was going to happen because their numbers were all the same. And it did.'

'Ah, this is way too weird. You're freaking me out.'

'I know. I've had to live with this for fifteen years.' Those stupid tears weren't far away again.

He suddenly slapped his forehead.

'That old bloke, the one that was run over, you saw his number, didn't you? That's why you wanted to follow him.'

I nodded. There was silence again for a while.

'My nan knows about you, doesn't she? You and her, you're the same, aren't you?' He shook his head. 'All this time, I just thought she talked a load of bollocks, like it was funny really. But she knew there was something different about you. You're a pair of witches! Shit!'

I sat up a bit, tried to breathe more evenly. There were a couple of ducks paddling along the canal, little brown things, oblivious. I watched them making steady progress upstream. How easy to be a bird or an animal, living from day to day, unaware that you're alive, unaware that one day you'll die.

Spider had got up, was pacing around again, up and down on the flat stones edging the canal. He was muttering under his breath – I couldn't catch the words – just trying to get his head round what I'd said, I suppose. He scooped up a handful of gravel, started chucking it at the ducks. Must have hit one, because they suddenly took off, little brown wings going like the clappers.

He swivelled round. 'Do you see everyone's numbers?'

I looked back down at the ground. I knew what was coming next. 'Yeah, if I see their eyes.'

'You know mine, then,' he said, quietly. I didn't say anything. 'You know mine,' he said, more insistently.

'Yeah.'

'Shit, man, I dunno if I want to know or not.' He sank

down to the ground, crouching, holding his head.

Don't ask me, I thought, *never ask me that, Spider.* 'I won't tell you,' I said quickly. 'I couldn't. It's not right. I'll never tell no-one.'

'What d'you mean?' He was looking at me now. As our eyes met, that bloody number was there again. 15122009. I wanted to rip it out of my head, blank it out like I'd never seen it.

'It would do your head in if I told you, freak you out. It's just not right.'

'What if someone hadn't got long to go? If they knew, they'd have a chance to do stuff they've always wanted.'

I swallowed hard. 'Yeah, but it'd be like living on Death Row, wouldn't it? Each day, one step closer. No way, man. No-one should have to live with that.' Except, of course, that we all do. We all know we're one day closer to the end when we wake up in the morning. Just kid ourselves that it's not happening.

Spider stood up, scratched his head and kicked some more gravel into the water. 'I need to think about this. You've done my head in today.' A siren started up from a street nearby. 'Let's get out of here.'

I handed his top back to him and we set off down the canal path. The gravel crunched under our feet as we walked past the graffiti-daubed walls lining the path. A lot of the buildings were derelict, but here and there some had been tarted up, turned into posh offices or restaurants or wine bars, shiny islands in a sea of grime. The sirens faded as we got further away, and there was an odd quietness about the place, like everything had ground to a halt.

When we got near the estate, we cut up to the main road. A couple of people had stopped outside the telly shop window, and we joined them. A dozen screens all the same.

The London Eye wasn't turning any more. There was a bit missing, like someone had taken a big bite out of it; one pod gone, the ones near it twisted and wrecked, rubbish all over the ground. Only it wasn't rubbish, it was bits of people and people's things. The camera lingered over some tattered blue material, what was left of someone's coat, and something flapping in the breeze: the frilly edge of a straw bag, shredded in the blast. Words slid along the bottom of each screen: TERRORIST ATTACK AT THE LONDON EYE . . . NUMBER OF DEAD AND INJURED UNKNOWN . . . POLICE WARN PUBLIC TO BE VIGILANT FOR MORE ATTACKS . . .

We watched for ages. Beside me, Spider kept saying, 'Shit, man. Jesus Christ.' The news was on a loop, the same pictures over and over again. As I stood there, I could feel stuff rising up inside me. I fought to keep it down, but in the end I had to find an alleyway and get rid of it: the sour contents of my stomach spilling out of me onto the ground.

Spider came to find me. 'You all right, mate?'

I coughed and spat, trying to get my mouth clean. 'Yeah,' I said. I got a tissue out of my pocket, wiped my mouth. 'Spider?'

'Yeah.'

'I could've done something. I knew something was gonna happen. I could've warned them, got them to shut the place down or something, I dunno.'

'Yeah, but what if they'd shut it and they'd all made for the tube, and it had happened there?' He was right, I supposed. One way or another, today was their day: the Japanese couple, the old lady, the guy with the rucksack. But there was this feeling crushing me, the feeling that I could have made a difference.

'You wanna come to mine?' Spider asked.

'I dunno, I guess I do.' I wanted to go somewhere safe. I wished I could say, 'I'm going to head home,' but nowhere felt like home.

I suddenly remembered Sue and the police – God knows who would be waiting for me back at Karen's. Yeah, Spider's was definitely the better option.

We shambled back to Carlton Villas and let ourselves in. Val wasn't on her normal perch; she was in the front room with the big TV on. She half got up when she saw us coming through the door.

'Terry, that you? Ah!' She collapsed back into the chair. 'I've been fretting all afternoon since the news came on. You all right?'

Spider bent over to give her the normal peck on the cheek, then wrapped his arms around her and folded his legs so he was crouching on the ground in front of her chair, hugging her. He held on tight.

'You were there, weren't you?' she said. 'I knew it. I knew it.' One hand rested on his back, the other clutched his head into her, nicotine-stained fingers buried in his springy hair. 'It's all right. You're safe now, son.'

I hovered in the doorway, feeling that I shouldn't be seeing this; it was just between them. After a minute or so, Val looked round at me. 'Come here. Sit down, love. You look done in.' I sat next to her and she took my hand. 'I'm so glad to see you both.'

Spider disentangled himself and sat back on his heels. He rubbed his arm across his face, but not before I'd seen the tears glistening there. 'We were there just before, Nan. I was going off on one because we didn't have enough money left to go on there, but Jem, she . . .' he hesitated, looked at me quickly, '. . . she said we should come away, it didn't matter. We were on Hungerford Bridge when it went off. We saw it, Nan, we saw it.'

'So you saved him. You kept my boy safe.' She held both my hands in hers now, looked deep into my eyes. 'Thank you. Thank you for bringing him back to me. He's a naughty boy, but he means the world to me. Thank you.'

I didn't know what to say. 'We were just lucky,' I mumbled, but Spider wasn't having it.

'No, it wasn't luck. She saved me, Nan, just like you said.' I flashed him a warning look, but the shock of the day and the relief of getting back home was loosening his tongue. 'She's like you, Nan. She knew something was going on.'

I made to get up, but Val tightened her grip on my hands. 'You felt something? What was it?'

I shook my head. 'I just had a feeling, that's all. I knew something bad was going to happen.' Her eyes were boring into me as she sat there, just waiting. My heart was beating like mad, the blood pumping through me, deafening me. 'I knew people were going to die.'

Val made a little sighing noise, like she'd been holding her breath. 'I knew there was something,' she said, quietly. 'I knew you had a gift.' She was still holding my hands, shaking them gently up and down, a gesture of comfort. 'You're here for a reason, Jem. You saved Terry for me. Thank you.'

Her eyes were glistening, and I thought, *You've got it wrong about me. Spider could have stayed where he was and he wouldn't have died today. I only protected him from getting hurt, he wouldn't have died today. I can't save him, I want to but I can't, and soon he'll go, and you'll think I've let you both down.*

But I couldn't say any of this, I could never tell them what was coming up for Spider. So I just sat there, and Spider, Val and I were all quiet, as the reporter on the TV broke the news that police were putting out an urgent call to trace two youths seen running away just moments before the explosion, both in hoodies and jeans, one black, very tall, one shorter and white.

I felt my stomach lurch. Whatever trouble I'd been in yesterday fell away. Spider and I were up to our necks in it now. We all looked at each other, and Val held onto my hand with one of her hands and reached out to hold Spider's with the other.

'You've done nothing. They've got nothing on you,' she said firmly. But we'd both had run-ins with the police before, and they weren't going to swallow any stories about second sight, were they? Spider looked at me over the top of his nan's head, and I knew what he was thinking. We couldn't stick around waiting to be picked up. It was time to run.

Chapter 11

'Listen, I've got to go out for a bit, like I said, do a bit of business, and then when I get back, we'll get going.'

'But—' I started to object, but Spider wasn't having it.

'We're gonna need money, aren't we? You get a bit of food together while I'm out, yeah?'

'Okay, but what if they pick you up now?'

'I'll be fine.' He put a jacket on over his hoodie, and crammed a beanie over his unruly hair. 'There, don't worry, Jem. Safe.' He formed a fist and held it out to me, and I did the same. Our knuckles touched. 'Safe, Jem, I'll be back soon.' He sloped out of the front door.

All this time, Val had been watching us and hadn't said a word. Now she got up from the chair.

'You'd be all right here, you know. They've got nothing on you. You didn't do nothing.'

I shrugged. They'd been heavy enough about the knife – this was something completely different.

'I'm not going to stop you, don't worry. You'll have to do

what you think best. Look,' she said, making for the door, 'if you are going you'll need some different clothes. Let me have a look in my room. You go through cupboards in the kitchen, take what you want.' I went through to the kitchen, and started opening cupboard doors randomly. There was hardly anything there – a few tins of peas, some beans, a box of instant mash. I took out a packet of crackers.

'Did you find the chocolate biscuits? I've got a packet of chocolate biscuits somewhere,' Val said, coming into the room with an armful of clothes. 'Here,' she said, handing them to me, 'try some of these.'

I took them back into the lounge, and sorted through, thinking that I'd rather die than wear them. She's small, like me, so we were okay size-wise, but – obviously – they all stank to high heaven of smoke and, to be honest, they were gross.

'What you pulling that face for? Not good enough for you?' She'd caught me. 'Look, you'll need a couple of T-shirts and you're going to need something warm. It's dropping cold at night now. This jumper,' she rummaged vigorously in the heap and pulled out a big pink thing with a huge roll neck, 'and a coat, or something. Here.' She threw a mint-green padded anorak and some gloves in my direction.

'I'll . . . I'll try them upstairs.' I stumbled up, and found the bathroom, dumped the clothes on the side of the bath and slid the bolt across to lock the door. I used the toilet, and then sat there for ages, just breathing, trying to get my head around what had happened, what was still happening. It was like things were slipping and sliding around me, and I was trying to catch up, hold everything together.

After a bit, I stood up and wriggled out of my hoodie. I'd have to try Val's things anyway. I put them on and faced the mirror. I looked like me in someone's nan's clothes. It was horrific. But I was going to have to do something, wasn't I? The filth who'd picked me up the other day would soon realise it was me they were looking for, even if Karen didn't ring them up, which I was pretty sure she would. They'd have a description then, wouldn't they? – even a photo. Karen had taken a couple of me with the twins when I'd first got there. They would be looking for a small, skinny girl, with long, mousy hair.

I opened the cabinet on the bathroom wall above the sink. Among the painkillers, pile cream, and indigestion tablets were some nail scissors. Without thinking twice, I took them out and started hacking at my hair. The scissors were crap, and I could only cut through if I pulled the strands really tight. As I snipped away, I was left with handfuls of hair. I let them fall to the floor. Halfway through I looked in the mirror. Christ, I looked bad. What the hell had I done? It was no good though; now I'd started I'd have to see it through. I didn't look in the mirror again until I'd gone all the way round.

Have you ever seen that film, *The English Patient*? Bloody boring if you ask me. Karen made me watch it at her house once, it went on for hours and she cried her eyes out at the end, silly cow. Anyway, one of the characters, the nurse, cut her hair off, ended up looking absolutely brilliant. She just cut it, ran her fingers through it, and there she was, like a model. Just like me. Except that I looked seriously bad. There was no way I could even go out of the house, let alone run away, looking like this. I looked at the bundles of hair lying on the floor with a sick feeling in my stomach. Was there any way to stick it back?

Val knocked on the door. 'You all right in there? Jem, you all right?'

I slid the bolt back and opened the door.

'Sweet Jesus!' Yeah, it was as bad as I thought it was. 'It's all right. It's not that bad,' she said quickly, trying to undo the damage, but we both knew she wasn't fooling anyone. It was tragic. 'I think it's going to have to all come off, love. I've got some old clippers somewhere. Let me look under the sink.'

She sat me on one of the stools in the middle of the kitchen. I felt like a squaddie, wincing as the clippers buzzed in my ear.

'Sit still, love, I can't do it if you move about.'

Eventually she stood back and admired her work. 'There, that's better.' I put my hand up to my head. It had all gone. You could feel the shape of my skull. 'Not too short, love, just a Number Four. Go and look.'

I went back up to the bathroom, stood outside the door for a bit while I got the courage up to look. The girl in the mirror stared back at me. She was a stranger. I was used to seeing my face curtained by my hair, half-hidden, now my features were laid bare – eyes, eyebrows, nose, mouth, ears, jawline. I looked about ten, a ten-year-old boy. I scowled, and the person in the mirror scowled back. He might be small, but you wouldn't mess with him. I was fierce. Intense eyes, strong cheekbones, and you could see the jaw muscles through the side of my face. It might have felt like my protective layer had been stripped away, but it was a pretty powerful look. I reckoned I could live with it. I ran my hands through, starting to enjoy the feel of the newly cut ends.

When I walked into the front room, Spider was back. His jaw literally dropped, I swear it did. 'Fucking hell, I've only been gone half an hour, what've you done?' He walked around me, examining me from every angle. 'Oh my God,' he was laughing. 'You look way cool!' He reached out and touched my hair.

'Get off!' I wasn't public property. He jumped back, holding both his hands up in defence.

'Okay, okay.' He was still laughing, then he sobered up. 'Listen, we need to get going. Sooner the better.'

'Where you going, son?' Val asked.

Spider shuffled his feet, looking down at the carpet. 'It's better if you don't know, Nan . . .'

'All right, but you'll ring me, won't you? Let me know you're okay?'

'Yeah, I'll try.'

Val had put some stuff together in a bag: food, a sleeping bag, a blanket. I went upstairs to fetch my 'real' clothes, and put them in a carrier Val had found for me. We stood around awkwardly for a minute, then Spider coughed. 'Come on, time to go.' He reached down and hugged his nan. She held him close. I tried not to think that this was probably the last time they'd see each other.

Spider picked up the bags, and moved towards the front door. Val caught my arm. 'Take good care of him, Jem.' Those hazel eyes looked deep into mine. I swallowed hard, but didn't say anything. I couldn't promise anything, could I? 'Keep him safe.' I looked away, and straight off she dug her fingernails into my arm. 'Do you know something? Do you know something about Terry?'

I gasped, she was starting to hurt me.

'No,' I lied.

'Look at me, Jem. Do you know something?'

I pressed my lips together, shook my head.

'Oh, Christ,' she murmured, her pupils widening in alarm. 'Just do your best, Jem.'

She let go of my arm and we walked into the hall. Spider had opened the door by a crack and was peering out.

'Okay,' he said, 'I think it's clear. Let's go!' He darted out to a red car parked halfway onto the pavement, clicked open the boot and chucked the bags in.

'What the . . .? Is this yours?' I spluttered.

He looked up and grinned. 'It is now. Get in, quick.' He was looking up and down the road, twitching like mad.

Val fumbled in her pocket and brought out a fiver. 'Here,' she said, trying to give it to Spider, 'take this.'

He smiled and closed her hand around it. 'Nah, don't worry, Nan, I got money.'

'I don't care, Terry. This is mine, it's all I've got. I want you to have it. Take it.' She shoved it into his pocket.

'What you gonna live on?' Even in such a hurry, he had time to think about her.

'Don't worry, I get my Disability money tomorrow. I'll be fine. You have it. Get some chips or something.'

'Cheers, Nan.' He bent to hug her again. Her eyes closed as she held him one last time. 'I'll be in touch, see you soon, yeah?'

'Yeah, all right, son.'

We got in the car, and Spider reached beneath the steering wheel with both hands, and rummaged about until the car spluttered into life. As we moved off, I looked behind. Val was standing on the pavement, just watching, hand half-raised. Her voice echoed in my head: *Do your best, Jem.* I wanted to tell Spider to stop the car there and then. I wanted to get out and run, and just keep running until I had a heart attack or someone caught me and none of it was in my hands any more. Deep down inside I knew there was nothing I could do to keep Spider safe – his time was coming, and it was days rather than weeks now.

'Stick the radio on, find some music.' His voice broke into my thoughts.

I looked across at him. He was fizzing with energy, loving the buzz of it all – running away, driving through London. If he'd been a dog, he'd have had the window down now, with his head out and his ears flapping in the breeze. I flicked through the radio stations. It was all rubbish, so I opened the glove compartment, looking for CDs. There was a pretty tragic selection: the Bee Gees, Elton John, Dire Straits. There was all sorts of other crap in there too – receipts, an old hairbrush, some papers. I fished one bit of paper out, just a boring bill. I was about to chuck it on the floor when something caught my eye. At the top, it was addressed to Mr J P McNulty, 24 Crescent Drive, Finsbury Park, London.

'Oh my God, Spider. This is the Nutter's car! What are you like?'

His eyes were shining. 'Couldn't resist it. Neat, eh?'

'Have you been up the school?'

'Yeah, just sneaked in. They were all in last lesson. Didn't take long – you might as well not lock an Astra.'

'He'll have reported it by now. They'll all be looking for it.'

'Yeah, I thought about that. Reckon we should avoid the motorways, all those cop cars and cameras. Give us a bit longer before we ditch it and get the next one.' I was impressed – he had thought about it. He kept glancing up into the rear-view mirror. Every time he did it, the car swerved a bit.

'What you doing?'

'Just checking we're not being followed.'

'We'd hear the sirens, wouldn't we?'

'It's not just jam sandwiches, Jem, there's unmarked cars too. There's all sorts . . .'

'Where are we heading, anyway?' I hadn't questioned this before, I'd just let Spider take charge – he seemed to know what he was doing.

'I don't think it's worth trying to get out of the country. They'll be watching all the ports. We just need to keep moving 'til we find somewhere we can lie low for a bit. I thought we'd head west – might end up at the seaside.'

The penny dropped. *His best day ever.* 'Weston-something or other?'

He smiled. 'Yeah. We could aim for there, anyway.'

'Where the hell is it?' I admit it, my knowledge of geography is nil.

'Out west, head for Bristol and keep going. I might buy a map book when we get some petrol. Not that I can read a map, but how difficult can it be?'

'You got some money, then?'

'Oh yeah, I got plenty of money.' He put his hand up to his jacket pocket. 'We got the cash, the wheels, we're on our way!' And he let out a ridiculous whooping noise, and laughed like a maniac.

And just for a moment, I forgot the bomb, and the police, and the fact that I was in a stolen car with a guy whose pockets were full of dodgy money. It seemed like after waiting for fifteen years, my life had finally begun. I was in a real-life adventure, and I was enjoying the ride.

Chapter 12

The road out of London was like something out of a science fiction film. We went up on a kind of ramp, drove through space-age office blocks fifteen metres up in the air. It was all concrete and glass and sky. We were part of a stream of cars, spewing out of the city. As I watched the tail-lights stretching out ahead, I thought about how each of those cars contained someone with their own story. People on their way back from work, glad to be heading away from the bomb and the mayhem, back to their two point four kids in the suburbs. None of their stories could be anything like ours, could they? Two kids on the run from the police in a stolen car. I was living out a dream, Spider and I were movie stars; it was exciting, dangerous, too cool to be true.

Spider pulled out to overtake a van. Out of nowhere there was a blaring horn, something was right on top of us in the outside lane.

'Shit!' Spider yanked the wheel and we veered back over to the left. The car in the outside lane drew level with us, the driver making gestures and shouting as he eyeballed Spider.

'Up yours, mate!' Spider responded. The bloke was going mad.

'Just leave it, Spider. Don't look at him. For God's sake, keep your eyes on the road, we'll crash!' Spider was driving wildly, his steering completely random. Eventually, the other guy accelerated away, still going nuts, and I breathed a sigh of relief.

'We don't want to draw attention to ourselves, just calm down.'

'Yeah, I know, but he was a complete wanker. Winding me up, man.'

'I think we should get off this road, find somewhere quieter.'

'Yeah, we'll take the next exit.' He was still agitated, but at least he had both hands on the wheel now.

Before long there was a sign showing an exit coming up. We moved over into the slip road, and the brakes squealed as Spider tried to slow down to take the bend as it curved round. A sign flashed up showing a roundabout ahead, but we were going too fast to see what it said. We joined the roundabout, but then we didn't know what to do. We hurtled round, looking at the exit signs: 'Hounslow . . . Slough . . . Harrow . . . Christ, where do we go?' We did the full circuit, felt like we'd never get off, before plunging down one exit with car horns going off at us left, right and centre. We carried on, the traffic nose to tail.

'Did anyone follow us, Jem? Did anyone else go round like us?'

'How would I know?'

'You need to look in the mirrors! It's not frigging brain surgery!' There was sweat beading on his forehead. I knew he was stressed, but he was being a tit.

'Shut up!' I yelled. 'All I can see is lights, they're all the same. How the fuck would I know if we're being followed?'

He wiped his hand over his forehead and into his hair. 'Where are we?'

'I dunno, just keep going. There'll be more signs soon.'

'I don't think the signs help much. We need a map.'

'Won't help me, I haven't got a clue about maps.'

'Well, we'll just have to learn. God, I need a break.' Spider turned into a side road and pulled over. He switched the engine off and stretched out as far as he could in his seat, then rubbed his face with his hands and exhaled hard through his fingers. 'Shit! That's hard, man.'

'Driving?'

'Yeah, there's so much to think about, everything's coming at you from all sides. Whoa.'

He wiped more sweat away from his forehead with his sleeve, put his head back and closed his eyes.

'Spider,' I said, slowly, 'you have driven before, haven't you?'

'Sure I have,' he said, his eyes still closed. 'I had a go in Spencer's car round the industrial estate.'

'But I thought you'd done this loads, nicked cars and that . . . ?'

'I have, Jem, but I was always the starter. They never let me drive.'

I looked at him sharply. 'I don't believe you . . . you're a headcase! We've just driven through one of the busiest places in the world, and you've only driven a car once before. Oh, my God . . .' I found myself laughing, relief teetering on the edge of hysteria.

He opened his eyes now. 'What? What you laughing at? I got us here, didn't I?'

I paused for breath. 'I'm not laughing at you. Honest, I'm not.' He looked so offended, I put a comforting hand on his arm. 'You did get us here. You were awesome. You were awesome, Spider. Here, let's have a look in the bag your nan got ready. Have a snack.'

He got out, went round to the boot, fetched the bag and slung it onto my lap. I fished into it. It was pretty pitiful – crackers, chocolate biscuits, some tins, but no tin opener. There was a packet of fags, at least, and something heavy at the bottom. I reached further in and put my hand around the neck of a bottle. I drew it out. Spider's face brightened up.

'No way, man,' I said, putting the vodka back in the bag. 'I don't think this would help right now.'

'I am thirsty, though. Anything else to drink in there?'

I rummaged about. 'Nah.'

'Slim pickings,' Spider said, and snorted with laughter.

'What?'

'It's just something you say, isn't it, when you haven't got nothing? It's just funny.'

For some reason, those words tickled him and he started laughing properly. It was infectious. I didn't even really know what he was going on about, but I started laughing too. We sat there, like a pair of idiots, helpless for a while.

When we stopped, it was like all the energy had gone out of us, we'd laughed it away. It was silent in the car. Reality was seeping in, like when you drink something really cold and can feel it making its way down your throat and inside you. Doubts about the whole thing were crowding in on me. We didn't know where we were going, we'd got nothing useful with us, everyone would be looking for us. I didn't want to be the one to say it, but I couldn't help myself.

'Perhaps we should go back,' I said. 'They might be easier on us if we went back and gave ourselves up.'

Spider shook his head. 'I ain't never going back. I can't, Jem.'

'What do you mean, you can't? All right, it'll be bad for a bit. They'll question us about earlier on, and we've taken the car now, but what's the worst they can do? Lock us up?'

'No, Jem, not the police – although they will lock me up this time, they've been waiting for an excuse. It's not them, though. Look.' And he reached into his jacket pocket and drew out a brown envelope, a big one folded over, and handed it to me.

'What's this?'

'Have a look.' I unfolded the end and peered in. There were notes inside, a dense wedge of notes. I put my hand in and pulled them out. I had honestly never seen or held so much money in my life.

'That's our future, Jem. Well, the next few weeks anyway.'

I held the notes in one hand and flicked through the other end with my thumb, like you'd flick through a book. There must have been hundreds of used fivers and tenners. Thousands of pounds. 'What have you done, robbed a bank?'

He chewed on a hangnail, looked at me without answering.

'What have you done, Spider?' I asked quietly.

He looked down, ran his hands through his hair. 'I didn't make my last drop-off.'

'It's Baz's money? You robbed Baz? Oh, my God, Spider, they'll kill you!'

He was back to chewing the edge of his finger. 'Not if they don't find me. That's why I can't go back. It's you and me now, Jem. We've got to do this. We've got to find somewhere new. Start again.'

I closed my eyes. There really was no going back. I felt a hand on my shoulder.

'You all right?' I didn't answer, didn't know what to say. 'I could drop you off somewhere, if you like. I can't go back, but you can. You could go back, Jem.'

I let his words sink in. He really meant it – he'd go on without me. But what did I have to go back to? The police, the Social, Karen? I opened my eyes and he was staring right at me, really looking at me. How many people in my life saw anything more than an odd, quiet little kid in a hoodie? How many people had really bothered with me? Spider was different: he was funny, mad, restless, reckless. He was all right.

'No,' I said. 'It's okay. I'll stay for the ride. Wouldn't mind having a look at Weston-Super-Wotsit.'

He grinned and nodded. 'Let's carry on down this road, find a petrol station and get some proper food, buy a map, get sorted.'

'Okay,' I said, 'let's do it.'

We did a twenty-three-point turn in our side road, and joined the main drag again. After about ten minutes, we found a petrol station, and drew up beside one of the pumps. After a bit of messing about, Spider found the catch to unlock the petrol cap, and did the business. We both went into the shop, and I used the toilet while Spider gathered armfuls of stuff – Coke, crisps, chocolate, some sandwiches. Enough to keep us going for a few days. People were looking at us a bit funny. *Shit*, I thought, *they'd remember two kids loaded down with stuff.*

The queue was achingly slow.

The guy behind the counter had the radio on. The music cut to a news report. 'London is reeling after a massive blast ripped the London Eye apart . . . seven dead, and many more injured . . . police are looking for two youths, one black and very tall, the other shorter and slightly built.'

My skin was prickling all over. I felt like there was a big neon sign over my head, an arrow pointing down, HERE THEY ARE. I knew Spider had heard it too, he was looking down, shuffling from foot to foot, and chewing at his lip. I was waiting for someone to say something, to grab one of us. It was agony. Every part of me wanted to dump the stuff and leg it, but I fought it. *Stay cool, stay cool.* We inched forward. The news finished and the music came back on as we reached the till. The guy didn't even look at us, just asked for the pump number, and scanned the stuff. Spider paid in cash and we ducked out.

As we made for the door, I spotted a camera high up in the corner. Just for a second I looked straight at it, and it looked back at me, an unblinking eye. *That's it,* I thought. They'd got a picture of me now, in Val's stupid anorak, and with my short hair. Before I got back in the car, I took off the vile coat and chucked it on the back seat. Spider was already starting the engine.

'Okay, let's go. Here, you look at the map, see if you can work out where we are.' He plonked a big map book on my lap.

I started to protest, but he cut in. 'Jem, we've got to get out of here. This is life or death. I need you to do this.'

I flicked through the pages until I found a big map of the south of England. I concentrated hard, trying to see a pattern in the web of lines on the map, then found London, and looked to the left. I felt a twinge of triumph when I spotted Bristol. There were loads of roads between the two, we just needed to find one of them.

'Just drive until we find a sign, Spider. I'll be able to tell when there's a sign.'

And so, haltingly, we found our way out of the city, stopping every now and then to check, turning round when we'd gone wrong. All the time I was listening out for sirens, checking in the wing mirror for cars behind. When I finally got where we were on the map, I held my finger there, moving it along as we travelled.

In Basingstoke, we pulled off the ring road and found a quiet street. Spider got out and took a leak, and then we had a sort of picnic in the car: sandwiches, crisps, Coke.

'I reckon we should ditch this car. It's too hot, every pig in the country's going to be looking for it,' Spider said through a mouthful of food, little bits of crisp spraying all around him.

I felt a twinge of regret. 'I kind of like it.'

'Yeah, I know, but they'll pick us up tonight or tomorrow unless we switch. Why don't we find somewhere really quiet and get some kip, then swap cars early in the morning. I'm done in.'

We drove around until we found a country lane, without streetlights. We pulled into a sort of lay-by, turned the engine off and killed the lights. It was pitch black, unnatural.

'I don't like this, Spider. It's too bloody dark. Let's find somewhere with some streetlights. This is too weird.'

'No, man. If it's light, people will see. We won't last five minutes. You won't notice the difference when you've got your eyes shut. Look, climb in the back, and lie down, you'll be all right there.'

'Where are you going?'

'Nowhere – I'll kip here.' His long limbs only just fitted in to the front, his head was brushing the ceiling.

'No, I'm all right here, I can tip the seat back. You get in the back, bit more space for you.'

So much for old-fashioned gallantry. He agreed straight away, and got out of the driver's door and into the back. He leaned over and rummaged about in the boot, then passed a blanket over to me.

I wrapped it round my shoulders and wriggled down, trying to make myself comfortable. I closed my eyes, but all I could see were the images from the TV: the space where the pod used to be on the Eye, bits of blue anorak, a shredded straw bag. I could see the queue again, those faces looking at me. I opened my eyes, but there was no relief, nothing to focus on, just the wretched blackness of a country lane. The darkness was so dense, there could be anything out there. There could be a bloody great bloke with a knife just a couple of metres from the car, and we wouldn't see him until he loomed up, pressed his hands and face against the windows, grotesquely distorted, yanked open the doors and . . .

'You awake, Spider?'

'Yeah.' I could hear him shifting around. 'I'm so knack-ered, but I can't sleep. My brain won't switch off, it's like I'm wired.'

'I'm scared. I don't like it here.'

I felt his hand reach round the side of my seat, patting my arm. I got my hand out of the blanket and intertwined my fingers with his. His hand felt like it was twice the size of mine – long fingers and knobbly knuckles. He gently stroked the base of my thumb with his, soothing me without words. I guess I must have nodded off, because the next thing I knew a grey, silvery light was filling the car through fogged-up windows, and Spider was getting into the driving seat.

'Time to go, Jem. We'll find some nice wheels and get some miles behind us before everyone wakes up.'

He turned the car around and we headed back to the suburbs of the sleeping town. I was flung forward as he slammed the brakes on suddenly. A fox was crossing the road in front of us, a big bugger. Spider smiled as it melted away into a hedge.

'Glad I didn't hit him. He's the same as us, Jem. A thief, out and about, nice and early. Respect, Mister Fox.'

We carried on, soon finding some quiet suburban streets full of parked cars. Despite it being God knows what time, Spider was wide awake, his eyes flicking along the rows of cars, sussing things out. After a bit, he pulled up and nodded towards the other side of the road, where a big estate car was parked up.

'That's the one, Jem. Get all the stuff in the bags. Let's do this quickly, and no noise.' He held his long, bony index finger up to his mouth, and winked. He was loving this.

Chapter 13

'Stay here, I'll just suss it out.'

Spider swung out of the car and darted across the road. He did a quick tour round the estate car and came back.

'Yeah, that's fine. No crook lock or nothing. Get all the stuff together, blankets and everything.'

'Just a minute.' I reached into the glove compartment and pulled out the letter to McNulty. I scrabbled about for a pen, and found an old pencil stub. In the smallest print I could manage, I wrote in the corner of the letter: *The end – 25122023.* A parting gift to the cruel bastard.

'What the hell are you doing?' Spider hissed at me. 'We've got to go before those net curtains start twitching. Come on!'

I dropped the letter onto the floor, gathered up my stuff and got out of the car. Spider was already at the driver's door of the new one, fiddling at the lock with some sort of tool. It gave a satisfying click, and he got in and opened the passenger door. I went round, chucked all the stuff onto the back seat and got in quickly, trying not to make too much noise as I shut the door. Spider was doing his thing under the steering column, and soon the engine sparked into life, and we were off, easing through the sleepy streets, nice and quiet.

It took us ages to get out of Basingstoke. What a complete nightmare, like they'd designed the roads to keep you trapped there forever. We drove round in bloody circles for about twenty minutes, until I spotted a sign for Andover – I'd seen on the map that that was one of the next towns west. As we headed away, Spider heaved a sigh of relief. 'Reckon they should bomb bloody Basingstoke, leave London alone.'

Even at half six there were plenty of cars around.

'Try the radio, see what's happening,' Spider said.

I didn't want to know, kind of wanted the outside world to stay outside, for it just to be me and Spider in a car, travelling, but I switched the radio on anyway and pressed a few buttons randomly until I found some news.

'The death toll from the London bombing has risen to eleven overnight, with twenty-six of the injured still being treated in hospital, two of them on the critical list. Forensic experts are now engaged in a painstaking search of the site, sifting the debris for evidence of the perpetrators and for clues confirming the identity of the dead. Police are still appealing for two youths seen running from the scene minutes before the explosion to come forward, and are set to release CCTV pictures at a press conference later this morning.'

'Switch it off, Jem. Don't say nothing about the car, does it? P'raps they haven't sussed it's us yet.'

'They probably wouldn't say everything they know, though, would they? It's not going to take long, is it? Karen will have reported me missing, and they've got the CCTV . . .'

'The best thing would be to find somewhere to hide out, camp out somewhere in the woods. Wherever there are people around, it's danger for us.'

My heart sank. What the hell did either of us know about camping out? Two kids from London? 'Spider, have you been camping before?'

'Nah, but how difficult can it be? We just need enough food and water, and some blankets, find somewhere sheltered. We'll be fine – commandos, yeah?'

I laughed. 'I'm not going commando.'

'No, you retard, living off the land. Catching stuff, eating berries. We can do that.'

'We'll be in bloody hospital by tomorrow night if we're picking stuff and eating it. We'll be poisoned. If we don't freeze to death.' I looked gloomily out of the window at the alien patchwork of fields and hedges. It was about as friendly as the surface of Mars: no shops, no houses, no people, no life. True enough, London was a dump, but at least it was some sort of civilisation, not like this endless, muddy, dull green wasteland. 'Why can't we just stay in the car? Park it out of the way?'

'Yeah, maybe you're right. Listen, I think we should drive for another half-hour or something and then park up out of sight until it gets dark. We're much less likely to get spotted in the dark.'

We carried on, past bleak, rolling hills, farms here and there. Every now and again, little clusters of houses and the odd shop sprang up – they had names, but you couldn't really say they were places. There was nothing to them. Some of the houses had straw on the roofs, like it was the bloody

Dark Ages or something. It reminded me of the Three Little Pigs, one of the stories my mum read me. Stupid little pig building its house out of straw, and the big bad wolf blowing it down. The wolf ends up boiled in a pot, doesn't he, the three little pigs safe in their brick house? I don't know why they tell children all these lies. It doesn't take long to work out that in real life the wolf always comes out on top; little pigs like me and Spider don't stand a chance.

'What you thinking about?'

I came to with a start. I hadn't been asleep, just thinking so deep I wasn't there for a while.

'Pigs.'

'You seen some?' He craned behind quickly, making the car swerve over to the right.

'No. Keep your eyes on the road! You'll kill us both. Anyway, not that sort of pig – real ones, well, storybook ones, oh, never mind . . .'

There was a signpost with a picnic table on it. We turned off the road and found a big lay-by, hidden from the road. There was a lorry parked there and we pulled up behind it, and both had a swig of Coke and some biscuits. A bloke appeared from the side and walked round the back of the lorry. He stopped to light a fag, then checked the fastenings on his wagon were done up. All the while I could see he was looking at us. He was pretending he wasn't, but you know, don't you, when someone's staring at one thing but looking out of the corner of their eye at something else? Instinctively, I slouched down in my seat as I watched him walk round to the cab door and haul himself up.

'Can you see him?'

Spider picked a bit of biscuit out of his teeth. 'What, that driver?'

'Yeah, can you see him in his cab?'

'Just in his wing mirror. Why?'

'What's he doing?'

'He's got a fag on and he's talking into a little radio thing.'

My skin was pricking all over. 'He's spotted us, Spider. He's ringing the police.'

'Nah, don't be daft. These lorry drivers talk to each other all the time.'

'But what if he is? What do we do?'

'We need to dump this car, get another one. Let's get out of here, anyway.' He started the engine and slipped easily through the gears as he accelerated away and back onto the main road – he was getting the hang of driving.

I looked behind. Way back, the lorry was lumbering along, following us.

When you looked, there were lorries everywhere – one a couple of vehicles ahead of us, and, every minute or so, one coming the other way. If he had spotted us, and had told all his mates, we were completely stuffed. They'd be able to trace our every movement. A truck was heading towards us, and as I looked into the cab, the driver met my eyes – just for a moment – and looked away. He had a headset on, and was talking as he passed us.

'Spider, we've gotta get out. They're on to us. That lorry just now, he looked at me. Did you see?'

'Nah, man, I'm keeping my eyes on the road, like you said.'

'Watch the next one.'

Another couple of minutes and another lorry approached. The driver definitely clocked us. Spider saw it too.

He cursed and swung into the next side road, steaming along a narrow lane. I was holding on to the door with one

hand and the dashboard with the other, praying we would-
n't meet something coming the other way. He slowed down
and eventually pulled up at a place where a little lane, not
wide enough for a car, met our road.

There was a signpost, a green one, saying *Footpath*. My
heart sank.

'Gather up the stuff, we're going to have to leg it.'

'No way. Where to? How . . . ?'

'We'll just take our stuff, go up this track, walk a few
miles, find somewhere to kip down, and I'll get some more
wheels as soon as I can. Nick something from a farm. Come
on, get the stuff together.'

We bundled everything we could into some plastic bags. I
frantically flicked through the map book, and tore out the
pages showing where we were now and all the places between
us and Weston.

'Yeah, good thinking, that's the girl.' Again, you could tell
Spider was buzzing with adrenalin. I guess I was too, but it
was like two sides of the same coin. He was excited, enjoying the adventure, I was eaten up with fear – they were closing in on us.

We couldn't get everything in the bags. I put the coat on,
easier than carrying it, and Spider draped a blanket round
his shoulders; then, with a backward glance to the car, we
started up the lane. God knows what we looked like – a pair
of dossers, I suppose. We weren't like hikers with rucksacks
and walking boots, just ordinary kids with plastic bags, and
a touch of the charity shop about us.

The bags were a bloody nuisance. One of them kept
bumping my leg, no matter what I did. I tried turning it
round, swapping hands, nothing worked. Bump, bump,
bump. The plastic cut into my hands, a cruel nagging pain.

And my feet and legs were all over the place. The track was so uneven; there were two deep ruts made up of stones, big ones and small ones, and a hump of grass in the middle, but all different levels. I started off walking in one of the dips, but my ankle was turning over on the stones, so I switched to the grassy bit. That was okay until it suddenly decided to slope or there was a hole or whatever, and then my ankle would go again. And all the time, bump, bump, bump, the bloody shopping bag. I got so sensitive to it, it felt like a sledgehammer hitting the side of my knee.

After going on like this for half the morning, I stopped and dropped both bags. I turned my hands over to look at the palms; they were bright red, criss-crossed with fat white lines where the bags had cut in. Spider carried on, oblivious. It was like he was listening to music; he was walking along to his own rhythm, nodding his head, his legs kind of springy – but, of course, he wasn't, unless it was just in his own head. After a few seconds, he realised I wasn't following and turned round.

'What's up?'

'I can't go on any further. I've had it. Can we stop for a rest?'

He looked at his watch. 'We've been walking for six minutes. If you went back to that bend, you'd still be able to see the car.'

I kicked one of the bags. 'I can't do it! I don't like walking!'

'We walk miles in London, along the canal and the streets. Miles, man. You can do this.'

'Yeah, but that's London, civilisation. They've got pavements and tarmac there. This is crap! My ankles hurt. And these stupid bags keep banging against my leg, and look at my hands!' I held them up towards him.

'Look,' he said patiently, 'we need to get as far away from that car as we can, find somewhere to hide out. Why don't we follow this path for an hour and see where we get to?'

'You're not listening to me! I CAN'T DO IT!' I let out a scream of frustration; I may even have stamped my feet. Then I picked up one of the bags with both hands and flung it. It sailed gracefully through the air and lodged in the top of a hedge, about two metres up.

Spider lurched over to me and put his hand over my mouth. 'Shh! You'll have them all running here, you divvy.' There was light dancing in his eyes, a broad grin on his face. He was laughing at me.

He was laughing.

At.

Me.

I went ballistic, lashing out with fists and feet, screeching and grunting. 'Don't you ever laugh at me! Don't you ever . . . !'

Instead of backing away or hitting back, he got his arms and legs round me, and kind of wrapped me up, and squeezed. My arms were held down by my side, my legs had nowhere to go. I was held in close, my face pressed into the smelly place under his arms, and he sort of sapped the fury out of me. I could feel it going, feel my body relaxing. His chin was resting on the top of my head, and we stood there for a bit, just breathing.

'You all right now?' he said after a while.

'No.' But I was, or at least I was better.

Spider released me and went to fish the bag out of the hedge. 'Let's have a bit of chocolate and press on. I'll carry your bags.'

I couldn't let him do that – I mean, I have got some pride.

'Piss off, I can carry my own bags.'

'Yeah, right.'

In the end we compromised and he carried the awkward one, and we set off again, up the track, as a soft yellow light filtered through the branches and leaves above us, and the sound of sirens drifted over from the main road.

Chapter 14

The lane ended with a gate and a stile. We put our bags down, leaned on the gate and peered over. The path seemed to go straight on, through the middle of a field. It dipped down, so you couldn't see the other side, but rising up beyond it were more and more fields, as far as you could see. I had never seen such a godforsaken picture of nothingness.

'Where the hell are we going?' I asked.

Spider shrugged. 'Away from the car we just dumped. Anywhere.'

'We can't go across there,' I nodded my head towards the rural wasteland.

'Why not?'

'Look at it, soft git! There's no trees, no hedges. Everyone for fifty miles around will be able to see us.'

'D'you wanna go back? Sit in the car till they find us, haul us out and spread-eagle us on the floor with a gun in the back of our necks?'

'What do you mean, a gun . . . ?'

'They think we're terrorists.'

I leaned my head on my arms and shut my eyes. I didn't know what I'd imagined being a runaway would be like, but this wasn't it. I felt so tired, an aching tiredness creeping through my arms and legs.

'Can't we just stay here for a while?' I said, my head still down, my voice muffled by my sleeves.

Spider shook his head. 'It's too close to the car. We've got to get further away.' He paused. 'Look, there's a clump of trees at the top there. We could get over to that, and then hide out until it starts to get dark.'

I looked up. There was a dark smudge hugging the curve of a hill about twenty miles away.

'What, that? Over there?'

He nodded. 'Yeah, take us half an hour, forty minutes tops. We can do it.' He got hold of all the bags and lifted them over the stile, then stepped over himself, his long legs making short work of it.

I sighed and followed. The wooden step wobbled when I put my weight on it, and I let out a squeal. Spider laughed and put his hand out to steady me. I grabbed hold and swung my leg over, then let go, swivelled round and gripped the top of a wooden fence post as I brought my other leg over. With my bum in the air, the bloody step felt like it was going to give way, and there was something squishy on my hand. I let go of the post and realised I'd put my hand on some bird shit.

'Bloody hell!' I could hear Spider laughing out loud behind me. 'It's not funny, I've got shit on me now!' I reached down with one leg, feeling for the ground with my foot. When I was finally on solid ground, I turned round to see Spider doubled up, laughing his guts out. 'What?'

'I've never seen anything so funny in my life! You're brilliant.'

'Piss off!' I made to wipe my hand on him, but he ducked away. I chased him around the bags for a bit, before he managed to grab my wrist and pull me down to the ground to forcibly rub my hand on a clump of grass. Most of the stuff came off, and I wiped the rest on my trousers. We sat apart from each other. My chest was heaving from the exertion, my lungs sucking in the air in great gulps, until gradually my body calmed down and my breathing got back to normal.

Spider rooted in one of the bags and swigged at a bottle of Coke, then passed it to me. It was warm, and a bit flat, but it tasted like nectar. Then we gathered up the bags and set off along the path, out into No Man's Land.

You wouldn't believe how uncomfortable I felt walking into that field. After all Spider's talk of guns, I kept thinking of the space between my shoulder blades, just waiting for a sniper to put a bullet there. The further we walked away from the stile, the more exposed I felt. I couldn't have felt more vulnerable if I'd been walking along that path stark naked. There was nothing around us, just grass and sky, more sky than I'd ever seen before, an obscene amount of sky. You don't realise in a city how much space buildings take up. When you take them away, there's just sky, huge and empty. There's nothing between the top of your head and deep space, and it's only gravity stopping you from drifting up and up, away from the earth. I was thoroughly freaked out. The only way I could tackle it was to look down at the path and put one foot in front of the other.

In front of me, Spider loped along with his familiar springy stride. I found myself studying the way he moved, his long legs going all the way up to his skinny arse. He'd always seemed so restless at school and round the estate, like it was difficult to contain his energy within those walls, those streets and buildings. Here, his legs seemed to eat up the miles. This tall black guy from London looked almost at home here. It was the right scale for him.

Not like me. Where he sprang along, I plodded, my head full of *I can't . . . I don't want to . . . I hate this*. As soon as we'd reached the top of one slope and I thought we were near the cover Spider had spotted, another hill rose up. They were like waves, stretching back as far as you could see.

Eventually we were walking along the edge of one field, with thick trees lining the other side of the path. There was the sound of water, and Spider stopped and put his bags down.

'Wait here a minute,' he said, took a quick run up, and vaulted over the barbed-wire fence.

'What are you doing?' I shouted, but he didn't reply, so I was left standing there like a prat. I sat down, facing the way we'd just come. If I saw people following us, what would I do? I didn't have time to think of an answer because Spider was soon back, looking smug.

'There's a slope and then a river, Jem. This is good news for us. We just need to wade along it for a bit, and then if they've got dogs they won't find us. They'll lose the scent. I've seen it in films.'

Well, I'd seen it in films too, but did that mean anything? There was no stopping him, though.

'Here, chuck those bags over, and then I'll help you.' I heaved them over to him, and then looked at the fence.

'I don't know . . .' I said, dubiously.

'Come here, put one foot on the wire, and your hand on

the fence post and then spring up. I'll get you.'

With no better idea, I just did as I was told. The wire bent under my weight, but I thought, *What the hell*, and tried to climb up. At that moment, Spider reached over and grabbed me under my arms and lifted me right over, plonking me down safely on the other side. We smiled and high-fived each other. Then we gathered up the bags and set off through the trees.

The ground dipped sharply down. Sure enough, there was a river at the bottom, only about four or five metres wide, fast-flowing and muddy.

'How deep is it?' I asked.

'Dunno, only one way to find out. Why don't we chuck the bags over to the other bank and then I'll go in, test it out?'

'Why don't you test it out first? If it's too deep, we can't get across, can we? So there'll be no point having the bags over there.'

'Jem,' he said, seriously, 'I think we have to get across. I don't think we've got an option. It'll be okay, I promise.' He picked up the first carrier bag, tied the handles together and started swinging it backwards and forwards, then with a bit of a grunt, let go. It sailed over the water and landed on the other side. He grinned, and set to work on the others. It was okay until the last one. He didn't quite get it together and it went too far up in the air and then straight down into the river.

'Bollocks!' he said and sat down, frantically scrabbling at his trainers and socks. He rolled up his jeans and then kind of slid down the bank and into the water. 'Jesus!' he screamed, voice high like a girl's. 'It's like ice!'

The bag had floated downstream about ten metres and got

stuck on something over near the other bank. He started wading towards it, the water just up to his knees. 'Chuck my trainers over to the other side and then do yours. You can come across, it's freezing, but it's okay,' he shouted.

I stuffed his socks into his shoes and lobbed them over, one after the other. Spider was making his way towards the bag. I crouched down to take my shoes off.

'Whoa!' Spider was halfway across the river, flailing his arms about. 'It's a bit slippy, you have to be careful,' he called.

'Okay,' I yelled back, and went back to unpicking the knot my laces had got into. Spider was splashing about, swearing, like normal, but I wasn't watching him. Finally, shoes and socks off, I stood up to throw them across. The plastic bag was still there, bobbing about as the water tried to pull it away from whatever was snagging it. But Spider wasn't. He'd disappeared.

Chapter 15

I looked up and down the other bank. Nothing. My eyes scanned the surface of the water – there was no sign of him. The unreality of it was overwhelming. I felt like something in my brain had slipped and shifted: I was alone, Spider had never existed, because if he had, how could he have disappeared like that?

Suddenly, away to my left, there was an extra movement in the swirling water. Something broke the surface – a knee, an elbow or something. Spider was thirty metres away already, being swept along in the current. I started running down the bank. Different bits of him were visible as the water turned him around like a rag doll – his arm, his back, the back of his head – but not his face. His face stayed underwater.

I was panicking, running as fast as I could. Branches along the bank whipped me as I ducked and dived my way through. I got level with him, screaming and running at the same time. He couldn't hear me. I looked wildly around for something to reach him with. I pulled at a long branch, trying to break it off, but I wasn't strong enough. He was away from me again. The thought of him helpless, breathing in water, made my own breath nearly stop. This wasn't meant to happen. His number, 15122009, it wasn't for a week yet. What the hell was going on? I started running again.

I got ten, fifteen metres ahead of him. There was no-one about. No-one and nothing to help us. I had no choice now. I plunged down the bank and into the water. It wasn't just the cold that shocked me, it was the strength of it. The river buffeted at my legs with terrifying force. It was only up to my thighs, but it was all I could do to stay on my feet. Down at that level, it was more difficult to see where Spider was. I searched the water frantically, and at last got a glimpse of a dark shape heading towards me. He was going to pass to my left; I had to go towards the other side or he'd slip right past me. I started wading across, but the water was getting deeper. I was so slow, grunting with frustration. Spider was only a few metres away now – damn it, I was going to miss him. I lunged forward. I was there, but my feet were on slime, and as Spider's body came barrelling into me, I lost my footing and went down into the water too.

Everything was mixed up now – up and down, water and air, Spider and me. Even as I thrashed around, I held on to his hoodie. Whatever happened to us now, it was going to happen to us together – I wasn't going to let go of him for anything. When my face broke the surface I gulped down some air. I kicked my feet around, desperately trying to find the river bottom, but the current was relentless. Spider was like a dead weight, bumping into me, pushing me under. I wanted to sort him out, get his head above water, but it was hopeless. It was all I could do to find some air myself. Still holding Spider, I got on to my back, so that my face was upwards. I tried to flip him over too, but I couldn't manage to. We were carried downstream, round a couple of bends. I was just wondering if we were going to carry on like this until we got to the sea when there was a sickening scraping feeling down my back, and I jarred suddenly to a stop. The jolt made me lose my grip on Spider for a second, but I grabbed him again.

We'd both stopped moving. The river carried on around us, but we were wedged on some sort of stony bar, sticking out from one bank into the river. Spider was lying face down on top of my legs. I hauled him off me and over onto his back, then gripped him under his armpits and pulled him up the spit and out of the water. He was heavy, a lifeless weight. I knelt next to him, looking at him with disbelief. His eyes were shut. He was gone.

This was all wrong – so, so wrong. It wasn't meant to be like this.

'Spider, wake up!' I yelled. 'Wake up!' Nothing. 'Wake up! You can't fucking leave me! You can't do this!' I brought my fist down on his chest in sheer frustration. His mouth fell open and water trickled out.

I drew myself up, leaned over him and pushed both my palms hard down into his stomach. More water came out. I did it again. And again. And again. Suddenly, a plume of water spurted out of him, like a whale's spout, and he made the most godawful noise I'd ever heard as he drew a massive breath into his waterlogged body.

I'd sprung away from him with the surprise of the water, and I just sat back on my heels for a while, watching his chest rise and fall on its own. He opened his eyes and seemed to be trying to focus, then he said, 'What you crying for? What's up with you?'

I hadn't realised I was crying, but when I wiped my hand across my face there were hot tears and snot there.

'Nothing,' I said. 'I'm happy.'

He closed his eyes and opened them again. 'I don't get it. What's going on?'

'You fell in the water. I got you out.'

'Right,' he said, 'that's why I'm all cold and wet then. I don't remember a thing. I thought we were walking through a field and then suddenly I'm flat on my back, soaking wet and you're crying – sorry, happy.' He started to sit up, looking about him like he'd just landed from another planet. 'Here, you're all wet too,' he said, then a big grin slowly spread across his face. 'You didn't give me the kiss of life, did you?'

'No. Shut up.'

'You did, didn't you?'

'No! I squashed your stomach down until the water came out, but I wish I hadn't now, you bloody moron.'

He reached over to me and ran his hand over my shaved head, the smile fading away as the situation sunk in. 'You saved me. You saved my life. Jesus, Jem, I owe you big time, man.'

I shrugged him off.

'Forget about it. I just did what anyone would've.'

'There isn't anyone else here, though, is there? There was only you. Only you could've saved me. And you did.'

'Just leave it, all right? It's not a big deal. Look, at least we're on the right side of the river now. We just need to walk back to our stuff. Get some dry clothes. I'm fucking freezing.' It was true. I was shivering violently, and so was Spider.

We helped each other to our feet, staggered up the bank and trudged upstream again. Spider was in front, like usual, but he kept stopping and looking back at me, then smiling, shaking his head and carrying on. And all the time my mind was racing ten to the dozen. So, the numbers were right, after all. It wasn't his day today. But if I hadn't been there, surely he would have drowned – he was nearly dead when I dragged him out of the water. Spider knew it: I had saved him. I'd kept him alive.

My head was spinning now. What if he'd been meant to die today, but I'd made things turn out different? For the last couple of weeks, I'd felt guilty about the old tramp. I'd never meant to hurt him, but there was no escaping it: it felt like we'd chased him into the road. But perhaps the numbers were a two-edged sword. What if I didn't just have a hand in causing death – what if I could save lives too? And if I had saved Spider today, could I save him on the fifteenth?

Chapter 16

Our bags were still lying where we'd chucked them. Spider fished out the one in the river with a branch, and we both found some dry clothes, turning our backs on each other while we got changed. I was too cold – almost panicky cold – to worry if he was peeking, and too busy getting myself dry to think of sneaking a peek at him. In the hurry to leave, I hadn't got any spare underwear from Val – frankly I didn't want to think about what she might wear under her clothes – so I kept my soggy bra and knickers on and just changed my jeans and top. I put on as many dry layers as I could find, with Val's coat on top, and we bundled our wet clothes together in one bag and set off again – cold, shocked and shivering.

Walking away from the river, we hit a series of rolling hills. They rippled like waves as far as you could see. Our adventure in the river had left me feeling dog-tired. My legs felt like lead as we trudged along. Not surprisingly, a bit of the spring had gone out of Spider's step too.

We were still aiming for a little knot of trees on top of a hill. I was beginning to think they were like one of those mirage things in the desert, disappearing just when you got near them, but eventually Spider got to the top of one hill and gave a little shout, 'Hey, we're here!' – and amazingly, we were. We scrambled down the other side and up the last rise, and into the relative cover of a little clump of woodland.

I sank down at the edge of the trees, and looked back at the way we'd come. I couldn't believe it was so far. 'Look how far we've walked! No wonder I'm knackered.' I flopped backwards, not caring what I was lying on.

'If we can see all of that, anyone there could see us. Let's go further in.' I didn't know what was happening to Spider. It was like he'd suddenly swallowed a sensible pill or something.

I groaned, struggled to my feet again and followed him into the middle of the wood. He'd gathered up all the bags and found a place between four tree trunks to settle down. Although you could still see out to the fields when you stood up, when you were sitting down the plants and bushes blotted it all out. We were hidden.

The ground was hard and uneven. Spider had spread out the blanket he'd been carrying. You could still feel lumps and bumps underneath you, but it softened it a bit.

Spider was sitting propped up against a tree trunk, but I lay down flat and looked up at the trees above me. It was weird. Although I knew the trunks were pretty straight, they looked like they were bending together over me as they stretched up into the sky. Their leaves were black against the brightness, making a lacy pattern, almost too complicated to look at. It was like they were hypnotic. If you let yourself go, you started to get all mixed up in your head, and you could imagine that you were high up, looking down hundreds of feet to the leaves below you. The wind was swooshing through the branches, making this amazing spaced-out sound – it could have been wind or water or even traffic – really soothing.

'I can't believe we just did that,' I said after a while.

'What?'

'Walked all that way.'

Spider snorted. 'Yeah, it's pretty cool what you can do when you have to. Perhaps we'll walk all the way to Weston.'

'How far's that?'

'Haven't got a clue. A long way, man.'

I groaned again, and shut my eyes, and let my mind focus on the noise, only the noise . . .

When I woke up, my head was aching and my mouth felt disgusting – dry inside and sticky round my lips. I had to struggle to remember where I was, and even when I sat up and looked around I wasn't sure if it was morning or evening. My watch said five past four, which I guessed was the end of the afternoon, but it could have been the next morning, I just didn't know. Spider was snoring away with his back to me, curled up like a baby. I could see the side of his face. Asleep, you could imagine him as a child – he was peaceful, kind of innocent. Just for a minute, I tested out the feeling: what it might be like to be someone's mum. It made me feel scared – there was no way that was for me. I could never handle that much responsibility, and besides, how could I ever look a child – my own child – in the face and see their death before they'd even begun? Some people aren't cut out for all that. I was one of them. No big deal.

I rubbed my eyes and my forehead, but the pain in my head carried on throbbing. I reached across and dug into the bags, looking for something to drink. The Coke was welcome, but I wished we'd got something hot to drink – a nice cup of tea or some hot chocolate. Something comforting. Spider must have heard me rummaging about in the plastic bags because he unwound and turned over.

'What time is it?'

'Just gone four.'

'God, we've slept the day away.' He sat up slowly. 'I feel rough.'

I passed the Coke over. 'We've not really been eating and drinking today.'

He took a long swig. 'Aah, that's better. Any sign they're following us?'

'Dunno, I can't hear anything.'

'We'll have a look in a minute. Let's have some food, then.' Once again, we delved into the bags and munched our way through crisps, crackers, biscuits and chocolate.

Spider stood up as he was eating, and walked around our little woodland, up to the edge on one side, and then across the middle to pick up another biscuit, and on to the other side. 'I can't see anything,' he said, chewing and talking at the same time. 'I was thinking we should walk on a bit further, but it's going to be dark soon. I think we should rest up here, set off early tomorrow.'

I wasn't going to argue with that. I didn't mind if I never walked anywhere ever again.

Having decided we were going to stay put, we were suddenly faced with twelve hours of nothing to do. It became impossible to relax, to sit still, and there was no question of sleeping. We both wandered around the wood for a bit, looked out at the view from various points. I stood for a long time watching banks of cloud roll across. They seemed to move so slowly, but if you fixed your eyes on one, then looked away for a few seconds, it had gone further than you thought. Bit like us, walking through the fields, going so slowly, like a pair of bugs crawling on the surface of the planet, and then looking back to find we'd covered miles.

'I've never seen so much sky,' I said. 'It did my head in, walking out in the fields with all that sky above us.'

'It's good when you get used to it. There's so much air, you can fill your lungs with it over and over again.' Spider flung his arms out wide. 'It's like this at the seaside. Great flat beach, and sea and sky. You'll love it, Jem.' He turned round to face me. 'We'll find a B&B, and have fish and chips every day. We can walk along the pier, write things on the sand, just have a laugh.'

He started clambering up a tree, but didn't get very far before his feet slipped down. He tried again, with the same result. The light was going from the sky, like the colour was being sucked out of it. The air temperature was dropping even further too.

'It's going to be dark soon,' I said with a shiver. 'What do we do then?'

'We'll just have to go to sleep.'

'It's only half past four.'

'I know, man, but what are you gonna do? Watch telly?'

The reality of it was dragging me down. I started thinking about the cold, the blackness. I didn't want to be out there in the dark. It had been bad enough in the car, but at least we had had four metal walls and a roof.

'Let's not stay here, Spider. Let's try and find somewhere else.'

'We haven't got time, mate. Can you see anywhere? It would take hours to find somewhere, and we'd be walking in the dark. We haven't even got a torch.'

Around us, the world was going from colour to black and white. Soon it would be just black. I had no idea what went on in the countryside at night – animals? – people with guns out hunting? – and I didn't want to find out. I was starting to lose it.

'Why haven't we got a torch? Why?! Wasn't it just a little bit stupid to come out here without a torch?'

'Are you calling me stupid? What about you? Look in the mirror, Jem. There's two of us out here and neither of us brought a torch. It's not just me!'

We were shouting in each other's faces now. His spit sprayed my cheeks, went into my eyes, but I didn't even care. I was so mad that he'd brought me here, put me in this situation.

'I can't look in a fucking mirror, can I? There's no fucking mirror! There's no fucking anything!'

'Look, we've just got to deal with it, okay? I'll try and find us a car tomorrow, but for tonight, we're here, and that's it.'

'I don't wanna be here, don't you understand, you moron? I don't wanna be here. We don't know what we're doing! We haven't got a clue!'

'For Christ's sake! You are vexing me with your attitude.' He was right in my face, wagging a long finger in front of my eyes. 'You can't be a little girl out here! You've gotta grow up, man! What's wrong with you? You were way harder back in London. Listen, I'm walking away from you before I do something or say something.' And he stalked off, shaking his head and flapping his hands about.

'Yeah, just fuck off!'

'You fuck off!' he shouted without turning round.

Of course, there was nowhere to go. We were stuck on a

tiny island. I could still see him, an agitated cartoon, silhou-etted against the inky sky. I wanted to scream, *Don't you fucking walk away from me!* but I bit my lip, tried to calm myself down, tried to disentangle the angry thoughts in my head and think straight. Whichever way you looked at it, we were in trouble. I went back to our camp and lay down on my side, pulling the coat over me and the blanket round me.

If I closed my eyes I saw bodies and bits: that old guy flying through the air, tattered pieces of bright blue on the ground, my mum. So I kept them open and stared at the odd pattern of branches, twigs and leaves at ground level in front of my eyes. I watched a bug of some kind struggle up the stem of a plant and totter about at the end, the little leaves bending under its weight. My skin started to itch at the thought of bugs and spiders crawling all over me all night. God, the countryside was disgusting.

I heard Spider crunch back through the undergrowth, then plonk himself down nearby and rummage in the bags. He had obviously fetched out another blanket because I could hear him shifting around where he sat, trying to get comfortable, then more rummaging, and the sound of some-thing scraping, something metallic.

I thought, *I'm not going to talk to him, he can do what the hell he likes, I don't care*, but every fibre of me was tuned in to him now, trying to work out what he was up to. After a gap, there was the unmistakable flick of a lighter and a little glow in the gloom. A tiny crackle as his fag took, and then a long breath out and a gentle sigh of satisfaction.

I sat up, and his voice said, 'I knew you weren't asleep. Here, do you want a drag?' The glowing tip of the cigarette moved towards me as he held it out. I took it and inhaled. There was something reassuring about the smoke – it felt normal, familiar, comforting.

'Sweet,' I said, but I didn't really mean the fag, welcome though it was – it just felt good to re-establish a connection. The way I saw it, we couldn't really afford to fall out.

We passed the fag between us for a while, not speaking much, just being in the moment. Then Spider said, 'Do you think there are any black farmers?'

'I dunno, shouldn't think so. Why?'

'I like this place. I like the feel of it under my feet. I like looking for miles.'

All this, based on one day, walking across some fields. 'Come on, Spider, that's not going to happen.'

'Why not? Do you need GCSEs to be a farmer? Do you need a degree? Do you need to be white?'

'I dunno, I dunno. I guess you need money, though. Loads of money.'

'I wouldn't have to buy a farm, just work on one. I don't think running around for Baz or anyone like him is much of a career. I don't wanna do that stuff. I need to find something else.' His voice was passionate in the dark. 'I've got out now. *We've* got out. I don't wanna go back. Wherever we end up, I want to start a new sort of life, not fall back into my old ways.'

What he was saying, it touched me. He was speaking from the heart.

'The Nutter was right, you know,' he continued.

'No way!'

'No, he was right. People like you and me, we've got the future all mapped out from the time we're born. Dole queue, checkout, building site, street. No future at all. I don't wanna be like that.'

'You going to go back to school, get your GCSEs?' I asked,

not believing it for a minute.

'Nah, think I've left it a bit late for that. But I want to do something. I want to be different. I don't want to be no cliché black boy, a statistic.'

The knot which had been forming in my stomach as he spoke gave a lurch, and tightened to a physical pain. It was breaking my heart to hear him talk about the future. How could I sit there and listen to him, to the boy with only a week left? What he was saying, it was right, it was inspirational. But it was way too late. If the numbers were right. If . . .

I knew I was on the edge of blabbing. I wanted to tell him everything – to share it, maybe work out how to change it. But you can't do that, can you? I could never tell someone their number, except bastards like McNulty, and he was probably too stupid to work out what it meant. I swallowed hard, trying to get back in control of my emotions. Change the subject, fill the void with words.

'How come you ended up living with your nan? Do you mind me asking?'

'Nah, man. No big secret. My mum pissed off with some bloke when I was still a baby. Don't even remember her. Don't reckon I missed out on anything – I've always had Nan.'

'She's cool, your nan.'

'Yeah. Daft old bitch.'

'Do you think you should call her? Let her know you're all right?'

'Nah, it's not safe to phone. They can trace them, you know. Nan'll be all right. She'll be cool.'

A picture of her standing by the side of the road as we left – was it only yesterday afternoon? – flashed into my head.

'I heard you tell Nan about your mum,' Spider said quietly. 'I'm sorry, and that.'

'Not your fault.'

'I know, but . . .'

'Probably better off without her. She was . . . complicated.' I lapsed into silence. I was a liar, and I knew it. Whatever life I would have had with her, I would rather have had that – had some sort of home – than the gypsy life I'd had since she died. Nobody's child.

We talked on and off for hours. Our voices sounded thin in the open air, but as long as we kept going, they fended off the unknown ghosts and monsters waiting out there, in the acres of dark stretching away in every direction. The gaps between conversations got bigger as we started to drift in and out of consciousness.

I reckon I was pretty deep under when an almighty screech woke me with a start. I opened my eyes, but there was little difference: open or closed, it was pitch black.

'Did you hear that?' I whispered.

'You'd have to be dead not to hear that.' Whatever it was went off again, a high-pitched screaming noise tearing into the night, so loud it felt like it was all around us, on us, in us. I was wide awake, too scared to move. Spider shifted nearer, I could hear him squirming through the leaves and stuff on the ground, smell him getting closer.

'What do you think it is?' he said in a low voice, very near to my ear.

'I don't know.'

'Do you believe in witches?'

'Shut up!' Yeah, right then I believed in witches. And ghosts and werewolves and all the other things that go bump in the night.

Another bloodcurdling screech, this time followed by a couple of loud hoots.

'It's an owl, Jem. I've never heard one before. Noisy buggers, aren't they? Where's a stone or something?' He sat up and rummaged around next to him, then stood up and launched something up into the trees above us. I could hear it clipping the leaves and branches. A few seconds later the screeching set up again, but grew fainter and fainter as the owl went off looking for somewhere less dangerous to perch.

'You're a true countryman, aren't you? Chucking stones at an owl.'

'Too right, they're always shooting something or setting their dogs on it, ripping something to shreds. I reckon I'd fit right in.'

The owl was still protesting, but a long way away now. Its voice seemed to emphasise how alone we were, the dark space all around us. As we listened, I felt the cold taking hold of me. We might manage one night out here, but we'd have to find something else tomorrow.

I was so awake now that sleep was out of the question. All I could do was lie there and listen and try not to think too much.

I thought Spider was asleep, but after a while I felt his hand inching over my blanket until he found mine. And we lay there, hand in hand, waiting for the light to creep back into the sky. And we were both awake when we heard a new sound thudding through the heavy night air – a helicopter.

Chapter 17

'Can you hear that?' I asked. Stupid question.

'Mm.'

'Do you think it's just a helicopter?'

He knew what I meant. Just a helicopter taking someone somewhere, going from A to B. 'I dunno.'

He moved away from me, crawling through the undergrowth. It was still dark, but there was a hint of blueness in the sky when we looked back the way we'd come yesterday. It was over there that the noise was coming from.

'It's just hovering there, Jem. Shining a light down. There's other lights too.' I could hear him worming his way back to me, then he was there, right beside me, rolling up his blankets. 'Come on, Jem. We've got to get a move on. Looks like they're on to us.'

'Spider, it's dark. We haven't got a torch, remember?'

'We'll just have to do our best. Better to move in the dark anyway.'

'Yes, but . . .' I was going to point out the mud, the fences, the barbed wire, but another noise cut in then. The sound of a dog barking. It was coming from behind us too. Lights, helicopters, dogs. I had a sick feeling in my stomach. This was a proper manhunt. I shut up and started bundling up my belongings.

We blundered out of the trees and set off down the hill. You couldn't see where you were putting your feet, and the ground was so rough we both kept stumbling and tripping. I put my right foot into a dip and staggered forward. I dropped my bags and flailed my arms blindly, trying to rescue my balance. My right hand found something to grab onto, but it dug into me as it moved under my grip, and I still fell forward. Something ripped across my face as I sank down onto the ground and let out a string of curses.

'Where are you?' Spider's voice came through the dark.

'I'm here! I don't know where I fucking am!'

'Don't move. I'm coming.'

He found his way back to me, at first nothing more than a dark shape against the darkness. As he came close, I could see his face was furrowed with concern. 'Jesus, Jem, you've fell in some barbed wire. Here . . .' He gave me his hands and pulled me up on to my feet.

I gasped and cursed again as he squeezed the wound on my right hand.

'Have you got a hanky or something?' he asked. I reached into my pocket and found an old tissue. He took it and gently wiped my face. It hurt like hell. My hand was screaming too. Spider ferreted about in a bag, pulled out one of his T-shirts and ripped a strip of it off. He wound it round my hand and tied it in a knot. He was taking charge again, doing his best, but even as he did it, my confidence was slipping away.

'We're stuffed, Spider, aren't we?'

'What do you mean?'

'They're gonna get us today. Worse now, the dogs will pick up the smell of the blood, won't they?'

'I dunno about that. I think that's sharks, the blood thing. Anyway, we've got a head start and we're the other side of the river. I reckon we should keep going, find somewhere to hide out. I think we need to be in a building, so the helicopter can't see us. They use those cameras, don't they? Pick up on your warmth, but I don't think it works through buildings. Here,' he picked up my bags, 'I'll take these. Are you okay to carry on for a bit?'

'Yeah, s'pose.'

He set off and I stuck close to him this time. It was taking ages to get light, because it was cloudy. I glanced behind me, but the top of the hill was blocking the view back. Stupid, anyway. Did I really want to see the people following us? I caught up with Spider again and we trudged across the fields.

If I'd felt exposed the day before, it was ten times worse today. If the helicopter came our way before we found somewhere to hide, we'd had it. The skin on the back of my neck was pricking, anticipating the thudding of the chopper blades getting closer and closer. We walked solidly all morning, sweating in our thick coats despite the icy wind, not speaking – there was nothing to say. We came across a couple of farms, but the buildings were all together: house, barns, sheds. Wouldn't take anyone long to search them. We needed something more remote.

It took us several hours to find a barn. It stood in the corner of a field, and was made of metal, great tall legs, a crinkly metal roof and no sides. It was on its own, beside another little knot of trees, no houses for miles. There were piles of hay stacked up like hairy yellow bricks, forming walls along two sides. Once we got nearer, we saw something else under there – a ramshackle metal fence with cows inside. They raised their heads as we approached, snorting and snuffling. I'd never been close to a cow before, only seen them on the telly – no joking, they were massive.

'No way,' I said to Spider. 'Not here. Not with those things.'

'They're behind a fence,' he said, doubtfully. I could tell he was as wary as me.

'Yeah, but look at it. It's only held together with string.'

The cows were still watching us, like they were expecting something. Then, without warning, one of them suddenly went berserk and butted into the one next to it, sending shockwaves through the lot of them, as they scattered and then regrouped.

That was it. 'We can't stay here. We'll get trampled.'

'There's nowhere else, is there, Jem? At least there's some shelter here. Look, if they get out we can climb up the hay, can't we? Cows can't climb, can they?'

'I dunno.'

We sat down on a hay bale and looked at the cows. A couple of them were still eyeballing us, but most of them had gone back to nibbling the hay. One of them lifted its tail, still eating, and a stream of brown liquid poured out. I have never seen anything so gross in my life. Instinctively, I held my hand up to cover my mouth, as my empty stomach heaved. I looked away, but Spider's jaw had dropped and he was staring at it in horror, completely mesmerised.

'That is one sick cow,' he said, eyes still on it. 'Either that or someone's been feeding it curry. Last time I had a curry, bloody hell . . .'

'Shut up!' I managed to say before the dry heaves silenced me again. Hunched up, I staggered out of the barn and stood a few metres away, bent over with my hands on my legs, trying to calm my stomach down and suck in some fresh air. After a bit, I could hear Spider walking over towards me.

'You all right?'

'No.' I felt his hand on my back. It rested there for a second then moved gently up and down, soothing me. I focused on his hand, where it touched me, and my stomach muscles gradually unwound. Even though I was feeling better, I stayed bent over for a while, not wanting to dislodge his hand. I'd never been one for physical contact, but this was comforting, warm. When I straightened up, Spider was just standing there, not looking at me but staring into the distance. He let his hand fall off my back. The wind was whipping across the fields, with a bit of an edge to it now.

'Better?' he asked, without turning his head.

'No, well, yeah.' I wanted to say thank you to him, for calming me down, making me feel better, but that would have been too soft. Instead, I followed where he was looking, back the way we'd come. 'How long do you think we've got? Before they catch up with us?'

'Dunno. I can't hear the helicopter any more.' We stood there for a bit, both straining to pick up the heavy, choppy drone. Maybe it was just the wind getting up, drowning it out, but the noise didn't seem to be there any more. I started shivering, and Spider put his arm across my shoulder.

'Come on. We'd better find the best place to hide. We need to get somewhere at the back, right behind that hay.'

Again, faced with something to do, Spider launched himself into it. Talk about bloody Action Man – he was throwing bales around, piling them up, shouting instructions at me. He was making a sort of tunnel; one minute he'd disappear, crawling on his hands and knees, the next he'd come backing out lugging another bale. Then he came out frontways, a big, stupid grin on his face.

'Here, get in.' I must have pulled a face, because he said, 'It's all right. Come on, or I'll come out and drag you in.'

I got down on my hands and knees, peered inside and then started to crawl in. It hurt when I put my hand flat on the floor, so I just leaned on the fingertips of my right hand and shuffled through as best I could. It was pretty dark inside, but not completely black, and the tunnel wasn't that long. After about five or six metres it opened out into a little room, or really a cave. There was just enough room for me and Spider to sit side by side. I couldn't see him properly, but I could smell him. The exertion of lugging the bales around, after walking for hours and the fact that he hadn't washed since God knows when – apart from a dunk in a river thick with mud – had increased the strength of his normal staleness to Olympic proportions.

'What do you reckon? Cool, isn't it? All we need to do is pull a bale across the entrance behind us and we're sitting pretty. Shall I go and do it now, see how easy it is?'

The thought of being sealed in there with him was too much. I lurched towards the tunnel again. 'No, it's all right. We can do that later, if we need to.' Emerging back into the barn, I breathed in deeply. Even the stench of the cow shit was better than Spider's rankness.

Spider crawled out of the tunnel, looking like a dog with two knobs. I didn't mean to pop his bubble, but my hand was hurting and I was tired and scared. I suppose I just said what was in my head, without stopping to think about it first.

'Spider, if they do find us here, we're stuffed, aren't we?'

His face changed instantly, like someone had switched the light off. And I hated myself for doing that to him.

'Yeah, Jem. If they find us here, we're cornered. We'll be like rats in a barrel.' He got to his feet and came and sat on a bale next to me. He leaned forward, resting his arms on his thighs, head down. His voice was low, intense. 'I won't go quietly, Jem. I'll fight them, Jem. I will.' I knew he had a knife with him. The way he was talking now, I was pretty sure he'd use it.

I could feel anxiety shooting through my veins. 'It's not worth it, Spider. If they really corner us, we should give up. What have they got on us, after all? We didn't do nothing at the Eye. They can't pin that on us. You've nicked some money, but I doubt anyone's reported that. We nicked a couple of cars. Big deal. If you start fighting – cut one of them – that's different. They'll throw the book at you.'

'Jem, whatever happens, they'll lock me up. You might be okay – you didn't nick the cars, did you? There's that knife thing at school, but little white girl like you, Karen and the Social on your side, no previous, they'll go easy on you. But they'll take one look at me – think about it, I tick all the boxes, typical young offender. They won't think twice, just chuck me inside for a few months, a year. Lost in the system.' He rubbed his hands through his hair. 'I can't do it, Jem. I don't wanna be locked up. I don't wanna be just another kid they've thrown away.' He smashed his hand down into the straw next to him. I'd heard him go off on one before, knew he could work himself up into a temper, but when I looked at him, his face was all screwed up like he was going to cry. He was angry, yeah, but he was scared too. 'I won't do it, Jem. I'd rather fight and die.'

'Don't say that, mate. Don't ever say that.' And all the time I was thinking, *Is that how it will happen?* I put my hand on his back and moved it up and down, like he'd done to me before. He was so skinny, I could feel every bone in his knobbly spine through his clothes.

He sniffed hard, wiped his sleeve across his nose. Then he sat up and looked straight at me. 'Is it today, Jem?'

I stared blankly at him, pretending I didn't know what he was asking. 'What?'

'Is today when it all ends for me? You know, don't you? Are they going to find us? Are they going to put a bullet in me like they did to that guy on the Tube?'

I felt tears pricking my eyes. 'Don't ask me, Spider. You know I can't tell you.'

'Oh Christ,' he whispered. He put both hands up to his mouth, like he was praying. He was breathing hard, eyes flicking left and right, panic in them as clear as day. It crucified me to see him like that. I couldn't let it go on, so I broke my rule.

'It's not today,' I said, quietly. 'Spider, are you listening? It's not today.'

He dropped his hands down and looked at me. His eyes were red-rimmed.

'Thank you,' he said, and he nodded. 'I shouldn't have asked, and I won't ever ask you again. I promise.' He looked like a little boy, so serious and solemn.

I wanted to put my arms round him and tell him everything was going to be okay. I suddenly thought of Val, the woman who had comforted him like that when he was little, and the words she'd said to me – was it only two days ago? – came ringing back into my head. *Take good care of him, Jem. Keep him safe.* This was all getting too much – I was in way too deep.

We ate the rest of our stuff perched on some hay bales. I turned my back on the cows, so they wouldn't put me off eating. We shared the last packet of crisps and had a chocolate bar each, and a last swig of Coke. We ate slowly, trying to make a meal out of hardly anything. As we swallowed the last mouthfuls down, we both knew. That was it. All gone. We were running out of options now. We'd have to take some action tomorrow. We had no alternative.

Once we'd eaten, there was nothing to do again. We talked a bit, but there wasn't much to say. We both knew we were in trouble, both feeling ground down by it. After a while, we crawled into Spider's hay cave, spread our blankets out and curled up a little way apart from each other.

It was dark now, really dark, but probably only about five. We lay there, talking a bit, listening to the cows. If you tried not to think about how revolting they were, how big, it was actually quite a mellow sound; you could hear them blowing air through their big hairy nostrils, moving about in the hay, munching away all the time. Every time one of them farted, Spider hooted with laughter. Easily pleased, some people.

I don't know how long we lay there. I couldn't get comfortable. The bales were quite hard underneath, and the spikes of hay were scratchy, even through the blanket. My skin, with two days' grime, was itching like mad, and so was my scalp. I felt sticky, horrible.

'I could do with a bath, or even a shower,' I said, wriggling where I lay, trying to scratch my back against the hay underneath.

'Doesn't bother me,' said Spider.

'Obviously,' I said.

'What do you mean?' he said.

'You stink, Spider. No offence, mate, but you do. And I

stink too now, and I don't wanna.'

While we'd been talking, a noise had been building up in the background. Now, in a pause, I could hear drumming on the tin roof. It was raining. The noise was incredible, water battering down on metal. I wriggled out of the tunnel and sat on a hay bale, pulling my top over my head and unbuttoning my jeans.

'What you doing?!' Spider had emerged behind me.

My jeans got stuck on my trainers. I yanked at the laces.

'I'm going to get clean. Come on, come outside.' Down to my bra and knickers. Bare feet.

I ran outside. It was lashing down. I could feel mud and crap splashing up my legs as great drops hit the ground. I didn't care. It felt fantastic. Fresh, icy pinpricks hitting my defenceless skin. I tipped my face up towards the sky, rubbed my hands over it and over my scalp, through the bristles of hair. The itchiness was going away. I smoothed the rain into my skin, all over, then stood, face up again, mouth open, catching raindrops on my tongue.

I looked across to the shed. In the gloom I could see Spider leaning against one of the metal legs, smiling and shaking his head.

'You've lost it, man,' he shouted. 'You've really lost it.'

'No,' I bellowed back. 'It's great! Come on out here!'

'Na-ah. Not me, man. I got wet enough yesterday.'

I ran over to him, laughing as my feet slipped in some mud and I almost went over. He backed away, but I grabbed his arm, then held both his hands and pulled him outside. Once he started to get wet, he gave in, started stripping off and throwing his clothes back into the barn. 'I can't believe we're doing this, it's mad!'

I ran back out, twirling round with my arms outstretched,

losing myself in the dark and the rain. Down to his pants, Spider picked his way out to me gingerly, curved over, stomach sucked in, his body trying to defend itself against the cold. He was so skinny. You could see his muscles, not because he was buff, just because there was no fat hiding them. He stood there with his arms across his body. He wouldn't look me in the eye. I was past shyness, carried away with the exhilaration, but he stood there, paralysed with self-consciousness.

'It's freakin' freezing!' he squealed. I laughed.

'It's refreshing!'

'It feels like needles!'

'Rub it in. Rub the water in, it's fine.'

He rubbed one arm, stiffly, then moved up to his shoulder. 'Oh yeah, you're right.' He started to get into it, running his hands over his hair, turning his face up like me, closing his eyes. He let out a whoop of joy, and I watched him as he smoothed the water from his face and shoulders and chest, and it struck me suddenly. He was beautiful.

I felt my whole body flush with the shock of it. It was like I was seeing him for the first time, seeing beyond what everyone else saw – the twitching, and swearing, the aggression and awkwardness.

I realised he was looking at me.

'What?' he said.

'Nothing.'

'Getting cold?'

'Nah, I'm all right.'

'You have to keep moving or you'll freeze!' He suddenly took off, leaping around like a lunatic, whooping. I joined in, dancing and skipping, laughing my head off. He grabbed my hand and spun me around, then pulled me in towards him and put his arm round my waist, and we waltzed around like a couple of maniacs. And all the time, the rain was thundering down around us. It was the maddest, maddest thing.

'Someone up there likes you,' he shouted into my ear.

'What do you mean?'

'They sent you a shower just when you wanted it, didn't they?'

'It's just rain. There's no-one up there.'

'How do you know?'

'Well, no-one's been looking out for me for the past fifteen years, why would they start now?'

We'd stopped dancing, but he still had his arm round me.

'I'll always look out for you,' he said. His words went straight into the middle of me. My stomach kind of flipped over. At the same time, my eyes starting stinging. There was no 'always' for this boy. I turned my head away, so he wouldn't see my tears.

'I mean it, Jem.'

'I know,' I said, unsteadily.

He brought his hand up to hold the end of my chin and gently turned my head back towards him. Our heights were so mismatched, my eyes were at the level of his chest. He tilted my head and bent down towards me.

I just had time to think, *This isn't happening*, before I felt his lips press gently on mine. I closed my eyes. His mouth moved slightly, and his nose nuzzled mine. I felt him start to move away again, and opened my eyes. His face was so close, it was sort of distorted, but the number was there, the same as ever. As he moved away, he became more familiar, his features morphing back into the Spider I knew. He frowned, let go of me and held up both his hands.

'Sorry,' he said. 'I'm sorry.'

'No,' I said, quickly. 'Don't be.' I reached up and cupped the back of his neck and drew him down to me, and we kissed again. And we lost ourselves in each other, gently exploring the faces and features we'd thought we knew so well. Standing in the rain, in the dark, in a totally different dimension.

Chapter 18

I lay back on the blanket, instinctively crossing my arms over my tits. He was trying to touch me there, to kiss me. I knew my arms were fending him off, I didn't want to, it was just so difficult. If we were going to do this, I told myself, I'd have to trust him, to let him in. I made myself lift up my arms, right over my head, so my hands were resting on the hay behind me. It was a wilful act – I was laying myself open to him. He got stuck in eagerly, kissing, nibbling and sucking. It was wonderful. And shocking. It was too new and too weird, and I found myself stepping away in my mind. I became an observer, and the absurdity of us naked in a smelly barn, the bizarre sensations all over my skin, inside me, the tension of it all, forced stuttering laughter out of my mouth.

Spider stopped what he was doing and looked up at me. His face was deadly serious – I'd never seen him so serious.

'You're laughing.'

'No,' but I couldn't hold down my nervous giggles.

'Did I do something wrong?'

'No, course not. It's just . . . I'm just . . . not used to it. I'm sorry.' The laughter drained away, as I saw how hurt he was.

'It's fine,' I said. 'I've never done this before. I'm nervous. It's fine. Come here.' I wasn't far from crying now, all my emotions way too near the surface. I drew him down to me, kissing him tenderly, urging him with my mouth to kiss me back. It was better when we were kissing. We relaxed in the softness of each other's mouths, the wetness. It brought me back into my body. I was there with him again.

He caressed me and stroked me, nervous energy trembling out of the ends of his fingers. He fumbled in the dark and we did it. We really did it – there, on an itchy blanket, with the dust from the hay and the smell of cow shit in our nostrils. The hay bales beneath us may have rocked a bit, but the earth didn't move. It was awkward, mechanical – all over in a minute or so – not worth worrying about. But afterwards, we were different. Not because of the sex, because of the closeness, the intimacy. We covered ourselves up as much as we could with the two blankets and the old green coat, and huddled together. The rain had washed away his sour smell, there was only a slight comforting muskiness as I nestled into him, with my head on his chest.

'Have you done that before?' I asked.

'Yeah, course. Loads of times.' His lie hung in the air. 'Well, once anyway.' I waited. 'Okay, I've done it once now. With you.'

I smiled, and held him closer.

Even then, after all that, he was still fizzing with energy, his hands so restless. He was running his fingers through my short, short hair, while the other hand moved over my arm, my stomach, my side. He shifted over, so we were face to face, and softly traced the line of my jaw with his finger.

'Funny, you seem more like a girl with your hair short. Can see your face.' He kissed my forehead, my nose, my chin, down in a line. 'Your pretty face.'

No-one had ever called me pretty before. I'm fairly sure no-one had ever thought it either.

'I thought I told you never to say anything nice to me.'

He snorted. 'Oh yeah, I promised, didn't I? That doesn't count, though.'

'Why not? A promise is a promise, isn't it?'

'Yeah, but that was before I fell in love with you.'

It was too much, too new. I reacted how I always had. I said the thing I always said.

'Fuck off!'

'Okay, forget it.' His hurt was so intense it was physical, a black moon hanging over us where we lay.

Oh my God, what had I done?

'I'm sorry, I'm sorry. I don't know how to behave.'

'It's all right, Jem.' But he'd let go of me, moved away.

'No, it isn't. I'm an idiot.' If I'd said it back to him, there and then, if I'd said I loved him. If . . . if . . . if.

Without his warmth, the blanket was hopelessly inadequate, and the cold that had been lurking in my hands and feet spread all over me, making me shiver violently. I sat up and began to cast about for my clothes, cursing yet again our lack of a torch. Whatever I found, I put on, no bra or knickers, only one sock, and that felt like Spider's, a jumper, my jeans; the rest would have to wait until there was some light. A metre or so away, Spider was doing the same. It felt like something was over between us. I'd killed it with my big mouth.

I curled up, but even with some clothes on, I was chilled

right through. When you think about it, if you're going to dance around in the rain with your clothes off in December, and then roll about in a barn, butt-naked, you're going to get cold, aren't you? I guess being hungry didn't help either. A metre away, I heard Spider shifting about as he bedded down. He sighed. Could have been just breathing out, but to me there was frustration, anger, sadness in that sigh. I wanted to reach out to him, but was frightened he'd just shrug me off.

We lay there in silence. Behind us, even the cows were quieter. They'd settled down in the hay and their own filth, and were just gently chewing and breathing. I was too cold to sleep, and there was no way I could even try with this wall of silence between us. I needed him.

'Are you awake?' I whispered, my voice nearly disappearing in the darkness of the huge barn.

'Yeah.'

'I'm freezing.'

'I know. Me too.' A pause. A long, long pause. 'Come here, then.'

I shuffled over to him as he turned over. He wrapped one of his long arms round my shoulders and I snuggled into him.

'I'm sorry,' I said. 'For earlier.'

'It's fine, Jem, shut up. It's in the past.'

'Yeah but . . . I didn't mean to say it. I didn't mean to hurt you.'

'I know. It's all right. We're all right. Lovers' tiff, eh?' He kissed the end of my nose, moved down to my mouth, and suddenly it was all right again.

And as we breathed in each other's breath and I buried my hands in his spongy hair, I thought, *Lovers, yes, we're lovers now*. We came up for air, and lay cuddling. My hands were still cold, and he took them and slid them under his clothes onto the bare skin of his chest and stomach to warm them up.

'Wouldn't it be good if you could start again?' I said. 'I feel like my life's stuffed up before I've even got started.'

'Tell me about it.' He turned over to face me again, and my hands moved round him, my arms enclosing him. 'But we *are* starting again, Jem. I reckon if I hadn't met you, it would have been dope and pills and smoking crack and injecting junk. Prison. Hospital. That's how it would have been for me, but you saved me from that. It's going to be different for us now.'

I dug my fingernails into his back, felt the tears pricking my eyes.

'Ow! What's that for? Leaving your mark on me?'

'No, just holding you tight.' And he held me too, and we had sex again, only it was making love this time, slow and tender. And I didn't just lie there, I was part of it; moving and kissing, stroking and sighing. It was like I was someone else, but I wasn't. This was me, the real me, and Spider was the only person ever to have found me, to see me for who I was. And I saw him too. He was beautiful.

Afterwards I lay in the crook of his arm, my hand resting on his chest, and he was still, not a twitch or a tremor. We were peaceful and calm together, and I fell asleep with his warm breath on my face and his heart beating next to mine.

Chapter 19

I was waking up slowly, still in a dream, not knowing what was real and what wasn't. I could hear the warm, deep noises of cows talking to each other. My nostrils were full of earthy, shitty air – animal and vegetable all mixed up. I was curled up on my side as usual, but my back was warm, there was something heavy lying across me and I felt enclosed. I opened my eyes to face a wall of hay. I looked down and there was Spider's arm draped over my waist. He was on his side, too, curved into my body.

It was just getting light. The cows were struggling to their feet, kicking the hay about – I guess that's what woke me up. I put my hand onto Spider's arm and hugged him in closer. That little movement woke him up, and he nuzzled the top of my head, planted a kiss.

'We'd better get up, it's morning,' I whispered.

Spider groaned. 'Okay,' he said. 'Just five more minutes.'

And so we lay together a little longer. I was awake now, my mind going over the night before. Was it real? Was I different? Spider fell asleep again, I could tell by the weight of his arm, his heavy, even breath on my scalp.

I started getting worried about someone finding us there. Surely someone would come up and see to the cows. They didn't just leave them for days, did they? I swivelled around under his arm, rubbed my hands up and down his chest to wake him up.

'Come on, we've got to go.' He opened one lazy eye.

'Whassahurry?'

'We need to get out of here, it's getting light.' I wriggled out of his arms and sat up. We hadn't slept in the hay cave, just lain down on top of some bales. There were bits of clothing all over the place, socks trodden into the filthy ground. Oh yeah, it was real.

I gathered up my clothes and did my best to brush the crap off them, then undressed in order to get dressed properly again. I felt more self-conscious in the cold light of day, and quickly put my T-shirt on, then squirmed about getting my bra on underneath it.

'What you doing that for?' a sleepy voice asked. 'I've seen it all now. You don't need to hide.'

'I know,' I said, 'I'm just cold. Anyway, get up. Here . . .' I balled up the sock of his that I'd been wearing and chucked it at him.

'Yeah, yeah.'

Once dressed, there was nothing to do but leave. Nothing for breakfast, not even a drink. The cows had lined up by their fence and were watching us curiously, their breath steaming in the cold morning air. We put the blankets in a couple of bags and left. There was no question about what we had to do today – we needed to find a bit of civilisation – so we followed the path back to the main road. Spider carried our plastic bags. As we set off he put them both in one hand, and gently scooped up one of mine in his free one. We walked along, side by side, not speaking. When the path narrowed, he went a bit in front, but didn't let go of me, and we carried on, me with my arm reaching forward, him reaching back. Sounds soppy doesn't it, like we'd mushed into sickly boyfriend-girlfriend stuff? But it wasn't like that. We were just together now. Properly together.

We walked along the road, sticking a thumb out every time we heard a car behind us. We'd got to the point now where we had to risk being recognised. Nobody stopped. They were all in a hurry, speeding along this little country lane like it was a race track, swerving out when they spotted us, taken by surprise. A couple of them sounded their horns, like we shouldn't be in the road at all. Where did they expect us to walk? In the ditch? Tossers.

It had stopped raining, but everywhere was soaked, and there were big puddles lying on the tarmac at the side of the road. My trousers got heavier as the water soaked up from the bottoms. It wasn't easy walking on a completely empty stomach. My legs were tired anyway, really tired, and my body was rebelling against what I was asking it to do. I kept belching, but I couldn't even taste yesterday's food – just sour, acid emptiness.

It had got to twenty past eight when we stopped. We couldn't sit down anywhere, it was all too wet, but we stood a few metres away from the road, up a track to a farm. Spider put his bags down and lit one of our last cigarettes. We shared it in silence, while water dripped onto us from the trees above.

'It's pretty grim, isn't it?' Spider asked eventually. I just nodded. 'I reckon we should risk using the phone. Get a taxi.'

'No way, they'll trace it. It'll be the end, Spider.'

'What else can we do? We're stuck in the middle of nowhere here.'

'I dunno – but they'll be waiting for us to use the phone, won't they?'

He dropped the fag end and ground it under his foot. 'I'm hungry, Jem. I'm cold.'

'I know. Me too.'

We lit another fag, and passed it back and forth, a small comfort in an otherwise bleak world. After a couple of minutes, we heard a car crunching down the drive behind us. We looked at each other. No time to move on, no point really. A massive four-wheel drive thing came round the corner. They hit the brakes when they saw us, then drove round us. I could see the driver as the car went past – a woman, early thirties maybe, quite smart, hair pulled back into a ponytail, and a bit of toast held in her mouth like a beak. There were a couple of kids in the back. They looked like dolls strapped into that massive car.

The woman looked at us – surprised, wary, a bit angry maybe – then drove up to the junction and turned left out onto the road. A few metres down, she stopped and reversed until she was level with us. The front passenger window went down and she took the toast out of her mouth and leaned across.

'Are you waiting for someone?' The voice was sharp, like she was accusing us of something. The crime of being strangers. The crime of being young.

Spider held his hand up. 'We just need a lift. Into town.' He was busking it now – neither of us knew if there was a town nearby, or where it might be.

She looked at us doubtfully, her mouth a thin, tight line.

'Right. I'm sorry, I can't help you.' The window went up again and the car set off.

'Bitch,' I said. Spider nodded and took another drag.

Three metres along the road the car stopped again and reversed. This time another car was coming up behind, and its horn blasted as it overtook her. The window came down.

'You'd better get in,' she said, briskly. 'I'm going into town. Put your bags in the back. One of you will have to go in the back, in the middle.'

Spider and I exchanged glances, then he opened the boot and slung the bags in. I pulled open the passenger door. The kids were staring wide-eyed, like their mum had lost her marbles. I tried not to look them in the eye – I can't stand that, seeing kids' numbers. Gets to me. They were in posh uniforms – blazers, shirts and ties, you know the sort of thing – and they were looking at me like I was some sort of alien.

'Um . . . 'scuse me . . . can I just . . . ?'

The boy, sitting nearest to me, swivelled his legs to the side and leaned back into his seat. I clambered past him and settled in the middle. The little girl, on the other side, shrank away from me.

Spider had closed the boot and was up front now. 'Thanks, thanks, really appreciate it. It's cool, it's cool. Nice car. Great. Cool. Cool.' His head was nodding in appreciation. I wanted him to shut up, not to sound too mad. 'This is really good of you. It's fucking freezing out there.'

I heard a sharp intake of breath from the boy. Out of the corner of my eye, I could see him, eyes like saucers, mouth open. The woman spoke very slowly, carefully.

'Listen, I'm happy to give you a lift, but not if you're going to swear. We don't do that in this car.'

Spider clapped his hand to his mouth. 'Jesus, I'm sorry.

I'm sorry. No offence, lady. All right, kids?' He turned around, flashing them a smile. 'It's not cool to use those words, is it? Not cool.'

I thought I heard a little squeak from the girl. I glanced at her. She was absolutely terrified. Quite possibly wetting herself. She'd probably never even seen a black man, let alone a six-foot-four, foul-mouthed black dosser. I guess you could find him intimidating at the best of times, but after a couple of days on the run and sleeping rough, he was a bit of a sight.

Spider's nerves were getting the better of him. He just couldn't stop. 'It's very good of you. To stop for us. Very good.'

'That's all right.' You could tell now she was regretting her reckless impulse, would never do it again. 'Where are you heading?'

My stomach flipped as I realised we hadn't agreed a story. After two days on our own, we'd suddenly plunged back into the real world. Spider just ploughed ahead, ad-libbing. 'We're heading to Bristol, going to stay with my aunt. She's in Bristol, yeah.'

'How did you end up at Whiteways?'

'Um, we've just been hitching. Got dropped by the main road. Been walking for a couple of days.'

As he was talking I noticed the lady's half-eaten bit of toast. She'd put it down by the gear stick and forgotten about it. Saliva jetted into my mouth. I couldn't take my eyes off it. Oh. My. God. I couldn't help myself – I leaned forward, stretched my hand out and picked it up, then sat back and crammed it straight in my mouth, folding it up so it all went in. It was cold and a bit soggy, and the best thing I've ever tasted. The salty butter made more saliva gush out, and some dribble ran down my chin as I chewed.

This was all too much for the boy. 'Mummy,' he squealed. 'He's eaten your toast!'

He?

'Oh,' came her reaction. 'Never mind, Freddy. I'd finished really.'

I wiped my chin with my sleeve, reluctantly swallowed; I could have kept it in my mouth for ever. 'I'm sorry,' I said. 'I was just . . . hungry.'

'That's quite all right,' she said, evenly. The little girl started crying, quietly whimpering next to me. 'It's all right, children. We're nearly there. Nearly there.' She didn't need to say 'thank God' – we all knew she was thinking it.

We were on the outskirts of a town now. I can't tell you how good it was to see houses, to know there were shops and cafés only a few minutes away.

She pulled up at the side of the road. 'School's off that way, I'll drop you here. It's only five minutes' walk to the town centre. And there's a station, too.'

'Right, thanks, thanks. You've been very kind.' I climbed out, past Freddy, who was holding himself so flat against his seat that he was almost two-dimensional. We got the bags out of the back and stood on the pavement as the car moved off into the traffic.

'How lucky was that?' Spider said.

'Mm, think we'll be the last hitchhikers they ever pick up.'

'What do you mean?'

'Oh, nothing. I don't think we were their kind of people.'

'Yeah,' he laughed. 'And I think they thought you was a boy. Need their eyes testing.'

'Spider, do you think they knew who we were?'

'Nah, she wouldn't have picked us up if she did, would she?'

With the traffic streaming past us, I was starting to feel more exposed than when we'd been walking across the fields. We'd been cut off from civilisation for two days. What had everyone been hearing about us? What had they seen on the TV, or read in their papers? In one of those cars going past, was someone reaching for their phone right now, dialling 999? I felt edgy, really edgy.

'We should find a shop and then disappear, Spider. We can't hang about.'

'Yeah, I know.'

He grabbed the bags and set off along the road, long legs striding along. I had to jog to keep up. We'd got to the first few shops, keeping an eye out for a corner shop or a little food shop or something, when we saw an A-board on the street: *Rita's Café – All-Day Breakfasts Cooked to Order.*

Spider had stopped. He was staring at the board, licking his lips. I could read his mind – I knew what he was going to say before he said it.

'I know we shouldn't hang around, but, Christ, Jem, I'm hungry. What do you reckon?'

We both knew we should stick to Plan A – go into a corner shop, buy some sandwiches, water, cereal bars, all that stuff, and then find a shed or a garage or somewhere and have another picnic – but there was no way either of us could walk past that place.

'Sod it,' I said. 'Even a condemned man has a last meal, don't they?'

That big grin broke out again, and I swear a bit of drool trickled down his chin.

'That's the girl,' he said, and he picked up our stuff and headed into Rita's.

Chapter 20

I've never been to Africa and seen a hyena ripping into the carcass of an antelope, but I reckon it would be pretty similar to the sight of Spider devouring a cooked breakfast. He used his fork like a shovel, didn't stop to breathe or anything like that, just continuously scooped it up and in, up and in. He looked up at me. I hadn't even touched mine.

'What's up with you? You're not telling me you're not hungry?' A bubble of egg yolk oozed out of the corner of his mouth.

'No, I'm just enjoying the look of it – it's awesome.' And it was. After all that time out in the wild, eating crisps, biscuits and chocolate, it was almost too good to look at: a couple of plump sausages glistening with grease; the perfect fried egg, pure white and pure yellow; rashers of bacon fried into crispy waves; a pool of beans, the juice slowly spreading across the plate.

He snorted, and his egg bubble grew and turned into a drip. 'You're mental. Get stuck in.' He waved a fork in the direction of the woman behind the counter, who I guess was Rita, and called out, 'Hey, could we get some fried bread with this?'

'Coming up!' she replied cheerily, clearly a woman who liked to see people enjoying her food.

I cut the end off one of the sausages, let out an involuntary groan of satisfaction as the first mouthful hit home, and then steadily worked my way through the plateful. Rita waddled out from behind the counter, bringing a plate of fried bread. She was one of those people who almost look wider than they are tall, her enormous chest – barely contained by a man's checked shirt – bulging out from behind her apron. Her legs were bare under a square-shaped denim skirt and she had fluffy slippers on, the pink fake fur globbed together in places where the bacon fat had spattered.

'Shall I top those up?' she asked, nodding at our mugs of tea.

'Cheers,' said Spider, moving his mug nearer the edge of the table. She shuffled over to the counter and fetched the big silver-coloured teapot. The brown liquid steamed as it arced into our mugs. The café was empty apart from us, and she didn't seem in any hurry to get back behind the counter.

'Been sleeping rough?' she asked. It wasn't an accusation, just a friendly question, the way she said it.

'Yeah,' we both said, together.

She eased herself down into a chair at the table across the gangway.

'Do you need to phone anyone, kids? You can use the phone here, free of charge.'

Spider rested his fork on the edge of the plate. 'It's okay, we've got mobiles.'

I couldn't help thinking of Val, perched on her stool in the kitchen, her ashtray piling up with fag ends, and the look in her eyes as we drove away.

'If there's someone, somewhere, waiting for news about you, you should give them a ring. Just let them know you're okay. Take it from me, lovey. I know what it's like to sit looking at that phone, willing it to ring. Breaks your heart, it does.' She wasn't looking at Spider and me any more; her eyes were directed at one of the pictures on the wall, but I could tell she wasn't seeing it. She was somewhere else, somewhere painful.

I kept quiet, pretended to be reading the newspaper that was lying on the table next to me. I didn't want to hear anyone else's sob story. Spider was too busy wiping the fried bread round his plate and posting it into his big gob to ask, but she took our silence as encouragement to go on.

'Happened to me, you see. My Shaunie. We used to row – everyone does, don't they? He used to go off for a few hours, come home when he'd cooled down. I never thought he'd leave for good.' Her face was shining damply, from the heat of the kitchen maybe, or the effort of telling us about her son. She wiped her forehead with the bottom of her apron. 'Anyway, that's just what he did. We fell out one day, can't even remember what it was about, and off he went. I wasn't too bothered, thought he'd turn up later. I got his tea ready and put it in the oven to keep warm. It was still there the next morning, dried up and stuck to the plate. Shepherd's pie and veg. That's what I'd cooked him. Always liked a bit of shepherd's pie. I rang the police. They weren't really bothered. Seventeen, you see. You can do what you like at seventeen. I rang his mates, all the places he might go. Nothing. He just disappeared. Never seen him again. I don't know if he's alive or dead.' Her voice wobbled, and she stopped talking and sat there taking deep breaths in and out.

Embarrassed for her, I kept my eyes on the table, on that newspaper, and for the first time, the words in the headline came into focus. LONDON BOMBING – WHY DID THEY RUN? And underneath, a grainy CCTV picture of people queuing in a shop. The camera must have been near the ceiling, because you were looking at them from above, couldn't see their faces, except for one person who was glancing up, looking straight at the camera. It was me, of course. In that service station. On the front page of the paper.

Spider had put the last bit of fried bread down on his plate.

'That's terrible,' he said. 'I'm so sorry.'

Rita nodded, acknowledging his sympathy.

'Here.' He held a grubby tissue out to her.

'S'all right, I've got a hanky somewhere.' She dug in her apron pocket, fished out a big white man's hanky and blew her nose noisily.

'Changes your life, something like that,' she said quietly. 'You don't like to go out, just in case the phone rings. You stop sleeping properly, always listening for that key in the lock. Think you're going mad sometimes, when you see someone that looks just like him from the back, or hear someone behind you laughing just like he used to, and you turn round and it isn't him.' Sweat was beading on her forehead again, and she lifted up her apron, completely covering her face for a second, and mopped it away. 'You got someone, somewhere, going through what I'm going through – you give them a ring.'

I could feel sweat pricking at my armpits and forehead as well, but for a different reason. Her words drifted over my head as I read the story beneath the headline: *These are the first pictures of the two young hoodies seen running away from the London Eye minutes before Tuesday's terrorist bomb exploded. Police are stressing that at this time the two are seen as key witnesses, who may hold vital information about the terrorist attack. They have issued an urgent appeal for them to come forward.*

Rita had stopped talking, and was sitting mangling her apron in her damp hands. Nobody spoke for a minute.

'Thing is,' said Spider, 'people can trace phone calls, can't they?'

'And you don't want to be found.' Her eyes flicked between the two of us, not judging, and I thought that her Shaun must have been an idiot to leave a mum like that.

I clocked her number. Fifteen, sixteen years to go. Would she see her son again, or would it be fifteen years of missed birthdays, lonely Christmases? I tried not to think about it – not my problem.

'Tell you what, if you left a number, I could ring for you, after you've gone,' she said. 'I could ring after a couple of hours, tomorrow if you like, just to let 'em know I've seen you and you're doing okay.'

Spider nodded. 'Yeah, yeah, that'd be cool. Give us time to be on our way.'

'I'll get some paper and a pen.' Rita hauled herself back onto her feet.

I leaned forward over the Formica table. 'Are you mad?' I hissed.

'What?'

'Giving her your nan's number?'

'Like she said, she can ring tomorrow, when we're long gone. It's sound.'

I didn't say anything, just pushed the paper across the

table towards him.

'What . . . ?' he started to say, then he saw the picture. 'Oh, shit.'

We both looked towards the counter. Rita had her back to us, feeling about under a heap of paper for a pen. I tucked the newspaper into my coat, and, without speaking, we picked up our bags as quietly as we could and got up out of our chairs, trying not to scrape them on the floor.

I looked back when I was by the door. Spider was still by the table. What was he playing at? He reached into his pocket and got a couple of fivers out of his envelope. *For Christ's sake,* I wanted to scream, *we haven't got time for that!* I eased down the door handle and pulled, praying that there wasn't a bell about to betray us. It was okay, and I slipped out, Spider close behind me now.

'Don't run, Jem. Just walk. Keep it cool.'

We were only a few metres away when we heard Rita's voice coming out of the open door. 'What the . . . ? Here, come back!' We quickened the pace.

'Don't look back, Jem. Just keep going.'

I didn't need to look back. In my mind's eye, I could see her standing in the doorway for a bit, watching us disappear, then turning back, picking up the notes, and holding them in her damp hand as she sank down into a chair. Breathing heavily in and out, thinking of us, thinking of Shaun . . . until she realised the paper was gone, put two and two together and reached for the phone.

Chapter 21

The High Street was full of police informers. Every passer-by was a pair of eyes and a mobile phone. While we'd been isolated in the country, I'd started to think we were just getting paranoid, that it was all in our heads, this need to run and hide. My picture on the front page of the paper told a different story. It was real. They were all out to get us. Walking along the road, it felt like it wouldn't be long now. Even in a sleepy little market town in the middle of nowhere there were hundreds of people out and about: people who watched the news, went on the internet, read newspapers.

Another thing was bothering me. Try as I might not to meet people's eyes, I couldn't avoid them all, and there they were again: people's numbers. Telling me stuff about strangers, handing me their death sentences. I wanted to walk around with my eyes closed, to blot the numbers out. I didn't want to be reminded that everyone around me was going to die. The reason was walking beside me, holding my hand. Spider. For the first time in my life, I had someone I wanted to keep hold of. The date on the paper – 11th December – was like a slap in the face. Only four days to go.

'Listen,' he said, urgently, 'we'd better buy some supplies quickly and then find somewhere to disappear. We're too obvious here.'

He wasn't kidding. There may have been a few people walking or driving along who were lost in their own thoughts, not bothered about us, but everyone else was clocking us. I guess we were a pretty odd sight: two scruffy kids, one ridiculously tall, the other looking like a midget beside him. And I reckon my hunch in the car had been right: most of them didn't see a black man from one year to the next. There were certainly no other black faces about today. It was like one of those programmes off the telly, only in reverse – you know, where some white guy goes into an African village and the kids rush up to him, touching his white skin and feeling his hair. Except no-one was rushing up to us. They looked at us and looked away. One woman, coming towards us on the pavement, glanced quickly up and then made her kid walk the other side of her, away from us. And I thought, *Sod you, whatever we've got, it's not catching, you stuck-up cow.*

We found a newsagent's. Spider unwrapped some tenners from his wad and sent me in. I grabbed stuff as quickly as I could: a few chocolate bars and crisps, but also some sensible stuff this time – water, fruit juice, cereal bars.

The shop, squeezed in between an antiques shop and a greengrocer's, smelt stale. It was packed from floor to ceiling with snacks and drinks, newspapers and mags, loads of porno ones. It was like a little bit of London parachuted into the middle of nowhere. The guy behind the counter was reading a newspaper as I went round choosing. You could tell he was watching me.

I put the stuff on the counter. There were fags behind him, so I asked for half a dozen packets, and then I spotted something else: three or four torches huddled together on the shelf. I bought two, and the batteries to go with them. He put the stuff in a couple of bags, watching as I fumbled with the money. *He knows,* I thought, as I stood there, *he knows.*

He took the money. 'Ta,' he said, in a gravelly voice, like his vocal cords had been ripped by fifty years of smoking. Then, as I turned to leave, he called out. 'Here . . .'

And I knew the game was up. What was he going to do to us? An old git like that couldn't stop me, could he? I kept walking.

'Hey, you!' He shouted louder. I turned round. 'You forgot your change.'

I went back and took it from him silently.

Outside on the street, I gave Spider one of the bags to carry and he grabbed my free hand in his. 'Come on,' he said, 'Let's get out of here.'

We ducked into a side alley between two shops. It twisted and turned behind houses and past some allotments, and then out onto a canal towpath. We followed it along for a bit. A wall sprang up on the other side of me, and a train rattled past beyond it. We came to a tunnel. The path was narrow, a damp, cold curved wall on one side, a railing on the other to stop you falling into the canal.

Spider let go of my hand. 'You go ahead. I'll be right behind you.'

It was difficult to see where you were treading, and my ankles kept turning over on the uneven path. Halfway along,

I started to really lose my nerve. A figure appeared at the end I was heading for, a big, dark shape blotting out most of the light. I looked over my shoulder, expecting to see someone behind us too – it was a perfect place to trap someone, nowhere to go, no-one to hear you scream.

It was okay, though, the way behind me was clear apart from Spider. Not a trap after all, just a bloke walking along the canal.

We came towards each other in the dark. I wasn't sure he'd even seen me, he just kept coming towards me in the middle of the path, like he was going to barge straight through me. He was silhouetted against the disc of light at the other end, his features blotted out. As he got nearer, I thought, *He's black, that's why I can't see much of his face in here.* Then he got within six metres or so and I saw with lurching horror that his face wasn't black, it was blue.

It was blue and crawling with tattoos.

I swivelled round.

'Run, Spider! Run, run, run, run!'

He caught the terror in my voice, didn't question me, just turned, and we ran. I could hear Tattoo Face behind me, heavy steps on the crunching gravel, breath rasping in and out of his lungs. It was so narrow in there, our bags were catching on the wall and the railing.

Spider slowed for a second and I drew level with him. 'Ditch the bags, Jem. Leave them there.'

I dropped what I had and he let me get past, then he threw the bags he was carrying back down the tunnel, straight at Tattoo Face. Even as I ran, I could hear the guy grunting, trampling plastic and cans under his feet. We were out into the open air now, belting back along the towpath the way we'd come only a few minutes before. We'd slowed him down with the bags, but not much. He was a big bugger, but he could shift. I didn't want to look behind, but I couldn't help it, and when I looked over my shoulder he was bearing down on us like a rugby forward.

'Here!' Spider grabbed my arm and hauled me off to the left. We ran down a rough slope until we reached another path, feeding off the main one. It led to a railway bridge: grim black riveted metal covered in graffiti. 'Come on!'

We clattered up the steps. As we hurtled across the bridge, a train went underneath us; must've been an express because it blasted through, filling my ears with the sound of high-speed metal. It masked the noise of Tattoo Face's footsteps, but as we started to go down the steps at the other side, I could feel the vibration of the bridge as he thundered across. He was right behind us.

The bridge led on to a street, terraced houses one side, railway the other. Houses meant people – surely he wouldn't kill us in front of witnesses. Would he? I started yelling, screaming as I ran, 'Help! Help us! Call the police! Help us!'

There was no reaction. Either the houses were empty or people, hearing the noise, just sank further down into their sofas, turned the telly up a bit higher.

Spider wheeled round. 'What you doing? Shut up! We don't want the police. We just need to get away. Come on!'

'He's going to kill us, Spider! We need help.' Did a curtain twitch? Was somebody watching us now?

'I'm not going to kill you!' Tattoo Face's voice rang out along the street. 'I just want a nice little chat, kids, that's all.'

I looked back over my shoulder. The big guy had stopped running. He was standing in the middle of the street, bent forward but looking up at us, hands on his thighs, puffing and blowing. He was struggling to get his breath, but he kept his eyes on us all the time. Of course, I saw his number. I'd seen it before, at the party. 11122009. Four days before Spider. The same date as the newspaper I'd picked up earlier. It was today.

There wasn't just adrenalin running through me now – this buzz, this awareness shot through my veins like the first hit of the most powerful drug in the world. What did it mean?

Whatever was going to happen next, Spider would get out of it alive, and Tattoo Face wouldn't. Of course, I didn't know about me. Perhaps Spider would be the only one to walk away . . .

Spider and I had stopped running too. We both faced him in the street and then looked at each other, not sure what to do.

'What do you want?' Spider called out to him.

'You know what I want. You've got something that does-n't belong to you. Something a friend of mine wants back.' The money. 'We can talk about it, nice and civilised, like. No need to make a show of ourselves.' He was walking towards us now, slowly. I could hear the blood thudding in my ears as he kept on coming. Then, to his right, someone opened a door. A middle-aged bloke, holding a big dog by its collar.

'What's going on?' he shouted out.

Tattoo Face stopped and turned towards him, held both his hands up. 'Nothing. Bit of a domestic, that's all. My son here's in a bit of trouble. I just need to help him sort it out. You know what it's like, don't you? Kids!'

The guy looked at him, trying to suss him out. 'Do I need to call the police?'

Tattoo Face smiled. 'No, mate. It's nothing like that. We'll sort it out.'

While they were talking, Spider leaned down and whispered, 'Back away,' and so, slowly, we edged down the street. Then, as they seemed to be ending their conversation, we turned and started to run again, fast, really fast, legs pumping away like mad.

'Here!' He was after us again, but we'd got a good start now. We belted down the street. Spider was ripping his jacket off.

'What you doing?'

'Here.' He flung it across the top of the spiked railings to our left, then cupped his hands for me to put my foot into and almost flung me over. I landed awkwardly, twisting my knee. Spider pulled himself up the other side, crouched on the top and then jumped down. He grabbed his jacket off the top and helped me up.

'Okay?'

I nodded, not wanting to admit how much it hurt.

'Come on, then,' he said, and set off, scrambling down the embankment.

I tried to follow at a run, but it was agony. I dropped down on all fours and sort of scuttled along, taking some of the weight on my hands. Spider looked back.

'What the hell are you doing?' He was down the bottom of the slope now, by the side of the track.

'I've hurt myself. My knee,' I said, wincing as I tried to stand up on it.

'Why didn't you say?' He started back up towards me, but I heard a thump behind. Tattoo Face was over the fence.

Panicking now, I scrambled towards Spider. He lunged forward, at the same time as I was literally lifted into the air, scooped up by a big muscled arm wrapped round my waist. There was something cold and hard against my throat. That bastard had pulled a knife.

Spider tumbled forward, then froze, like a sprinter waiting for the gun. 'No, no, man. There's no need for that. Put the knife away. Come on, we can talk. We can talk about this.'

'We don't need to talk any more. You need to give me the money, and I'll let your little friend go.'

Spider got to his feet. Tattoo Face tightened his grip on me. I could hardly breathe. To be honest, I'd been so surprised when he'd grabbed me that I'd just hung there like a doll; now I struggled in his arms, until he dug the blade further into my neck. 'Don't come any nearer.'

'No, no, it's cool.' Spider backed away. He was down on the tracks again.

'Spider, just give him the money.' My voice didn't sound like mine.

He looked at me for a second, his face a picture of agony.

'I can't, Jem. This is our future. You and me. This is a hotel room and a big double bed. It's a pint or two in the pub and fish and chips on the pier. How can we have that, how can we have all that, without any money?'

I had a big lump in my throat. He'd got this all in his head, what he wanted for us. Christ, it wasn't much, was it? But we'd never have it. We'd never have even that. I started to cry. They were hot tears of frustration and longing, tears of hatred for the ticking clock.

'I'm sorry,' he said. 'I'm so sorry. I never meant any of this to happen. I never meant you to get scared. You're right, Jem. It's only money. We'll get some more. Let her go,' he said to Tattoo Face, 'and you can have your money.'

'Yeah, right, soft lad. I wasn't born yesterday. Give me the money and I'll let her go.'

'We'll do it together, yeah?'

'No, you'll give me the money,' Tattoo Face said, evenly, 'and then I'll let her go.'

Knowing Spider, I knew what was coming next. I could see it all in my head in slow motion, but Tattoo Face couldn't. He let out a great cry of dismay as Spider got the money out of the envelope, took the rubber band off, drew his hand way back and then flung it up and forward, launching the roll into the sky.

Tattoo Face's grip slackened. He dropped the knife, dropped me and hurtled down the embankment to the railway track.

I ran towards Spider and we met halfway. He gathered me in to him, pressing me into his chest, clutching at my hair.

'It's all right. I've got you. I've got you, Jem.' His voice was thick, he wasn't far from tears himself. 'Let's get out of here. Leave him to it.'

The air was full of notes. They were still falling all around us as we picked our way up the embankment. I looked back at Tattoo Face, bent over picking up note after note. You could tell he was mad, really mad, muttering to himself as he puffed and panted his way along, face down.

Spider had both arms round me. When we got to the top of the slope, he helped me over the fence again. I waited for him to join me, but he was standing there, one hand on the railings.

'Come on, let's get away from here,' I said.

He looked over his shoulder. I groaned.

'No, please, leave it. It's only money.'

'Just a hundred quid, Jem. Think what we could do with a hundred.'

I reached through the railings and grabbed his sleeve.

'Spider, don't.'

He unwound my fingers and kissed them.

'I'll be back in one minute,' he said and started back down the slope.

'Spider, no! No!' I screamed. He was down on the tracks now. Tattoo Face looked up at him.

'Come back for more, have you?'

'I just want a little bit. My cut – it's mine anyway.'

'You're not having any, you little shit. You go back to your girlfriend, right now, or I'll give you a good hiding.'

Spider squared up to him. 'I'm not frightened of you.'

'Funny, that's what your gran said when I paid her a visit.'

'You what?'

'I just wanted to know where you were. Bit of information. She wasn't very co-operative, your gran. Gave me a bit of lip, just like you. Still, she wasn't saying anything by the time I left her . . .'

'You bastard! What have you done to her?' Spider launched himself straight at him, charging head down into his stomach. He knocked Tattoo Face off his feet and they rolled together down the embankment onto the tracks. They were tumbling around, wrestling and landing real punches on each other with the sickening noise of flesh slamming into flesh. Behind their animal grunts and groans, there was other noise building up in the background; the rumbling of a distant train, and sirens, lots of them, getting nearer and nearer.

'Spider!' I screamed. 'Just get away from him! Get away!' I don't know if he heard me or not.

Suddenly, there was so much happening at once. Two police cars and a van swung into the road, screeched to a halt and spewed out teams of uniforms. They swarmed over the fence. Fifty metres down the track, a train came in to view, rattling along, blindly.

'Spider, get out now!' My voice was impossibly thin against the chaos around me. He didn't hear or he wasn't listening. I couldn't watch. I turned away and sank down to the ground, knees hugged in, eyes tight shut.

All around me people were shouting and screaming. There was an ear-splitting squeal as the driver of the train rammed the brakes on. It seemed to carry on for hours. I waited until the noise stopped. I would have to look: I needed to know. I tried to make myself breathe – three breaths in, three breaths out – before I turned around.

Through the railings, I could see the train. It had ground to a halt with the last carriage level with where I sat. The police had Tattoo Face in an arm lock. He was still putting up a fight, even with three of them trying to get him under control. There was no sign of Spider – without wanting to, my eyes scanned along the track under the train. The police were obviously thinking the same as me – some of them were walking along beside the end carriages, peering underneath. My mouth was dry. 'Oh, please, no,' I breathed to myself.

There was movement on the far embankment, something scuttling from bush to bush. I thought it was an animal to start with, then glimpsed it again. It was a person on hands and knees: it was Spider.

He was making his way up the slope and away to the right. When the bushes ran out, he got down on his stomach and crawled on his elbows. I got to my feet and started walking along the road in the same direction. I was limping, but I didn't notice the pain. I kept my eyes on Spider and soon enough I caught him looking over towards me. I gave him the thumbs up and he mirrored me. At the top of the embankment now, he scrambled to his feet and vaulted over the fence.

Below him, someone shouted out, 'Oi! That's the other one! Stop him!'

Spider broke into a run and I did, too – well, as much of a run as I could manage. We ran parallel to each other for a while, and then he disappeared from view, hidden by a wooden fence. We caught up with each other at a road bridge, a few hundred metres further on. He grabbed my hand, and we went for it, blindly running wherever our legs took us.

Chapter 22

We had nothing to carry any more, nothing to slow us down, and adrenalin was surging through us again. After a few twists and turns we found our way into a park. This was better: only a few people around, a couple of old ladies with their dogs. We walked along the paths, looking for somewhere to hide. Spider kept sending me into gaps in the bushes.

'Go in there and have a look.'

'You do it!'

'Don't be like that. You're smaller than me. Go and suss it out.'

I got ready to squeeze my way in, moving the branches out of my face. 'People like you sent people like me up chimneys a hundred years ago. Just 'cause I'm small,' I called behind me.

'No, mate, people like that woman who gave us a lift would have had us both cleaning her house, or polishing her shoes, or wiping her arse. 'Specially me. I'd have been someone's slave.' Point taken.

That opening was no good, but we found one a couple of minutes later. If you bent down and ducked under the bushes with thick rubbery leaves, there was a space behind, next to an old wall. It was big enough for us both to sit down and the ground was dry. No-one could see us. We would be all right here for a bit.

We sat down next to each other, our backs leaning against the wall. The instant my bum hit the ground, all the strength went out of me. I was so, so tired. I closed my eyes.

'Ciggy?'

'No. Nothing.' I didn't want to think, or feel, or see things any more. I didn't want to run or to hide.

'You all right?' His voice came to me through a thick fog. I'd nearly fallen asleep, just in that instant. I opened my eyes.

'I'm just tired.' He put his arm round me, pulled me in towards him.

'Did you hear what that bastard said?'

'About your nan?'

'Yeah. I should've killed him, Jem, while I had the chance. I was so mad, I just went for him. I forgot about my blade – should've pulled that and finished him there and then.'

'What good would that have done? Killing him? It would've just meant more trouble for you.'

'I don't care. He don't deserve nothing different for what he done. He had no right . . .'

'I know. But I'm glad you didn't. Anyway, he—' I was going to say, *Anyway, he's going to die to today*, but I stopped myself just in time. Surely, if Tattoo Face was going to die, it would have happened; Spider would've knifed him, or he would have split his head open on the rail when they were wrestling, or the train would've hit him. I was certain I'd seen his number, certain it was today. I didn't get it. I wasn't sure

167

any more – were the numbers just in my head or were they real? If I'd just made them up, that was cool – I could ignore them, try to change them, whatever. I could stop the clock ticking Spider's life away. If they were real, though, that meant Spider's nan was okay – she had years to go. It was all getting muddled up in my head. Whatever the truth of it, though, there was one way I could comfort Spider.

'I think she'll be okay, your nan.'

'You reckon? I don't even know if she's still alive.'

I turned round to face him. 'Spider, I know she'll be okay.'

'Because of her number?'

'Yeah.'

'But what if you're not the only one to see numbers? What if someone else sees completely different ones? What if her number's changed?'

'They don't.' I hesitated, checking Spider's number again – yeah, it was still there, still the same. 'They don't change.'

'So, the date we'll die is set from the minute we're born. Is that what you're saying?'

He was starting to piss me off now. I was trying to make him feel better, and he was giving it all these questions. Questions I didn't have answers for.

'I'm not saying anything.' I couldn't keep the irritation out of my voice. 'You're the one saying it all.'

'But I want you to say it, 'cause it doesn't make any sense to me.'

'What?'

'How everything is fixed for us. It's like it don't matter what I do because the end will be the same.'

'P'raps that's how it is. Things happen.' I wanted him to stop it, but he was like a dog with a bone.

'So everything's pre-set? It's all meant to be?'

'I dunno.'

'That bomb was meant to go off. That bastard was meant to beat up my nan. That's not right, Jem, is it? That can't be right.' He was raising his voice now. He'd taken his arm away from me and was waving it around. He seemed bigger than ever in this confined space.

'Course it's not right.'

'It don't make any sense.' A bit of his spit hit my face. He was well worked up.

'That's what I'm saying.'

'What?'

'Nothing makes any sense. Nothing means anything. You're born, you live, you die. That's it.' My philosophy in a nutshell.

That shut him up for a while. We sat, side by side, backs against the wall, both of us with our arms folded. But while I was still, Spider was shaking his head from side to side – it made his whole body move, his shoulder joggling into mine. Knowing, as I did now, how still he could be when he was happy and relaxed, it was disturbing to see him so agitated. He was out of his mind with worry. It felt like my fault. I wanted to reach him; I wanted to take his distress away.

'Spider, listen. Perhaps I'm wrong.' I was scared of what I was about to say. The words crept out of me like quiet little mice.

He was still shaking away, caught up in his own dark, mad world. I sat up on my knees, facing him and put my hands on both his shoulders. 'Spider.' He couldn't hear me. I moved my hands up to his face, held him firmly, slowing but not stopping his movement.

'What I said. That's not right either.' At last he was

listening. His face was still and he looked up at me, his eyes haunted and sad.

'Why not?'

'It's not all random, it can't be.' I took a deep breath. 'Because I was meant to meet you, and you were meant to meet me.'

His eyes filled with tears. Without saying a word he unwound his arms from around his ribcage and wrapped them around my waist, burying his face in my shoulder. Kneeling there, I held him to me, and stroked him, his back and his hair, and we cried together. There were no words to say what we were feeling; the tears said it for us – terror, relief, love and grief all mixed into the salt.

Later, much later, we disentangled ourselves and sat up. It was getting dark, and in our leafy cave I could only see Spider as a vague shape now.

'We need to get out of here, Jem,' Spider said. 'We couldn't have brought more attention to ourselves if we'd bloody tried earlier on.'

'Yeah, I know.' I had no energy left. My hand was hurting, my knee was hurting. I didn't want to be found, but it would be so easy just to curl up here, in Spider's arms, and wait for the inevitable.

'The best way to get out of here fast is to get another car.'

'And then what?'

'Drive to Weston. We must be bloody close now. You'll love it.' Even in the dark, I could tell he was smiling again. I wanted to feel it with him, I really did, but I couldn't. I felt cold inside, miserable, scared.

'What are we gonna do at Weston, Spider? They've got TV and papers there too, you know, and police and sniffer dogs and—'

He put one of his long fingers up to my lips. 'I told you. We're gonna eat ice cream and fish and chips and walk along the pier.' He was saying it like he believed it. Perhaps he did.

I gently took hold of the hand that was shushing me and laid it on my open left palm, softly tracing along his bony fingers with my other hand.

'What you doing?'

'Nothing. You've got lovely hands.'

'You're soft, you are.' He leaned across and kissed me tenderly. 'Okay,' he said, like his mind was suddenly made up. 'I know you're tired, so you stay here, and be ready to run when I come back for you. I'll find us some wheels, don't worry. I won't be long.' He started to crawl out under the branches.

'Spider.'

'What?'

'Be careful.'

'Course. Be ready, okay? I'll only be a few minutes.' And he was gone, the branches swishing for a minute where he'd pushed his way through. I watched as their movement slowed and stopped. And I sat in the gathering dark, and waited.

Chapter 23

I sat there, listening hard, with every bit of me ready to jump up and run. I was waiting for his footsteps, for the leaves to rustle, for a whispered instruction. In the background each noise was heavy with significance – the hum of traffic, the odd shout far away, a couple of sirens. What the hell was going on? Where was he?

Two minutes turned to ten. Ten minutes turned to twenty. As time went on I started to get glued into my position – hunched up, cuddling my knees. I made myself breathe slowly, almost in a trance, trying to suspend everything until Spider came back for me.

How long was it until I realised he wasn't coming back? I don't know, but gradually it seeped through me like the freezing rain that had started soaking down from the leaves above and up from the ground below. Something had happened to him. Because I hadn't seen it, I didn't feel shock, not then; it was like something even darker than the night all around settling on me, in me, a chill going right through to my bones. I didn't move or make a sound, I carried on sitting there, curled into a ball, only rocking a little, backwards and forwards.

I must have gone to sleep, because at one point I woke up lying on the ground with one thought in my head, *he's gone.* I was cold and wet, curled up in the dirt. I held both hands up to my face, covering my nose and mouth. My own breath warmed my face as I whispered over and over, 'Oh my God, oh my God.' I had no idea what to do – too scared to cry.

My whispered words filled my ears, but suddenly I was aware of other voices filtering through, and another sound, a swishing and flicking noise. Somebody was going through the bushes with something.

'Got one of them, the other won't be far away.'

'Not often you catch a terrorist, is it?'

'Do you think he is? A terrorist? Kid like that?'

'Could be, get them young, these days, don't they?'

'He didn't look very bright to me, when they took him to the station.'

'Don't need to be bright, do they? Better if they're not. Fill their head with stuff, they'll believe anything, these black kids. You don't know what's going on with them, do you?'

That was it then. He was banged up in the nick somewhere. I could feel stuff rising up into my throat. I swallowed hard. The voices were getting nearer. There were lights too. Torches moving this way and that.

'We'll do this park, then move on to the scrub land by Manor Road School.'

'Right-oh.'

I straightened my body out and tried to flatten myself against the wall. The slapping sound of the branches and leaves being hit was only a few metres away. I held my breath

– stupid thing to do, but you don't always think straight when you're backed into a corner.

Suddenly, something ripped through the bushes, thirty, forty centimetres from my face, showering me with the water from the leaves. A stick – they were poking around with sticks.

'Go under too, run it along the ground.'

'Okay.'

The stick came back in, sweeping along the surface of the ground. It started far enough away, but swished towards me, tracing a semicircle. I sucked my belly in as far as I could. The stick passed within a centimetre of me, before moving away again. The air inside me, already under pressure, was squashed further by my stomach. It felt like I was going to explode. I kept my mouth shut and breathed out through my nose, trying to control it, unable to stop a little explosion of snot. It sounded like a nuclear bomb to me, but it was nothing against the smacking of the leaves, the sound of those tossers' voices. They missed it. I could hear them moving further away.

I can't say I relaxed, but my breathing got easier. My mind was still panicking, though; I was alone, now, really alone. Spider and I, our adventure, had only lasted for three days, but it felt like I'd always been with him. We'd packed the amount of living most people do in a lifetime into those days. More than that, I'd learned to rely on him – let's face it, he'd done most of the thinking, the decision-making, ever since we agreed to cut and run. I was going to have to think for myself now.

I sat up slowly, even now trying not to make any noise. Those two, with their sticks, might have gone, but who was to say there weren't more like them? I knew that this place was safe, or relatively. I could wait here for as long as I needed to. But what was I waiting for? Spider wasn't coming back.

I tried to think what he would want me to do. But if I pictured him now, I saw him fighting, arms and legs flying everywhere, I saw him being held down, pinned to the ground, I saw him bruised, curled up in the corner of a cell. I didn't want to think of him like that – I wanted to see him loping across endless fields, or close to me, wrapped around me – but the wounded Spider, the captured and confined Spider wouldn't stay out of my head. It was no good, I'd go mad if I stayed here. I was going to have to move, and keep moving.

The way to keep faith with him was to carry on our journey. He'd spoken of Weston like some Holy Grail. He believed in it – he believed there'd be happy times for us both there. And if he believed it, so would I. I'd carry on, and I'd hold on to the hope that I'd see him there. Somehow, he'd know that's what I was doing, and he'd meet me there. I didn't know how, but I did know when – before the fifteenth, before the end, we'd be together again.

I waited until I couldn't hear anything above the background buzz of traffic – no footsteps, no deep voices, no helicopters, no dogs barking. After the exhaustion and despair, I felt an edginess kick back into me. I was anticipating the moment I emerged from the bushes, trying to picture myself crawling out into a dark, empty park. Part of me really wanted to get on with it, part of me was shit-scared.

I crept forward on my hands and knees, sticking my face out gently between the leaves, trying not to think about all the dogs that must have peed there over the years. It was too dark to see much; the swings and slide in the kiddies' play park were just ghostly shapes on the other side of the grass. It was all clear, but I hesitated for a minute. It felt sad leaving our hideout, the last place we'd been together. Was I just imagining it, or could I still smell his rankness, clinging to the leaves?

'Goodbye, Spider,' I said, quietly, in my head. 'I'll see you in Weston.'

Chapter 24

I hurried as fast as I could along the path, back towards the town centre. I was peering into the darkness ahead of me, looking out for danger. I didn't even notice the figures coming across the wet grass until it was way too late.

'Oi! There's a lot of people looking for you, including my dad,' a voice called out to the left of me. It was young, female, with the sort of accent you only get on telly, like a yokel in a sitcom. I stopped in my tracks and turned to face whoever it was.

'And?' Give them a bit of attitude, don't show them any fear. I could see them now, three kids emerging from the gloom. Kids like me, about my age, jeans and hoodies.

'And I reckon he'll be earning good overtime. I could tap him up for a few extra quid this week.' The other two laughed. Two more girls, with nose studs and lip rings. They walked up to me, looking me up and down.

Maybe before I would have started running, or at least hunched my shoulders, stared down, but now I stood my ground, looked right back at them. Their numbers came up, of course. They all had another sixty, seventy years – the piercings a sign of middle-class rebellion, nothing more, these girls were heading for comfortable lives, maybe even a husband and two point four children.

'You don't look like a terrorist,' said the first one again. 'Did you do it?'

'Course not.'

'What are you runnin' away from, then?'

'Don't like the cops. No offence,' I added, thinking of her dad.

'None taken.' She almost smiled. 'But you ran away from the bomb.'

'Yeah, just one of those things, you know.'

'Not really. What things?'

I didn't have the energy to lie. 'It just . . . I just . . . I felt something bad was going to happen.'

'And it did.'

'Yeah.'

'Do you often feel things, what's going to happen, like?'

'Yeah, sort of.'

'So you know whether we're going to turn you in or not?' I hesitated for a second or two. I wasn't going to beg.

'I don't think you are,' I said, evenly.

'Why shouldn't we?'

'You don't look like a grass.' It was a compliment, intended to flatter. It worked.

'No, I'm not. You're right there.' A pause. 'You're not going to last five minutes goin' up that way, though. Not through the town centre. Too many people. Where you goin' anyway?'

'S'posed to be heading west, Bristol way.' I didn't want to

say Weston – that was our secret, Spider's and mine.

'On the bus?'

'Walking.'

'Walking! Get off! Are you hungry?'

My eating pattern had been so odd, I didn't know if I was or wasn't. When I thought about it, my last real meal had been breakfast, and that seemed like years ago.

'Yeah, a bit.'

'Hang on, I've had an idea. Come on, we'll cut down the back to mine.'

The other two looked at her like she was mad.

'Wait a minute, that's not such a good idea, is it?' one of them said.

'Shut up – it's a great idea, last place they're going to look.'

'. . . but you'd be in a shed load of trouble if they did . . .'

'But they won't, it'll be cool.' She cut off any further discussion by turning round suddenly and starting to walk back across the grass. 'Come on!' she hissed.

I set off after her, with the others following me. I didn't know whether to trust her or not, but I didn't really have another option. We walked along quickly, in silence. She led us down back alleys and footpaths, between garden fences and alongside playing fields. Eventually, she stopped and we all caught up with her.

'I'll just go in and check what's goin' on. Wait yere.' And she disappeared round a corner. The three of us left behind didn't have anything to say to each other. They were pretty wary of me, and I was too tired to bother.

'It's okay,' she said. 'Dad's still out and Mum's glued to the telly. We'll go in the back way.'

The other two looked at each other.

'Britney, you're mad. We're going home.'

'You're bailing on me?' They nodded. 'All right, suit yourselves, but listen. Don't say nothing to nobody. I mean it – nobody.'

'Of course not.'

'See you tomorrow, then.'

'Yeah, see ya.' They trooped off down the street.

'Can you trust them?' I asked.

'Course, they're sound. Anyway, they know I'll kill them if they don't keep quiet. They wouldn't dare. Come on.'

We went round the side of the house and in through the back door, then straight through the kitchen and upstairs. A little plaque on the bedroom door had a border of roses and the words *Britney's Room* in the middle. Underneath were more recent additions: a skull and crossbones, a big sign saying *Keep Out*. Inside, the walls were painted dark purple and there were posters and pictures cut out from magazines all over them – Kurt Cobain, Foo Fighters, Gallows. The bed had loads of cushions on it and a sort of blanket, which was black and fluffy. It was all pretty cool really. I thought of my last room, at Karen's, my few bits and pieces all smashed up.

'You can sit on the bed, or the beanbag, whatever.' I perched awkwardly on the edge of the bed. Britney sat next to me.

'So,' said Britney. 'I'm Britney and you're . . . Jemma?'

'Jem,' I said.

'Right.' Now that she'd got me there, into her room, she didn't look quite so tough. In fact, she was pretty nervous, making me think the front she'd shown out in the park was just that, front. Underneath she was as worried as the rest of them. After about a decade of sitting in silence, she found some music to put on and then decided to fix some food, leaving me on my own.

I sat there and looked around. It was a cool room. As well as all the posters, there was a real dressing table with make-up and jewellery stands on it, and framed photos all over the place: pictures of family and pets. There were a couple of her with a boy, younger than her – in one of them he had thick, curly hair, in the other he was bald, but still with the same big grin on his face. So there was a brother somewhere, was there?

The central heating was stifling after a few days in the open. I was starting to sweat, and I was pretty sure I was smelling rank too. I took the green coat off, but I was still uncomfortable. I stripped off my hoodie and dropped it on top of the coat on the floor. Lying in a forlorn heap on the rug, they looked disgusting. They were filthy, and looking down, so were my jeans and shoes. Even though Britney's room wasn't exactly tidy, I felt really out of place, like a turd on a carpet.

Britney came back into the room, with big pizza on a plate and a bottle of Coke and some glasses. The smell of the food made me feel hungry and sick at the same time. She held a plate towards me, 'Just cheese and tomato, that all right?'

'Yeah, cheers.' I took a slice, not sure if I could actually eat or not. She was tucking in, looking at me and trying not to look at the same time. I nibbled a little bit off the end of the slice, chewed it slowly, and swallowed. It was fine, it settled in my stomach and stayed there, so I ate the rest of the slice and picked up another one. We sat there eating and drinking. It was bizarre. It was like how you'd imagine teenage kids to be, sitting in someone's bedroom eating pizza and drinking Coke. But we weren't having a laugh, talking about boys and make-up. We were sitting there, both aware of the silence, trying to think of something to say.

At the back of my mind, there was still the fear that it could all be a trap. So I asked her, right out.

'Why are you doing this? Being nice to me?'

She put her pizza down on the plate. 'I've never met a celebrity before. Well, not unless you count that one from *Eastenders* who switched on the Christmas lights a couple of years ago, and she was a bitch.'

'Celebrity?' I said. 'What do you mean?'

'Well, perhaps not celebrity. Famous, anyway. The whole town's talking about you. The whole country is. There's all sorts of rumours about you on the internet, pictures too, sightings – There were quite a few this side of Salisbury Plain. I thought you might turn up here. Most Wanted, that's what you are.'

'I'm just a kid. I haven't done anything.'

'Yeah, but they don't know that, do they? Even if you didn't do anything, you might have seen stuff. You could be a witness.' She took another bite of pizza. 'Did you see anything?'

I thought back to that afternoon. It seemed like a year ago. Before we nicked those cars, before we walked miles, before we slept out in the wood, before we found that barn . . .

'You all right? You've gone a right funny colour.'

I guess the heat and the food and the tiredness had got to me, the room was starting to swim around.

'I feel a bit dizzy.'

Britney jumped up from the bed next to me and took my plate. 'Here, lie down. You'll be all right.'

I lay down, but that was worse. Before I could get up and make for the toilet, I was sick, pizza and Coke on her fluffy black cover. She was horrified, and to be honest, so was I. She'd been kinder to me than I had any right to expect, and now I'd wrecked her bedroom. I sat up properly.

'I'm sorry, I'm so sorry,' I mumbled. God, no wonder I never got asked anywhere.

'It's okay, I'll get something.' Britney shot out of the room, while I got up and opened a window to try and let the smell out. I leaned against the window frame, breathing in some cool night air. When Britney reappeared with a bucket and sponge, I took the sponge from her hand, dipped it in the bucket and started trying to remove the mess from all that fake fur. It was a pretty hopeless job.

'Listen, why don't you have a shower, while I do this? Don't worry about the noise, Mum'll just think it's me.' She showed me where the bathroom was and started the shower running.

'Wait a minute, I'll get you some clean clothes.' She disappeared and came back with a little heap of clean, folded things, including a big thick towel. 'Don't take too long. Mum's programme finishes in ten minutes.'

She disappeared again and I locked the door behind her. The room was filling with steam. I wiped a hand towel over the mirror above the sink. There was someone in there looking back at me, but I didn't recognise her. She was nearly bald, big rings under her eyes, looked about twenty, maybe twenty-five, sick down her front. I turned away and stripped off my dirty clothes, then stepped into the shower.

Soft, warm water rained down on me. I breathed in the steam, turned my face up into the flow. I reached blindly for the nearest bottle of shampoo and poured a handful, rubbing foam into my scalp and all over my body. As the lumps of froth slid down my skin and gathered in the shower tray, I could feel myself getting cleaner. I scrubbed under my arms, round my groin, and I suddenly thought, *I'm washing him away*, and felt sad. For the last twenty-four hours, I'd been carrying the smell of Spider with me, on my skin, inside me. All that was spiralling down into the drain.

I switched off the shower and stepped out wetly. I wrapped the clean towel around me like a dress and then bent and towelled my head dry with the end of it.

There was a gentle tap on the door. 'You okay?' Britney hissed.

I slid back the bolt and opened the door a fraction. Our faces were surprisingly close together, and we both jumped back a little. 'I'll be out in a minute,' I whispered. I closed the door and quickly dried off and got dressed. The clothes were great, the sort of thing I'd wear anyway. Bit big, but wearable. I gathered up my old things and the towel and padded along the hallway into Britney's room.

She'd done the best job she could of clearing up, but you could still see where I'd thrown up.

'Sorry,' I said again.

''S'all right. Feeling better?'

'Yeah.'

'I was thinkin', the best thing would be for you to get some sleep here, and leave when it gets light.' I looked at her. Was she mad? Or just keeping me here until her dad got in?

'No, really I should go.'

'You won't be able to see anything. Set off early – you can do a couple of hours before anyone's up.'

She was right, but I just couldn't see myself bedding down in a cop's house for the night.

'Won't anyone come in here?' I asked.

She smiled. 'No, they wouldn't dare. One: I've told them not to. And two: they're scared what they'd find. Not that they would find anything; no drugs, no condoms, no pills, not even cigarettes. Just me. P'raps that's what they're scared of. They don't really get teenagers, my mum and dad. You could stay, see, you'd be perfectly safe.'

It was almost like she was pleading with me. She didn't seem to understand that she was the powerful one here. My safety was held by a little silver thread, a cobweb. She wouldn't have to cut it, just blow and it would stretch and break. She only had to raise her voice and shout to her mum and it was all over for me.

'What about your brother?'

'Oh . . . no, he died last year.'

Me and my big mouth.

'I'm sorry. I just saw the photos. Sorry.'

'It's okay. You wouldn't know, would you?'

Well, I thought, *the bald head might have given me a clue*.

She was busying herself sorting out blankets and pillows.

'How long is it since you slept in a bed?' she asked.

I had to think hard. 'Three nights.' The warmth from the shower, the sheer luxury of being inside had softened me up. I couldn't face going out into the dark and the cold. Not tonight.

'You sleep there then, I'll be all right down here.'

She got down on the beanbag and started to wrap the blanket round her.

'Don't be so soft. It's your room. I couldn't.'

'Course you could. You need some sleep. Some proper sleep.'

'No, I couldn't. It's not right. I'd rather go than kick you out of your own bed. I mean it.'

'Okay then.' She struggled up and climbed into bed, and I curled up in the beanbag, instantly regretting it. It was bloody uncomfortable.

Britney put the lights out.

'Night, Britney,' I said.

'Night, Jem.'

Waves of tiredness and nausea were sweeping through me. I was scared of being sick again. The events of the day were filling my head – this morning I'd woken up with Spider's arms round me. It seemed like years ago. It was too much to deal with.

The streetlight filtered through Britney's thin curtains, and I lay awkwardly, eyes wide open, taking in the room. What would it be like to be this girl? To have a mum and a dad, a cool bedroom, mates to hang out with? And a dead brother. However cosy things seemed, the facts of life were the same. You couldn't escape death: it would get us all in the end. Which brought me back to Spider. Where was he now? Lying there, I ached just to know he was okay, I ached to be with him.

Somewhere an alarm clock was ticking steadily away – the noise filled the room, each tick a hammer blow to my head. Three days to go.

Chapter 25

I lay awake in the soft gloom of Britney's room. Britney, curled up on her bed, had her eyes closed. She was breathing evenly, but I couldn't tell if she was asleep or not. I was exhausted, but wide awake. I didn't want to bother her, but it was pretty much torture lying there.

After about fifteen minutes, I was relieved to hear her voice, a soft whisper in the dark.

'You awake?'

'Yeah.'

'Me too.'

'I just can't sleep.'

'Look, get in here. Put your pillow down that end – we can top and tail.'

There was no way I was going to get any sleep on that bean-bag, so I did as she said, gratefully tucking in, curling my legs up, so as not too take up too much space. A few days ago, I'd never have done this, got into bed with a stranger, but now it felt okay; okay to be close to someone, okay to trust them.

'I used to do this with my brother, when we were little – top and tail – and my mum would read us a story. You got any family?'

'I live with my foster mum, and two little boys, twins.'

'What's she like? Your foster mum?'

Straight away, the words shot out – sheer reflex. 'Karen? She's a bitch.'

'Yeah?'

Then, just for a minute, I thought about Karen. What was she actually like?

'Well, I suppose she's not a bitch. She's been pretty kind to me, tried to help. Except . . . it wasn't the kind of help I wanted. She doesn't get me, doesn't understand.'

In the soft darkness, Britney nodded in agreement. 'Tell me about it. I don't think my parents were ever young – I think they were born middle-aged.'

'But they're all right, though.'

'Yeah, they're all right. They've been through a lot. S'pose I should cut them some slack really.'

'Britney, tell me to shut up if you like but . . . but . . . if you'd known that you only had a few years with your brother, would it have made a difference?'

She sighed, and I thought I'd overstepped the mark again, but then she said, 'We pretty much did know. At least my parents did – they didn't tell me until near the end. But I don't think knowing exactly when would've changed anything. Even with him ill, we still did things, had fun – between treatments, we went places, had holidays, all the usual stuff.' She paused, but I didn't jump in – I could tell there was more to come. 'And we sorted out the important stuff – Jim knew I loved him and I knew he loved me. Not in a stupid way, hearts and flowers, just normal, brother and sister. He could still wind me up something proper, right up until, until . . .'

'Sorry, you don't have to . . .'

'No, it's okay to talk about it. Death is so normal, I don't know why everyone gets so hung up about it. We all have to deal with it. Most people that you talk to have lost someone, but nobody talks about it.'

It was easier talking in the dark. I didn't feel so self-conscious, the words just tumbled out. Or perhaps it was just Britney, she was a good talker and a good listener. I felt like I could say anything to her.

'My mum died,' I heard myself blurting out, 'when I was seven, but I don't feel anything like you do. I just feel . . . I dunno . . . empty, angry. Like she left me. She chose to leave.'

'Was she ill?'

'No. Overdose. It was an accident. At least I'm pretty sure it was. I don't think she wanted to die, but then again, I don't think she was that bothered about staying alive. The next fix was the most important thing. I've always known that, but I've never said it to anyone – I was always way down her list, never first. She chose heroin over me.'

'But she didn't make a choice, Jem. You've just told me – she was addicted. It was out of her control. She was ill, like Jim was ill.'

'I still hate her for leaving.'

'That's a long time to hate someone. Perhaps you need to let it go.'

I let her words sink in and felt them settle within me. Sounded like she'd been watching too much *Oprah* to me. Life's not that simple. Not so easy to move on when the anger you've got is what keeps you going.

But it wasn't the only thing I had now. Spider – the need to see him again, the need to save him – had given me something else.

There was a noise then, a sharp bang from downstairs, and we both jumped out of our skins.

'It'll be Dad home – I'll just go and see.'

Britney clambered out of bed, put on her dressing gown and went downstairs. She left the door slightly ajar and I picked up the alarm clock from her bedside table and angled it in the light coming in from the landing, until I could make it out. Two-fifteen. Their voices were floating up the stairs now; Britney's soft burr and the deeper base notes of her dad. I could only make out a few of his words, but the ones I heard made me jump out of bed and crouch down behind the open door, my heart jumping around in my throat.

' . . . went berserk . . . eight of us . . . bloody strong . . .'

I opened the door a bit further, straining desperately to hear more. The voices downstairs were competing with Spider's words in my head: *I won't go quietly, Jem. I'll fight them, Jem. I will.*

What had he done?

' . . . died in his cell . . . investigation . . .'

Oh my God. He'd kicked off like he said he would. I'd told him not to. I'd told him it wasn't worth it. How could this happen? How could everything be brought to a big full stop, three days early? I wanted to scream out – I didn't care any more if I was found. If Spider was gone, I had nothing left. My whole body was a scream, my skin electric. We'd been cheated, cheated of our last few hours, cheated of the chance to say goodbye – it was unthinkable.

The voices were nearer now, right outside the door. I

190

hadn't noticed them come upstairs.

'Goodnight, love. Try and get some sleep. I'm just going in the shower.'

'Okay, night, Dad.'

Britney came back into the room. She was carrying a mug, and gave a little gasp as she spotted me behind the door. I saw her eyes widen and she quickly held her index finger up to her mouth. She closed the door, and I slumped back against it, silent tears running down my face. She crouched down next to me.

'What is it?' she hissed.

I couldn't get any words out.

He was gone.

It was all over.

'Listen, tell me in a minute, when my dad's in the shower. Get back into bed – I've brought you some tea. Here.' She'd put the tea down and now she was helping me to my feet, and shepherding me back to bed.

I couldn't drink the tea, it was all I could do to keep breathing, black grief pulsing through me. After a minute or so we heard the bedroom door go, and the shower start up. Britney shuffled forward in the bed, and put her hands on my legs.

'It's okay to talk now, but quietly, still. Now what on earth is it?'

'He's dead, isn't he? I heard you. He's dead.' The words were distorted, blurry, but somehow she understood.

'No, you turnip, it was the other one.'

'What?'

'The other bloke they arrested. A big bloke, Dad said, covered in tatts.'

Tattoo Face?

'He went mad in his cell, started smashing everything up. Took eight of them to stop him, and he died in the middle of it all.'

'He died?'

'They don't know if someone hit him, or if he had a heart attack or whatever. All hell's broken loose down the station anyway. Dad was one of the eight – he's been suspended for the time being.'

Tattoo Face, not Spider. 11122009.

'Britney?'

'Yeah?'

'Do you know when it happened? What time?'

'Just before midnight. Just before the end of Dad's shift.'

It was like things were slotting back into place again. The ground had shifted beneath my feet for a while, rules bending, but now we were back on solid ground; sickening, nightmarish, but solid ground. The numbers were real. Spider was still alive, but he only had three days to go.

'You okay?'

'Yeah, kind of.'

'Need a hug?'

I didn't answer but she leant forward anyway and put her arms round me. I stiffened, and she must have felt it, but she didn't let me go.

'It's all right,' she said. 'Everything will be all right. Here, have some of that tea.' She handed it over – hot, sweet tea, best thing I'd tasted for a long time. I drained the lot and we both lay down, curled up at opposite ends of the bed, legs hooked in to each other's. The tea had soothed me, my mind was so full I couldn't think any more. I was properly exhausted now; I could feel waves of sleep starting to wash over me.

'Britney?' I said quietly into the darkness.

'Mm?'

'Thanks.'

'You're all right.'

'I mean it.'

'Shuddup, and go to sleep.'

That made me smile, it was like listening to a reflection of myself. And I did go to sleep, an instant, dreamless sleep, away from the world for a few hours, away from the tick, tick, tick of the clock.

Chapter 26

I reached for the alarm clock and held it in front of my face. Nearly half six. It was still dark, but wouldn't be for much longer. I shifted round in the bed, trying to work out how I felt.

'Are you awake?' Britney's voice hissed.

'Yeah.' Truth was, I felt pretty rough. I'd had a few hours good sleep, but I felt tired, a bit queasy.

'We'll have to be really, really quiet.'

'Okay.' We were both in our clothes anyway, so we got up in the dark, and padded downstairs.

'I'll go in first, make sure we don't startle Ray.'

Ray?

She opened the kitchen door, and I could hear her whispering to someone. So it was a set-up after all. I should have known it was too good to be true. People will always let you down. I looked down the hallway. I could easily let myself out of the front door.

'It's okay, come on.' Britney was beckoning me into the kitchen.

I took another look at the front door, but something told me to trust her. I walked towards the square of light coming from the other end of the hall. She was bent over in the kitchen, holding the collar of an enormous dog, a great big hairy German Shepherd. I don't do animals. Never had a pet, obviously, don't know anything about them. The way some people fuss over them and talk to them, it's just odd, isn't it? They don't see them for what they are: something other, different, not human.

'Close the door behind you,' Britney hissed. 'This is Ray, he's Dad's work dog.'

Christ! I was shut in a room now, three metres by two and a half, with a bloody police dog.

'He was looking for you yesterday, too, weren't you, Ray-ray? You've found her now, haven't you? Clever boy! Say hello to him,' she said to me, 'he'll be fine.'

'Hello,' I said, trying not to look him in the eye, or wind him up in any way.

Britney stifled a giggle. 'No, not like that, stroke him, on his shoulder, not his head. Go on, he'll know you're a friend.'

'Is he going to bite me?' She smiled and shook her head.

I edged towards him, waiting for him to lunge forward and grab my arm in his massive jaws. Slowly, slowly, I leaned forward and put my hand on the fur at the bottom of his neck, and rested it there. I could feel his solid body underneath, warm and full of life, and the fur itself, it was fantastic; clean and soft. It felt like I was touching a lion. I moved my hand gently. 'Hello, Ray, you're a nice dog,' my words as wooden as my movements. He sniffed at my leg and then quickly, almost violently, rubbed his huge, hard snout up and down my jeans, almost knocking me over.

'What's he doing?'

'Nothing. He likes you. He's putting his scent on you. Just let him.' I wasn't going to argue, and so I stood there and let him mark me as one of his own. Not so bright, after all, dogs. He hadn't got a clue he was cosying up to the enemy.

Britney was busy in the corner with her back to me. When she turned round, she proudly held up a backpack, black with all sorts of stuff sewn on to it, and badges.

'I've put some things in. Your clothes and a bit of food, some water. I've got a blanket here, too, but it won't fit in. I'll tie it on with some string.' She fished in a drawer, found a ball of twine and started wrapping it round the rolled-up blanket. I didn't know what to say.

'Is that your bag?'

'My school bag.'

'Won't you need it?'

'I'll just get another one, say the strap broke. It's okay.'

From upstairs, there was the sound of the bathroom door going. We looked at one another. I wanted to go, there and then. Britney held her hand up to stop me. After the bog flushed, a man's voice rang out from the landing.

'Who's that down there? Britney, is that you?' My heart was up in my mouth again. Britney opened the kitchen door and shouted up.

'It's okay, Dad, it's me. The dog was whining. I'm going to take him out.'

'Okay. Thanks, love.' She came back in, finished tying the blanket on to the bag, then clipped the dog onto its lead and made for the back door, beckoning me to follow her. I closed it carefully behind us, shocked to feel the cool air on my face again. I'd felt out of place indoors, stifled, but now I was heading back to an outdoor life the uncomfortable reality of it came back to me.

She led me along the back alleys. She was holding the dog, and I had the backpack on. We walked in silence. The paths were so narrow it was single file anyway; dog, Britney and me. After a few minutes of twists and turns, we got to a stile between two fences. Britney unclipped Ray, and he jumped over, like it was nothing. We both clambered over after him. Off his lead, in the open field, he was more unpredictable. I kept expecting him to come to his senses and go for me like he was meant to do.

'Is he all right, like that?'

'What?'

'Just running about.'

'Yeah, he's fine. He'll come back when I call.'

'I mean, is it safe?' She got what I meant this time.

'Course. You're his friend now, he won't go after you. He'll have a look for some rabbits in a bit, once he's had a crap. The path goes over to that corner.'

I'd expected Britney to turn back once we'd got to the fields, but she walked with me a little way, the dog falling behind and then bounding up to us. We didn't say much – we'd pretty much said it all last night – but it was fine, walking along together.

'Where are you heading?' she asked, after a while.

'I can't really tell you. It's better if I don't. Not that I don't trust you.'

'No, it's all right, I understand.'

'It's a place we talked about, Spider and me. Even though he's banged up at the moment, I'm going to keep heading there. I'm going to do it on my own, and I think, I believe, he'll meet me there. Somehow, he'll make it.'

'I hope he does, Jem. I'll be rooting for you.' We walked a little way further, then she said, 'That's the canal there. If you go over that stile, there's a bridge the other side. Cross over and then follow the path left and you'll be on the tow-path. It'll go all the way to Bath. 'Bout twelve miles. I'd better take Ray back – they'll all be getting up soon.' So this was it, the place where we were going to say goodbye.

'Thanks,' I said, and I really meant it.

'That's okay.' She turned her head away, looking towards the canal. 'Good luck, Jem. I'll always remember you. It's been well cool.'

I kind of wanted to reach out to her, but I didn't know how to do it without it being embarrassing. I think she felt the same and we both stood with our hands by our sides looking at the ground, until it just felt silly and pointless. Then I nodded to her, tried to catch her eye.

'Better get off,' I said, 'I'll remember you too, Britney.' And I walked down the path and over to the stile.

As I climbed over, I looked back. She hadn't moved, was just watching me go. I waved, and she waved back, and it felt good, having someone saying goodbye properly, not just leaving without anyone knowing. She kept her hand up for a second, then called her dog and turned away. I jumped down from the stile and, hitching up the bag on my back, walked over the bridge.

Chapter 27

The towpath made everything simpler. There was one way to the next place and I didn't need to make any decisions or choices, just keep walking. With Spider nicked, I knew now that it was a question of when, and not if, I was picked up too. To be honest, I felt pretty calm about it all. The worst had happened already – losing Spider, being left sleeping rough in the middle of nowhere, being left without money. And I'd survived the first twelve hours. Well, I'd done better than survive: I'd made a friend. How cool was that?

I walked all day, past handfuls of boats, little knots of houses. There were joggers pounding along the flat path, and people on bikes. I just ignored them, head down, putting one foot in front of the other, no eye contact.

Funny, it was probably the first day I'd walked all the time, not hiding out and resting. I guess all the emotion and not eating much was catching up with me and I was in pretty poor shape, but I kept going. I was like a zombie, too tired and numb to think much any more, just following the track, on and on. It was so much easier walking with a backpack. Jesus, Spider and I had made things difficult for ourselves – grabbing stuff that came to hand, cramming it into plastic bags. What a pair of retards. My eyes started stinging, just thinking about him. Where was he? What were they doing to him now? The only way I could cope was to keep going, one foot in front of the other, on and on, heading west.

I could tell I was getting near to the city when the towpath started getting busy: there were family groups, kids on bikes or scampering along with their dogs, older couples arm in arm, enjoying a Saturday afternoon stroll in the winter sunshine. Eyes down, I still picked up on their wariness, the mothers shepherding the kids away.

One little tot blundered into my legs and stood staring up at me. I almost felt my hair stand on end. This little thing looked right into my face, with big, brown, trusting eyes and two trails of snot coming out of his nose. 432053. He was going to die in his forties, this kid with no idea what death was yet.

I sidestepped, my legs shrugging off his sticky grasp, and pressed on, while behind me his parents scolded him gently in a 'don't you just love him?' kind of way. Two minutes down the path, I fancied I could still feel the damp warmth of his hands through my jeans.

I was feeling edgy again now. People gathered together were dangerous. The odd one or two, you could deal with, but crowds were something else. I tried to pick up the pace, but I didn't have it in me. All day I'd felt the need to keep going, to get there, wherever there was. Now, I was worn out and getting scared again. The sun was starting to drop behind the hills.

The landscape around me was changing as the light began

to go. Pale buildings clung to the hillsides to left and right. Streetlights were popping on, giving the stone an orange glow, picking out the shape of the city's fingers reaching out into the fields. Soon there were buildings closing in on both sides. I was almost in Bath. Today, I wanted the light to stay. I didn't want to be alone in the dark.

I never used to be frightened of anything – reckoned that life had thrown about the worst it had at me by the time I was seven – but the last few months had shaken all that up, the last few days especially. All I wanted now was to find somewhere safe to bed down for the night, to curl up and sleep. I wanted to switch off, blank out the world for a while. A deep chill swept through me. Is that what my mum was doing when she was shooting up? Escaping for a few hours? Was it all too much for her? Looking after a kid on her own? Living in a grotty flat? Let down time after time? I'd never understood it before. Why she'd do that. But I was beginning to see how attractive a bit of oblivion could be – it was just that I didn't want to find it the way she had . . .

There was something strange about this place. Where I come from, canals are dirty places, running along the backs of warehouses and factories. This was different. It was edged with white-painted metal gates and fancy bridges, with carvings in the stone.

Soon the path left the canal and led to a road. I was actually on a hill – weird when you've been walking on the flat all day. The road went up and down to the left and right of me, while the canal carried on flat, underneath it, on the other side. I crossed over, and peered over the stone bridge. Couldn't see a great deal now, but could make out the shapes of boats tied up. Not sure there'd be anywhere to kip down along there. I'd be better off if I could find a park, or the bottom of someone's garden. I set off up the road and then turned right into a quieter one. It was like something off the telly, a film set, with a cobbled pavement and tall houses.

It was the time of day when people had their lights on but hadn't yet drawn their curtains. Every second or third front window was like a little TV screen, bright in the gathering gloom, drawing your eye in. People on their computers or watching the telly, some sitting reading.

Made me feel lonely, seeing a snapshot of other people's lives. They were warm, secure, there were cooking smells wafting out, soon be dinner time, they had people, they belonged. I made myself move on – no good thinking what other people had, I needed to find somewhere to sleep.

On the other side of the road, the houses stopped. A fence ran along the edge of a field. I started looking for a place to get through, didn't fancy getting caught up on more barbed wire. I was so tired, I felt like I was in a daze. A breeze got up, its icy edge cutting through my clothes. I needed to find somewhere to shelter, or else be found frozen solid in the morning.

I crossed the road to follow the line of the fence. A few metres along, there was a stile and I climbed over – or rather hauled myself, my legs pretty much shot after a full day's walking. As I clambered down the other side, first thing I did was put my foot in something. A big, slippery pool, stinking to high heaven. Oh great, cows again, but not safely penned in this time.

The grass sloped upwards into the blackness. I followed the fence along for a bit – it was flatter and you could see a bit better there with the streetlights – until I reached the corner of the field and there was no option but to climb, away from the road and into the darkness. The sky seemed to have disappeared, blocked out by the hill, and, I discovered, a clump of trees. They were the other side of the fence, but there was a gate, so I hauled myself over again and blundered up, bushes tearing at my jeans, until I found a flatter bit underneath the trees – actually a bit of a dip in the ground, a hollow. I checked for cowpats as best I could, and sank down.

I curled up like a baby in the blanket Britney had given me, wrapping it around my body and over my face. It hardly kept the wind off me at all. As usual I thought I'd never sleep: my head was full of Spider, always Spider. Was he asleep now? Was he lying somewhere, awake like me, chest rising and falling? How many breaths did he have left? But when I'd stopped shivering and my body's own warmth started to heat the space inside the blanket, I drifted off, the darkness around me sweeping into my head, switching the thoughts off.

Chapter 28

There was someone chasing me, so close I could hear his breath, feel it on the back of my neck. I was running faster than I've ever run. My chest was bursting, and I was running, running, but he'd got me, there was nowhere left to go. It was too much, I couldn't cope with it any more. I wrenched myself back to the surface, becoming aware of my surroundings, opening my eyes slightly to see the grey light of dawn.

Just a dream after all. But the noise was still there, someone near me, so near I could hear the breath in and out, in and out. Spider? Just for a minute, I thought he was next to me again. Oh Jesus. I rolled over slowly. There was a dark shape right on top of me, an animal of some sort, snuffling around. Cows? I'd thought they were in the other field. But it wasn't a cow, it was a dog; a big, black dog with its nose in my backpack.

I froze. Ray may have been a sheep in wolf's clothing, but I still didn't trust dogs and this was a big one, tall and skinny, but with bulging muscles in its shoulders and back legs.

Another noise broke in now, a woman's voice. 'Sparky! Come here! Come *here*!' I saw his ear twitch. He'd heard her, but the last of the bread Britney had put in my bag was more interesting. The owner of the voice came round the corner now: wellies, furry coat and scarf. When she saw us, she broke into a run.

'Oh, shit! Sparky, come here!' He looked up, then dipped his head again. Time was running out for him. One last chance to grab a mouthful. The woman got her fingers into his collar and yanked him right away. 'I'm so sorry, so sorry. It's the food. He's a terrible scavenger. Oh God, he's eaten your food. I'm so sorry.' Her voice was anxious, posh.

There was an awkward silence. I was still lying on the ground, woozy with sleep. The woman and her dog loomed over me. She was waiting for me to say something, worried about my reaction. I sat up and shuffled away from them on my bum.

'I'm sorry, he woke you up, didn't he? Scared you. He wouldn't bite you. It was just the food. Look, I only live down there, you could come and have some breakfast, a cup of tea.' It didn't look like she meant it; she was probably just trying to say something to make things better.

'No,' I managed. 'S'all right.'

'He's eaten your food. I could bring you something . . . ?'

'No, honest. I'm all right.'

'I don't think I've got any money on me.' She reached into her pockets. 'Oh, look, you could buy some breakfast with this.' She held out a handful of change towards me. I just wanted this all to stop. I wanted her to take her bloody dog and her middle-class niceness and her do-gooding pity away.

'I don't want your fucking money, I'm all right.' That did the trick.

She recoiled visibly, tightened her grip on the dog's collar. 'Right, okay. Okay. Sorry.' She backed off, then bent to clip on the dog's lead.

They took a wide semicircle below me on the hill and went through the gate into the next field, where they stopped for a moment. The woman unclipped the dog, dug about in her pocket and then looked back at me. Then the dog took off suddenly, stretching out its legs and tearing across the field. The movement rippled along him, like a wave, as if he was a little black racehorse. She set off walking after him along the path, and I stood up to watch them go. He circled around her three times, then trotted up close and followed along, steaming gently in the morning light. Watching them made me feel lonelier; hadn't thought it was possible.

My gaze shifted from the two of them, getting smaller as they reached the other side of the field, to the view beyond. The wind from last night had disappeared completely. The sky above was a clear, pale blue, the last few stars still visible. Beneath, clouds of the whitest, fluffiest cotton wool streaked across the scene at ground level. Honey-coloured spires and towers stuck up through them; islands in a billowing sea. I'd never seen anything like it. Somewhere beneath the fog, people were sleeping and waking, farting, scratching, having a morning piss, but on the surface it looked like Disneyland.

I'd been nervous about going into the city. Now I felt a strange burst of confidence. Nothing bad could happen in a place like this, could it? I rolled up my blanket and tied it on to my backpack. My fingers were clumsy with the cold. All my things, and the clothes I was in, were wet from the dew.

I set off down the hill towards the gate, my feet adding another set of prints to the two trails of the woman and dog.

As I reached to open the gate, I saw a little pile of coins on the top of the post. She'd left her change after all. I put it in my pocket. It felt grubby taking her money, different to Britney giving me her stuff. It felt like charity, and I didn't want to be nobody's charity case.

I went through the far gate and crossed the street. No-one about here. I cut down an alley between two terraces, heading into the city centre. The path went under a railway bridge and then suddenly I was back in the twenty-first century, and right by a main road with cars and lorries flashing by, their lights disorientating me, their noise ringing in my ears. I was still only half awake. I looked at the slowing stream of traffic, and darted forward.

A horn blared out to the right of me, injecting adrenalin into my bloodstream, making my heart jump and my legs run faster. Where the hell had that come from? I needed to keep my wits about me. I ran for a minute or so, then slowed to a walk, over a bridge spanning a thick brown river. The other side there were hotels and bars, and then shops, not real ones, but the sort tourists would go into. Rip-off shops. They all had Christmas lights and decorations in the windows – sparkly, twinkly tat. Nothing was open.

I looked at my watch. It was only ten to eight. Right in the centre there were a few people around; window cleaners, someone emptying the bins, people letting themselves into shops, or hurrying along, chins tucked down into their scarves, some smelling of their first cigarette of the day as they passed. No-one gave me a second glance. It's the time of day when you don't want to be bothered with anyone else. If you're out that early, you've got something to do, or somewhere to be, and you just get on with it.

My knee was still giving me gyp, but I didn't want to stop

anywhere, so I walked through the city. There was a group of dossers on some steps, swigging Special Brew for breakfast.

'All right, love?' one of them called out, holding his can towards me. *He thinks I'm like him*, I thought, *a friendly greeting to another dosser. And he's right, that's what I am.*

'All right,' I said, my eyes flicking back down to the pavement avoiding his automatically, and kept going, stepping over the cans lying round the bottom of the steps.

I walked down the main drag, under swags of Christmas lights, and right at the bottom found the only place that was open – McDonalds. I'd got enough money for a cup of tea and an Egg McMuffin. I always used to like that smell, the smell you get in a McDonalds, but as I waited for the guy behind the counter to fetch my order it was making me gag. I took my stuff outside, grateful for the fresh air, and wandered back up the street.

There was an archway leading to a square with loads of seats and a huge tree planted in the middle. I was right in front of the big church with the tower. As good a place as any. I sat down and put my drink on the bench next to me.

I unwrapped the muffin. The egg yolk had broken and was oozing out of the bun. I was hungry, but I couldn't eat that. I put it down on the bench, picked up my tea instead, and eased the plastic lid off. I took a sip, the hotness in my mouth making me realise just how cold I was.

I looked at the massive building on my left. Notices at either corner said *Bath Abbey*. There was a big, wooden door in the middle. Above it was a gigantic arch-shaped window. All the way up either side there were horizontal lines carved in the stone, with figures perched on them, looked a bit like people on a ladder. Actually, that's what they were; stone ladders with stone people climbing up. Some of them had bits missing, made them look like a smudged drawing, but the ones that were whole had wings. Angels? They were definitely trying to get up there, although some of them were the wrong way up, looked like they were about to drop off. Daft buggers, why didn't they just fly?

I drank my tea, and studied the weird carvings. The drink was warming me, making me feel more like a human being. I picked up the muffin, which was cold now, the liquid egg congealed. I took a little bite, but my stomach lurched as I chewed. No way. I spat my mouthful back into the wrapper.

There were more people around now. They were making for the area to the side of the abbey; through a makeshift arch I could see some little wooden huts, some sort of market. I could sense the sideways glances, the unease, and started to feel exposed again. Better to move on, find somewhere more out of the way to sit, until I'd worked out what to do. I stood up and hitched my bag onto my back. I was about to walk away when I thought better of it, picked up the empty cup and the vile muffin in its wrapper and put them in a bin a couple of metres away.

'Thank you,' a guy in a long coat and scarf said as he walked past, 'for keeping the Abbey churchyard tidy.' He held his hand up in a kind of greeting and breezed over to a little door at the side of the main one, a big bunch of keys jangling at his waist. I turned away, and made for an alley to my left, out of the square.

There was someone in uniform at the other end.

I swivelled round and headed back to the archway where I'd come in.

Two men in suits were striding towards me – could have just been office workers on their way to work, but they were looking straight at me.

Shit, this was it then. All those people I'd thought were taking no notice, one of them had clocked me, perhaps loads of them had. Or that woman in the fields. Bloody busybody. I wanted to shout, *No!* To hear it echoing round this square. I glanced over my shoulder to see if there was anyone behind me. The guy with the keys had got in now, was just swinging the door shut. I ran towards him.

'Wait, wait. Please.' He looked up, startled, then put his hand round the edge of the door, stopping its movement.

'Help me, please. I'm scared. Please let me in.' My voice was breaking. His pale blue eyes searched mine, and then looked beyond me. He hesitated for an agonising second, then grabbed my arm and pulled me inside. I stumbled into the darkness, while he pushed the heavy door with both his hands until it slammed shut. Then he drew the bolt across. From the other side came the sound of footsteps and hands thudding onto the wood.

Then shouts. 'Open up! This is the police!'

As my eyes got used to the gloom, I could see my rescuer turning around and leaning on the door. He put his hands up to his mouth. 'What have I done?' he gasped, looking straight at me. 'Dear Lord, what have I done?'

Chapter 29

He looked at me.

'Are you all right?'

I nodded.

'Are they really the police?' He meant the thugs banging on the other side of the door.

I nodded again.

'I should open up really, let them in.'

I closed my eyes – after all that, he was going to turn me in anyway.

'You look exhausted. Do you need a bit of time? Compose yourself?'

I didn't know what that last bit meant, but I did want some more time.

'Yeah.'

'Go through that door into the abbey and have a seat. I'll tell them what's going on.'

I wasn't sure.

'It's all right. Go on.'

I pulled on a big metal handle and opened the inside door. I stepped through, expecting more gloom, but the church itself was flooded with light. I was in the tallest space; columns of stone reaching up and up to the ceiling, which seemed to be propped up with huge stone fans. Lower down the windows were made of coloured glass, but up high they were clear, the sky beyond now a brilliant blue. I took my bag off and sat down on a wooden bench. It dug into my back. Behind me I could hear the bolts on the main door being slid back. Any minute now, those guys would burst through. I didn't want to see it happen. I closed my eyes again, and waited. There was the sound of voices, but I couldn't catch all the words. The door banged back into place, the bolt went across again. Then footsteps, and the inner door opening.

'They'll wait. They're not happy, but they'll wait. I said you'd claimed sanctuary in the Lord's house, and that they could not trespass here. A white lie,' he said, with a little self-conscious laugh, 'made with the best of intentions.'

I opened my eyes and looked at him blankly. It took him a while to twig that I hadn't a clue what he was talking about.

'It's what you want, isn't it? Sanctuary? A place of safety,' he explained. He was younger than I had thought when I first saw him. Late twenties maybe. Thin, with wavy brown hair crinkling over from a side parting, Adam's apple bobbing nervously up and down, and pale, pale eyes.

'Yes,' I murmured, 'somewhere safe.'

He frowned. 'Do you mind me asking why the police are chasing you? I mean, you don't have to say, not if you don't want to.'

'They think I've done something bad, but I haven't.'

'Something serious?'

'They think I blew up the London Eye.'

The frown deepened.

'Oh. I see.' He swallowed and the Adam's apple went into overdrive. 'You're the one, the girl from London that they're all looking for. That is serious. You really need to talk to them,' he said gently, 'clear it up.'

'Yeah, but they're not going to listen to me, are they? They just want someone in the frame, guilty as charged, case closed. You've seen them, they think I done it, but I never did. I never . . .' My voice rose, echoing up and through the space.

'They certainly want to talk to you, but not as a suspect, as a witness.'

'They're going to frame me, and they've taken my friend and . . .'

'Okay, okay. Look, the rector – my boss –' he added, quickly, 'will be here soon for Matins. I'll discuss it with him. I need to get the church ready. Do you mind waiting here while I get on? Or you could come round with me. I don't mind.'

The back of the bench was boring into my back. I didn't want to sit there for any longer than I had to, so I got up and followed him as he bustled about the place, switching lights on, unlocking doors, and lighting candles.

'I'm Simon, by the way.' He half turned and offered me his hand. I took it in mine, and we shook awkwardly. His hand was warm, delicate and surprisingly soft for such a thin man. 'And you are . . . ?'

'Um, Jem. I'm Jem.'

'Jem. Nice to meet you.'

Funny thing to say – suppose it was the way he was brought up, manners and everything. I didn't know what you were meant to say back, so I didn't say anything.

'Your hand's very cold. Been sleeping rough?'

'Yeah.' We'd got to an area at the front of the church on the right hand side, separated from the rest by a sort of wooden screen.

'If you sit in the chapel here, there are some warm air vents underneath the benches. Help you thaw out. I'll carry on round, but I'll be back in a minute, Jem.'

I sat where he'd shown me, on a cushioned ledge at the edge of the room. At one end was a table, with a gold cross on it. In the middle was a small black pillar with a candle on the top. There was writing round the edge. I got up to have a look: *Dona nobis pacem*. No idea what that was all about. Why write something in a language like that, something only posh people understand? It's like telling the rest of us to sod off, isn't it? I read the words to myself, sounding out their strangeness.

I started as I realised someone was standing in the chapel entrance.

'It's only me,' Simon said. 'I didn't mean to interrupt. Carry on praying.'

'Not praying,' I said, 'I was just . . . reading it.'

He smiled. 'Of course. They're lovely words, powerful.' I didn't have time to ask him what they meant as the sharp sound of a door opening echoed down the church. I flashed a worried look at Simon.

'Don't worry, that'll be the rector. Wait here.'

He disappeared back into the church. I stood up and went over to the wooden screen and looked through one of the gaps in the carving. A man had come in through a side door, a small man, but solid-looking, balding and with glasses – more like a bank manager than a vicar. He was looking left and right, his eyes sweeping around like searchlights.

Simon trotted up to him, and I listened as the man boomed, 'What in the name of the Lord is going on here, Simon? There are armed police outside the abbey. The whole place is surrounded.'

Simon held his hands up, like he was fending off the force of the man's voice.

'She's a child, Rector. She came to us for help, sanctuary.'

'I was frisked, Simon. Frisked! Before they'd let me into my own church.'

'Oh . . . I see.'

'Well you can stop smirking, this is serious. We must stop this right now. We must hand the girl over. Where is she?'

I shrank back further into the corner of the chapel.

'She's in the chapel, but . . .' – immediately, the sound of footsteps coming towards me – '. . . but, you can't just throw her out. She's a child.'

'She may also be a mass murderer, Simon. And I can do exactly what I like in my church. I am the rector, after all.' They were very close now.

'It's God's church.' The footsteps stopped. Their echoes faded away into the vaulted roof, and there was silence.

'I beg your pardon?'

I knew that tone. *That's it*, I thought. Simon was in real trouble now, and so was I.

'I mean, that is to say, this is the House of God. Of course, we look after it, but really it isn't ours. I mean, we're the guardians, but . . .' His stumbling words trailed off.

'And your point is . . . ?'

'Surely . . . surely, we must search our hearts and do what Jesus would do.'

How lame was that? I thought. *I'm done for.* But I wasn't, because Simon had found the perfect line, had said the one thing that could save me.

'What would Jesus do?' the rector said slowly. 'What would He do? Where is she?' His tone was gentler now.

'I'm here,' I said, stepping out from behind the screen.

He looked at me, and I saw his future: forty years or more, the comfort of growing old, respected, a somebody. I don't know what he saw when he looked at me; his face gave nothing away, but after a bit he said, 'Come, let us pray together, then.' He walked to the front of the chapel and knelt down.

'I'm sorry, I—' I started to say, but Simon held his finger up to his lips and shook his head, then he shepherded me beside him and we knelt down too.

The rector launched into a prayer, a string of stuff I didn't understand, like he was talking to someone – asking them stuff – but of course there was nobody else there, just us three. And then he was quiet. I didn't know what I was meant to do with myself. I held my hands in front of me, palms together, feeling ridiculous. I didn't know whether to have my eyes open or shut, and I shot a sneaky glance along the row to see what the other two were doing. They were kneeling up like two angels on a Christmas card, eyes firmly closed, in a world of their own. My knees were getting sore, especially the one I'd twisted getting over the fence. I shifted about to try and get more comfortable, and then sat down properly, wondering how long it would be until I knew my fate.

Hours later – or was it minutes? – and without saying anything to each other, they both opened their eyes at the same time and stood up. I got to my feet too. The rector stepped towards me and took both my hands in his.

'You're welcome in God's house, child. You have sought

sanctuary with us, and you will find it here. For the time being.' Behind him, Simon was beaming. 'This isn't going to be easy, for any of us. Before we go on, I need you to answer me honestly. Do you have anything with you, any weapons?'

I shook my head. 'Nothing.'

'No guns or knives? Explosives?' he said, eyeing my backpack, which was lying on the floor.

'No.'

'Do you mind if I, or Simon here, have a look?'

I did mind, as it happened. It wasn't really my stuff, it was Britney's, and it was all I had in the world, but I wasn't really in a position to argue. I undid my bag there and then and tipped it out, the contents spilling out onto the tiled floor: food, bottles of water, my fags, some spare knickers from Britney.

'We don't allow smoking in here. I'm sure you understand that.' I shrugged.

'And your pockets? Would you mind turning out your pockets?'

I dug my hands into the pockets of my coat and my jeans and added old tissues, my lighter, the last bit of change to the heap on the floor. Fifteen years old, and that was everything I had in the world.

'I'm afraid we'll have to search you.' I shot him a warning look. *Now we're getting to it*, I thought, *any excuse for him to stick his fingers where I didn't want him to. Dirty old man.* If they started anything, I was ready to defend myself. Neither of them looked like much of a threat to me.

'Simon,' the rector said, 'will you do the honours?'

Simon looked more frightened than me. He stepped forwards. 'I'm sorry about this.' He gently patted my shoulders, and then his hands moved under my arms and down my body. He crouched and patted each leg in turn, his face turned away from my crotch, but colouring up all the same. When he'd finished there were beads of sweat on his forehead – sheer stress, I should think. It was a pretty safe bet that he didn't get that close to a woman too often.

'No, that's fine,' he said, straightening up. 'Nothing there.'

'Good. Now, gather up your things and, Simon, if you show our guest . . .'

'Jem,' Simon said quickly.

'If you show Jem into the vestry, I will speak with the police and explain that this isn't a siege. We need to open up, there'll be people queuing outside for Matins.' He bustled off towards the main door, keen to put his day back on track.

Simon showed me into a side room, where there was a table and some chairs, and a rack with loads of cloaks and things hanging up.

'Just put your things down here.' He was having trouble looking me in the eye since he'd frisked me. 'Tell you what, I'll put the kettle on. No milk, I'm afraid, but I could make us a black coffee or tea. I'll just get some water.'

He disappeared into the toilet but left the door open. The tap was running for a long time, and I could hear the squelching of soap as he washed his hands, before the unmistakeable sound of the kettle filling up. I know I was pretty grubby from sleeping rough, but I had a feeling it wasn't just a bit of mud and grass he was washing away.

He smiled straight at me when he emerged. 'That's better. Now, tea or coffee?'

Chapter 30

'I'll talk to them on one condition: they must let Spider go, my mate. I need to see him. He hasn't done anything. If they let him go, I'll talk. You can tell them that.'

The rector let out his breath like a burst of steam. 'Must we really go backwards and forwards like this? You are in serious trouble, young lady. If you have done nothing wrong, if you have nothing to hide, then you should talk to the police. Nothing bad will happen to you if you tell the truth.'

I snorted. 'Yeah, right.'

His nostrils flared. 'I don't like your attitude. Appalling things have happened. Innocent people have died. We need to get to the truth. We need to find those responsible. It's not a laughing matter.'

'I'm not laughing,' I said, 'but I'm not talking to them. I don't trust them. Why should I? They've taken my friend away.'

'He was a suspect,' he said, his mouth slowly shaping all the words like he was talking to a very young kid or a foreigner. 'Of course they've taken him away. And if he has done nothing wrong and he tells the truth, they will let him go again. Perhaps . . .' his voice softened, 'perhaps we don't sometimes know people as well as we think we do. It's possible that your . . . your friend didn't tell you everything. That you got caught up in something you knew nothing about . . .'

'No!' I shouted, my voice echoing through the place. 'It's not like that. You're like the rest of them. You're twisting things, trying to make him into something he's not. It wasn't him at the London Eye. It was me.'

They were both looking at me intently now. 'Go on.'

'I didn't do nothing. I just knew that something was going to happen that day. I could see that lots of people there were going to die.'

'How did you know?' He was waiting for me to tell him I did it, I planted the bomb.

'I can see the day, the date when people are going to die.' They looked at each other quickly. 'I could tell you both yours, your last days, but I never will. I never tell people, it's not right. But when I saw that all those people had the same day, that day in London, I was scared. I didn't want to be there, so we ran away.'

'What do you mean, you can see the date . . . ?'

'If I look at someone, I see a number. It's kind of inside my head and outside at the same time. The number is a date.'

'How do you know what the number means?'

'I've seen enough death. I know. Anyway, I was right, wasn't I, about the London Eye? I was right to run away.'

They looked at each other.

'Why didn't you go to the police, tell them what you knew?'

'Why do you think? It's all so simple, isn't it? Tell the truth and it will all be all right. Maybe it's like that here, but it's not where I come from. They see a black kid with some money, they see a dealer. They see a couple of kids, just chilling somewhere, hanging out, they see a couple of muggers. They need to collar someone for a crime, they collar someone – one of the usual suspects, anyone who fits the picture, doesn't matter. Truth and lies, it all gets mixed up. No-one would believe me.'

'It's certainly . . . unexpected,' the rector was picking his words carefully, 'what you're saying. But if that's what you believe, then you should tell them. They will be able to do tests that can exonerate you, test your clothes for traces of explosives.'

'Fit me up, you mean.'

His turn to get angry. 'No!' he shouted, slamming his fist against the door. 'That's not how it works in this country. There are processes, checks and balances. You must trust the system. It's what keeps this country civilised.'

I closed my eyes. What can you say to people like that, part of the system themselves, or so naïve they believe all that establishment bullshit? I couldn't argue against them, anyway. I didn't have the words that would make them listen, respect me, didn't know their language.

They let the police in to see me, of course, and as usual they brought a social worker with them. The feeling that Simon and the rector might protect me from all that had faded during the lecture about our 'civilised society', but it still felt like a betrayal. I didn't answer their questions. The only thing I said, over and over, until I thought it would drive us all mad, was, 'I'll talk when you bring my friend here. I'll talk when I've seen Spider.'

They tried all the usual stuff: good cop, bad cop; kind cop, irritated cop; sympathetic cop, threatening cop. None of it touched me – I let their voices wash over and around me, while they got more and more frustrated. They brought in a doctor, too, but I didn't talk to him either. I was pretty sure once I started telling him about the numbers, he'd have me sectioned before I could blink – carted off to a secure ward somewhere, locked up, tranquillised.

There was the sound of movement outside. The door opened to let another woman in: Karen. To be honest, it took me a few seconds to remember where I'd seen her before. The last few days had been so intense, it was like I'd lived a whole different life since I'd left her house.

'Jem!' she said, and half-walked, half-ran across the room with her arms open. She gathered me to her, and all at once I was back in her kitchen, in Sherwood Road, and I was who I used to be, before all this happened. She held me for a long time. There was a lot of emotion from her, in that hug; it surprised me, kind of repulsed me too, but I didn't pull away. It was like she'd really missed me – I would have thought she'd be glad of the peace and quiet for a few days.

Eventually, she let go and moved away a little. 'How are you? Are you all right? I've been so worried. If you'd only told me. . .' There was pain in her face, concern.

'I'm all right,' I said, but I was betrayed by the wobble in my voice.

'You look tired, you're very pale.' She stroked my cheek with one of her pudgy hands. 'It's all right now, Jem. You can come home with me. I expect the police will want to question you again tomorrow, and I'll be with you, but you can come home tonight.'

Home. The thought of Sherwood Road, the estate, the

twins, everything back to normal.

'I'm not going, not without Spider.'

'Of course you must. Jem, you've been through a heck of a lot. Let me look after you for a bit. Give yourself a break.'

'I'm going to stay here.'

She frowned. 'I don't think you can, Jem. It's not somewhere where people live.'

'I can stay, and I'm going to. I'm going to stay until they bring Spider back to me. You're not going to take me away. You can't make me.'

She had her hand on my arm now. 'No-one's going to take you anywhere you don't want to go. I'm just asking you – asking, Jem – that you come home.'

I shrugged her arm away. Instantly her face crumpled with hurt feelings.

'I'm not going, Karen. I'm staying here.'

She sighed and shook her head. 'You're not so tough, Jem. One day you'll realise that, and I'll be there for you.'

She gathered up her handbag and went to join the others outside. I couldn't hear what they were saying, but I didn't care. They could talk about me all they liked. Whether he knew it or not, Simon had given me something precious, something powerful, a single bullet to defend myself with: one word, 'sanctuary'.

They came back in; Karen, Imogen – the social worker – Simon and the rector.

'We can't leave you here on your own,' said the rector, wearily.

'Why not?'

'You're a fifteen-year-old girl. It's not appropriate.'

'I've been on my own for days.'

'Be reasonable, Jem,' Karen chipped in.

'I'm not moving. I can sleep right here. It's safer than on the street.'

They looked at each other.

'I need to get back,' said Karen. 'I've got a neighbour keeping an eye on the kids, but . . . I suppose I could see if she could sleep there.'

Karen looked at Simon and the rector, who nodded. 'If you can stay, Karen, we'll make up a couple of beds for you.'

Karen made a couple of phone calls and there was a bit more faffing about. They were doing that adult thing of talking like I wasn't there. The rector started mouthing off about me vandalising the place, but Karen stepped in.

'I'll be here. I'll vouch for her. Anyway, she's not a violent kid at heart. She got into trouble at school, but I think there was provocation there. She wouldn't be destructive here.'

I just sat still, picking at a flap of loose skin on the side of my thumb. I looked up and Karen caught my eye. She looked at me evenly, but I knew we were both thinking of my room back at hers, smashed to bits the night before I left.

The rector's wife, Anne, had appeared with a couple of duvets and some pillows, and she and Karen made up two beds on the floor. She'd brought some food, too: packets and parcels that she left on the table.

Then, the rector, Simon and Anne started saying their goodbyes. Simon was telling Karen about the domestics and I tuned out for a while. When I tuned back in, he had lowered his voice, but I could still hear.

'If you're in trouble,' he was saying, 'if you need them, there's a spare set of keys in the vestry. In the desk drawer. The key to the side door has some yellow tape round it.'

'Okay,' said Karen. 'Thanks.'

They filed out quietly, down the abbey, leaving through

the side door. Beyond them I got a glimpse of the outside world. There was quite a crowd there, and a shed load of policemen. As the door opened, a barrage of flashlights went off, like strobe lights at a disco. Christ, what was going on? There were people shouting, it was completely full on. The abbey contingent looked shaken, and I ducked back out of view behind the door.

The last one out was Simon, the big bunch of keys jingling in his hand. He paused as he was swinging the door shut, leaving a five centimetre gap. 'Goodnight, ladies. Sleep well.' His face twitched into a smile, and he closed the door, the big metal key scraping round as he locked it, an oddly liquid sound.

On the other side of the windows, the sky was flashing like bonfire night, lighting up the inside of the abbey too. I leaned against the door, listening to the noise outside.

'Right,' said Karen. 'Let's see what Anne left us, shall we? This is going to be fun, isn't it, like camping? Ever been camping, Jem?'

Chapter 31

We unwrapped the parcels of food. Anne had brought us sandwiches, home-made cake, crisps. Karen made us both a cup of tea and we sat either side of the table.

I was waiting for the probing question, the time Karen would want it all explained to her, but for a while she was happy to chatter away about the twins and the media fuss – there'd been reporters camped outside their front door apparently. I thought she was going to ask about the numbers, all the rumours flying around, but, of course, she asked the question a mum would ask.

'So what's going on with you and Terry – Spider – then? More than mates now, is it?'

I didn't want to talk about him, not with her, but I realised that I did want her on my side. Maybe she could help me see him again. So, I didn't tell her to mind her own business, which is what I wanted to do.

'Just mates,' I mumbled, 'good mates.' A hateful warmth was spreading into my cheeks. God, it's hideous when your body betrays you. She saw it, and started smiling.

'But you like him,' she said, coyly.

I was bursting inside. Yeah, I liked him. I thought about him every minute of every day. I ached without him. I loved him. All those things I could never say out loud – except, maybe, to him.

'Yeah, I really like him,' I said, trying to keep my voice even, willing the hot skin on my face to cool down and get back to normal. 'And I really need to see him again. It's important, Karen. I need to see him.'

She smiled at me, a twinkling, sympathetic smile. 'I know what that feels like. I was young once, too, you know.' How many more middle-aged clichés was she going to roll out today? 'You will see him again, Jem. The police are holding him at the moment, but nobody thinks either of you planted that bomb. They want to talk to you as witnesses. And then there's stealing cars and whatever else you've been up to in the last few days. And we still haven't heard what they want to do about you taking that knife to school . . .' She sighed. 'I'm not saying it isn't a mess, Jem, because it is, but we can sort it all out. You just need to co-operate with the police, and then, eventually, they'll let you see Spider again.'

'Eventually's no good,' I blurted out.

'You've got to learn to be patient. I know it's difficult . . .'

'We haven't got the time to wait. It has to be before the fifteenth!'

'Don't be silly. You're both fifteen. You've got all the time in the world.'

'No, we haven't. You don't understand.'

'Then you'd better tell me.'

Faced with no alternative, I did. I told her about the

numbers, like I'd told Spider, the day the London Eye was blown to bits.

She looked uneasy all the way through, fiddling with the foil food wrappers, and when I finished, she laughed, a really nervous little whinny.

'Come on, Jem. You don't believe that, do you?'

'It's not what I believe or not. It just is.'

She snorted and looked down at her fingers, restlessly squeezing and shaping the tinfoil.

'That's not real, Jem. That's not real life.'

'It is, Karen. It's been my life for fifteen years.'

'Jem, sometimes things get muddled up. I know how tough it's been for you. You've been through so much unhappiness, and change. I knew that when I agreed to take you on. Sometimes, when things are confusing anyway, we try and make sense of it our own way, we find ways of coping . . .'

She still didn't understand. 'I didn't make it up! Do you think I want to live like this?'

'All right. Calm down. You didn't make it up on purpose, I know. I'm just saying that sometimes the mind plays tricks on you.'

'So I need a psychiatrist?'

'No, you need a proper home. There is nothing wrong with you that some stability – love, even – wouldn't cure. All things I'm trying to give you.' Her eyes flicked up to me, nervously. She was used to me throwing things like this back in her face.

The thing was, even as I was almost screaming with frustration, I could see where she was coming from. If someone else had told me my story, I'd have thought they were taking the piss, or were schizo or something. I wouldn't have believed them. Karen's world was one of routines and rules. She had her size seven feet firmly on the ground. Of course this didn't make any sense to her. She was looking at me now, just waiting to be kicked, and I would have a few weeks ago, but what would be the point?

'I know you are, Karen,' I said. 'I know.'

And she pressed her lips together, in a tight little smile, a grateful acknowledgement of the effort it had cost me to say that.

''Nother cup of tea, love?'

I nodded.

'Yeah. I'll just stretch my legs while the kettle's on.'

'Okay.'

I got up and walked out into the abbey, surprised again at its sheer size, the space above me. All over the floor were stones with writing carved into them. I was standing on one: the marker for someone, dead for two hundred and thirty years. The walls, too, were a patchwork. Words that had lasted for hundreds of years – describing people nobody remembered any more. I was surrounded by bones and ghosts.

I looked around the abbey, stopping here and there to read the stones. It should have creeped me out. It didn't. I liked it – I liked the honesty of seeing people's numbers. The stones told the facts: birth date, death date. The numbers were fine – it was the words that were more troubling. *Departed; Laid to rest; Taken by her Maker; Gone to a better Place.* I stopped in front of this last one. Was it wishful thinking, belief, or even certainty? If I'd written that memorial, I would have rubbed out the last four words. Just *Gone*.

That's all there was, as far as I could see. How could anyone possibly know any different?

It made me wonder where my mum was now, or where what was left of her was. What had happened to her after they'd taken me away in that car? Had she been buried somewhere, or cremated? Had there been a funeral, and had anyone gone? Or do junkies, dossers and slags just get chucked in a skip? All of a sudden, I really wanted there to be a grave somewhere for her. I wanted her messy, messed-up life to have ended properly.

Then a chill ran through me. What would they do for Spider? It seemed impossible that just over twenty-four hours from now, he'd be needing a gravestone. How could someone so alive, so fizzing with energy, just stop?

I felt a tide of panic rising up inside me. Despite what Karen thought, Spider's life could be measured out in hours now, minutes even. I'd seen his number so many times. It didn't change. It was real. He would die in jail, or some police cell. Beaten up, probably. Unless he was ill. Perhaps he was ill right now, already in the grip of something that seemed trivial, that nobody knew would be fatal. I couldn't possibly wait these next hours out, until someone came to me, told me the news. I needed to step up the pressure, somehow get them to release him.

'Tea's ready.' Karen's voice echoed into the church.

I wandered back into the vestry, determined to find a way to see him again. I'd been like a cork in the sea all my life, tossed around from home to home, no say in what happened to me. I had to take control.

We had our tea and got ready for bed. Karen carried on chatting away, trying to make it fun. By then, I was so tired, I was nearly falling over. I let her tuck me in and then listened as, huffing and puffing, she got into her bed.

'It's quite comfy, isn't it?' she said, in a cheery, making-the-best-of-things kind of voice.

'Er . . . no. But it's better than sleeping under a hedge.'

'That what you've been doing?'

'Mm.'

'Well, you get some kip now, and tomorrow we'll talk more about you coming home, and having a proper night's sleep in a real bed.' Her duvet rustled as she shifted about. 'Honestly, Jem, you're quite right, I don't think I could sleep more than one night here – the floor's so hard . . .' But no more than five minutes after that, she was gently snoring. She was well away.

Perhaps I would have slept on my own, but the steady noise of her rumbling breaths in and out seemed to fill the room. It was irritating beyond belief. I was jealous, too. How could this woman just drift off so quickly like that? My head was full of the last few days, racing ahead to the next few days. After half an hour or so, I knew I'd have to get up or kill her where she lay. Even to me, the murder option seemed a bit extreme, so slowly I peeled down my duvet and stood up.

I remembered Simon's whispered words to Karen before he left, and tiptoed over to the table, quietly easing out one of the drawers. The keys were in there all right, a big, thick bunch. As I made to pick them up, they moved against each other, a metallic, oily noise. I stretched the bottom of my hoodie out and wrapped them up, smothering their tell-tale sound. Then I padded out of the vestry, into the dark cavern of the abbey.

Chapter 32

It wasn't pitch black in the church. Streetlights from outside filtered in through the stained-glass windows. Once your eyes adjusted, you could see the shape of things; pews, statues, pillars, all in shades of grey. I knew the doors at the far end and at the side led outdoors, but I didn't want to leave – I was pretty sure I'd have more negotiating power while I stayed inside the church. But I did want to explore. I picked a door in the corner, to one side of the altar, and started trying all the keys.

The third one worked. I opened the door, which led through to a little room full of junk – well, it looked like junk; bits of old stone and wood. It was darker in here but I could just make out another door on the far side. Again, I had the key to this one. It was darker still inside there, the light just picking out the bottom of some stone steps twisting up round a central pillar. I hesitated for a minute. This was starting to creep me out. I didn't think I could go up there in the dark. I stepped inside and rested my hand on the cold stone wall. There was something knobbly there too, a switch. I flicked it on and the staircase was lit up, disappearing up and round.

'Come on,' I said, trying to gee myself up. My words bounced off the stone. It's bad at the best of times, isn't it, talking to yourself? Sounds even madder in a church.

I started up the stairs. My legs were pretty wobbly, my knee still not very good, but I took it steady, just one step after the other. You could only see a few steps ahead, and once you lost sight of the bottom, it felt like it could go on for ever. Everything about it was cold; the stone through my socks, the walls, even the air was colder here. I was starting to think I should go back for my trainers and my coat, or just go back full stop, when I got to the top. The stairs just finished, a blank wall in front of me, but there was a door to the side. Again, the keys did the job. I swung the door open and was met with a blast of cold air. I stepped through and smiled, couldn't help myself: I was on the roof.

I'm all right with heights – lucky, that – but as I stepped out onto the roof, a wave of sickness swept over me and I felt light-headed, dizzy. I was breathing hard from the climb. I sat down and hung my head forwards. The sharp air hurt my lungs. I tried breathing in through my nose, warm it up as it went inside. That helped a bit. Slowly, slowly I got back to normal. A little stone wall ran down each side of the roof. Like everything else round here, it was carved into a pattern, big holes in it. Even sitting down, I could see through to the rooftops all round me. Holding on to the stone, I pulled myself up.

God, it was beautiful, even I could see that. A different kind of city. From up here, you couldn't see the street-level grime; it was all roofs and chimneys, spires, squares and arches. The orange streetlights made the pale stone look warm, the buildings were almost glowing, even though it was freezing outside, and you could see strings of lights criss-crossing the little streets. In the yard next to the abbey, there was quite a crowd, some of them sitting down on benches or the ground, others gathered near the tree, with policemen dotted among them. Amazing how stupid tourists can be, hanging around outside on a night like this.

The tower rose up from the other side of the roof. Keeping my head down, I scuttled along until I reached another door. Again, my keys didn't let me down, and I was through, fumbling for the light switch. Another staircase, but this time with rooms leading off it. The first one I came to was full of ropes hanging down from the ceiling. The ends were all tied up on one side of the room, and I didn't twig what they were until I saw a photo on the wall, labelled *Abbey Bell-ringers 1954*. They were bell-ropes, and my fingers twitched at the thought of untying them, giving one of them a good yank.

There were more doors leading off this room.

I chose one with another staircase. Up and up, trying each door as I went. One room was different from the others. There was a wooden walkway across, suspended above a stone floor which dropped away on both sides, with odd ridges sticking up. Took me a while to realise why it looked like the negative of the roof downstairs. That's exactly what it was – the other side of the fan shapes in the abbey ceiling. The hairs on the back of my neck were standing up – I felt like I was in a secret world.

Another door at the end of the walkway. This one revealed a tiny room, a dead end. The far wall contained a big round white disc, lit up by the soft streetlight. There were markings round the edge and two sticks – a clock's hands. I was behind the clock on the abbey tower. There were stone ledges running along either side wall. I sat down on one, keeping my face turned to the clock – it made me smile, I've never been anywhere so weird. It was like sitting inside the moon. Then one of the metal rods feeding into it clicked, and the minute hand shifted round. Another minute gone, and, with a wrench to my guts, Spider was back in my head.

All over the world clocks were marking each second, minute and hour. On and on. Thousands, maybe millions of clocks. If I'd had a brick to hand, I'd have launched it through the round, white clock face, sending the glass spraying out into the night. I'd smash every clock and watch in the world. But would it do any good? Don't shoot the messenger, that's what they say, isn't it?

And sitting there, it came to me I was blaming the wrong thing. I was looking outside, when anyone could see that there was someone at the middle of all this. Me. I was the only one to see the numbers. I saw something that no-one else saw. My eyes, my mind, me. Whether they were real or imagined, the numbers were me and I was them.

Without me, would they even exist?

The lever running along the wall gave another lurch and the minute hand thunked forward again. Suddenly, I had to get out of there. The room would suffocate me, if I stayed a minute longer. I sprang up and started running, across the walkway, back to the stairs, and then on and up, blindly, to the top.

Although it was cold on the staircase, the iciness of the open air was a shock again. There was nothing up there, just a flat roof and an empty flagpole. Another stone wall ran round the edge. The view was even better up here – the orange lights of the town sprawling up into hills all around.

There was a swimming pool on one of the roofs, turquoise water lit from below. And immediately below me, another pool, square and green, with statues round the edge and steam gently rising up from it. From here, it felt like you could dive off the tower right into it. You could dive down and wipe it all away; the memories, the pain, the guilt. All you'd need to do was climb up on the little wall and jump . . .

From far down below, a voice drifted up to me. 'There she is!'

In the abbey yard, floodlit faces were turned upwards now. This far away, they all looked the same, a crowd of puppets. And it struck me, they weren't tourists down there, they were actually waiting to see me.

Someone screamed, their terror drifting up to me a split second after it had left them, infecting me, suddenly making me afraid. The ground below seemed to be moving, the people merging into a random pattern, swimming and shifting in front of my eyes.

My legs gave way and I sank down. Who was I kidding? I couldn't jump off there – my strength and my nerve had gone. My legs were so wobbly now, I couldn't even manage the stairs. So I bumped down them on my bum, one at a time. I've no idea how long it took – I didn't lock the door behind me, just bumped and crawled my way all the way down into the abbey, and then across the cold floor into the vestry.

I curled up in my makeshift bed, next to Karen, and shut my eyes tightly, but the numbers were still there: Mum's, Karen's, the old tramp's, the bomb victims'.

And Spider's.

Chapter 33

'It's all right, Jem, it's only us. Simon and me.'

I swam up to the surface again, through the green, green water of sleep towards the light. A woman's voice was speaking to me, and from somewhere a long way away my memory started to put the pieces back together. I sat up, rubbing the sleep out of my eyes, swallowing back the sour stuff at the back of my throat. Anne was over by the table, and Karen was already up.

'I've brought some juice,' said Anne. 'Shall I put the kettle on as well? You and Karen can have a cup of tea. Simon, would you like one?'

There was a shakiness in her voice that I couldn't put my finger on. She was trying to sound normal, say normal things, but the tremor in her voice made her sound afraid. What was she afraid of?

I felt embarrassed, these people seeing me in bed, at a disadvantage. I swung my legs out onto the floor and heaved myself to my feet. Just for a moment, it went red and then black behind my eyes, and I clutched the edge of the table to stop myself falling.

'Stood up a bit quickly?' Anne had her arm half around me, supporting me, although she held me away from her body. I got the feeling that if she could have used tongs, she would have. 'Sit down here, that's it. You don't look like you've been eating much. Try a bit of toast. Here.' She unwrapped a foil parcel.

There was a little pile of toast inside, cut into triangles. I couldn't do it, couldn't eat any – it actually turned my stomach to look at it. I'd only just woken up. I brought the edges of the foil together, hiding its contents away again.

'Um, I'm not hungry yet. Maybe in a bit.'

'Have some tea, then. Here we are.' She put four mugs down on the table, and joined Karen and me.

Simon stayed standing. He was paler than ever, and seemed intent on hovering there. He kept licking his lips, frowning. Finally, he came out with it.

'You were seen, last night, Jem. On the tower.'

'You what?' spluttered Karen.

'Jem was out there on the roof, on top of the tower. She must have taken the keys. It was a very dangerous thing to do – to go up there on your own. Questions are being asked. Stephen will be in shortly.'

'When was this?' Karen asked.

I sighed. 'When you'd gone to sleep. I couldn't get comfortable. Too many things to think about, so I had a look round. Haven't you ever wandered about here on your own?' This to Simon.

'Yes, of course,' he said, 'but that's different. You're still a child, and I'm an adult, I'm . . . responsible.' Standing there, shifting his weight from foot to foot and wringing his hands,

it was difficult to imagine anyone his age looking more innocent or vulnerable.

I liked him, I really did, but there was something about
that word – 'responsible'. I burst out laughing.

His pale blue eyes widened with the shock of being
laughed at, and then brimmed with tears. What was I doing?
This was the guy who rescued me, the one who gave me
sanctuary just in the nick of time.

'Sorry,' I said, quickly, 'I didn't mean to laugh. And I
shouldn't have used those keys. I didn't mean to get you into
trouble.' He was watching me carefully, blinking back the
hurt I'd caused. 'Simon, you've been really kind to me. I'd be
completely in the shit without you.' He winced, but kept
looking. 'I couldn't help exploring last night. It's an amazing
place.'

His face softened. 'Yes,' he said. 'It is.' He picked up the
keys, which were lying on the table. 'I'll go and check everything's locked up, and get things ready.' He scuttled out,
while Anne poured more tea.

'The police will be back soon,' she said. 'You should eat
something . . .'

I stayed quiet, folding the top of the foil over, sealing the
parcel. I wanted to tell her to leave me alone, I'd eat if I felt
like it, but a little voice inside me was telling me to shut up,
that she was trying to be kind. So I said nothing, which for
me was a big deal. I expect Anne just thought I was rude. I
glanced up at her and she was standing there, looking hurt,
like I'd rejected her or something. For Christ's sake, it was
only a bit of toast.

There was something else, though. It was the first time
our eyes had actually met, and though I tried to ignore it,
there it was, plain as day. Her number. 862010. Less than a

year to go. And suddenly her nervousness started to make sense. At some level, whether she understood why or not, she was scared of what I knew. She looked at me, a rabbit caught in the headlights, then swallowed hard and turned away.

Sure enough, the police came back, and the social worker, Imogen. There were other people, too: men in dark suits, who sat at the back of the room, listening. Karen sat in on the questioning, as the police went over and over the same ground as the day before. I stalled them for a bit, while I worked out what they really wanted to know; yes, there were questions about the day at the London Eye, and about Spider, but there was other stuff too. Someone had obviously told them about the numbers. At this point, the police took a step back and the men in suits came and sat at the table.

'We've been hearing stuff about you, Jem. Interesting stuff. Like the reason why you ran from the Embankment. They're saying you can predict the future. You can tell when people are going to die. That right?'

I looked down, saying nothing. One of them produced a set of photographs from his briefcase.

'Look at these photos and tell me what you see. How long has this one got? Or this one? Can you tell me?'

They went on and on, until I was hearing that edge of stress and frustration in their voices again.

Then I spoke.

'I can tell you. I can tell you everything you want to know.'

They sat up then, looked quickly at each other – little triumphant glances – and then back at me.

'Yes, I was there at the London Eye, and I'm pretty sure I saw the bloke who was carrying the bomb. I even spoke to him. I can give you a description. I can tell you about the guy with the tattoos, and why he was chasing us. I can even tell you about these pictures.' They were excited now, almost drooling. 'I could tell you, and I will, if you bring my mate, Spider, here. I'll make a full statement, and then we want a car, and some money, a thousand should do it, and we want you to leave us alone and let us get out of here.'

The guy in the suit leaned forward. 'I don't think you realise what trouble you and your mate are in. You're looking at some serious charges here. You're not in a position to negotiate.'

He didn't faze me at all. I'd thought this all through – they needed me to talk. 'Actually, I think I am. I know you want to sort out the bombing, don't you? And you'd love to know whether your Prime Minister's got a future, wouldn't you? Is he here for the next ten years or going to be taken out by a sniper's bullet? Does that interest you?'

'We'll need to talk about this.' He scraped his chair back and went outside with the others. Karen stayed behind.

'What are you doing?' she asked. 'What are you saying?'

'I told you yesterday. You just didn't believe me.'

'Jem, this has got to stop. These tall tales – it's gone far enough now, Jem. Stop saying these things. Let me take you home and look after you.'

'No! It's not gonna happen. I need them to bring Spider here, and I'm not budging until they do.'

She sighed, and I could tell she was about to launch into another weary lecture, when the door opened again. The men in suits were back.

'Okay,' one of them said, 'it's a deal.'

My stomach flipped over. I couldn't believe it – I'd won.

'You'll bring Spider here?' He nodded.

'After you've given us a full statement.'

'And you'll provide us with a car and some money like I said?'

He nodded again, but there was something in the way that the two policemen behind him looked at each other that made me suspicious.

'I want it all in writing,' I said, quickly. 'I want you to sign it. A legal agreement.'

And that's what I got, there in black and white. I would tell the police what they wanted to know, and they would bring Spider to me before the fifteenth of December and provide us with safe passage out of the abbey. Not being great at reading, I took my time, but it seemed okay. I asked Karen to check it too, but she refused.

'This is stupid, Jem. I don't want anything to do with it.' She watched while I signed the paper and then announced, 'I'm going to get back to the boys now. They need me too. I'll come back tomorrow.'

She gave me a big hug before she left. 'Imogen and Anne will be here with you. And you're to ring if you need anything.'

'Okay,' I said. To be honest, I felt a little twinge as she left. We didn't exactly see eye to eye – perhaps we never would – but she meant well, I could see that now. But I had to stay focused – everything was going to plan. All I had to do was tell them what they wanted to know, and then they'd have to keep their side of the bargain.

They'd have to bring Spider here.

Chapter 34

I gave them exactly what they were waiting to hear. I kept some of it back, of course. None of their sodding business what had happened between Spider and me. That was between us. But everything else, plus some 'information' of my own about people in the photos they showed me.

They talked to me, with a tape recorder going, and then they wrote it all down and got me to sign it. I had no problem putting my name to it. This was all part of the plan, taking me one step nearer to where I wanted to be.

'So when do I see Spider?' I said when I'd signed the statement.

'It'll take a bit of arranging – they're still interviewing him. He was taken back to London, Paddington Green.'

'Now just wait a minute . . .'

'No, it's all right, love. I'm going to take your statement back to London, see how they're getting on, and then I'll be back. I'll bring Dawson back here.'

So it was going to be a few hours then. Nothing I could do about that.

They gathered their stuff together, clipped their briefcases shut and were gone. On the way out, they shook hands with me, like we were business partners or something. That's a good sign, I thought. They're showing that they've made a deal with me. I had to trust them now – what else could I do?

By now it was lunchtime and Anne, the rector's wife, had brought me some scrambled egg on toast, kept warm under a wrapping of silver foil. She didn't eat with me, but kind of hung around, like she was waiting for something. Eventually, she squeezed some words out awkwardly.

'Jem, can I talk to you?'

I shrugged. Didn't bother me one way or the other.

She went up to the door and closed it, so that we were alone together in the vestry, just me and her. *She wants to persuade me to leave, I'm causing her husband too much trouble*, I thought, but I was wrong.

'They're saying . . . they're saying that you can tell when people are going to die.' Her face was creased into a frown as she searched my face.

I tried not to look, but I couldn't avoid her eyes, her need for contact was too strong. 08062010.

'Oh?' I said, willing her not to ask me.

'I'm ill, Jem. I've got an illness. I haven't told Stephen, so please . . . don't . . .'

Hearing her speak the rector's – her husband's – name made him more human; made me think I might have been wrong about him earlier. Yes, he was going to live for another thirty years or so, but maybe he wasn't going to be spoilt for the rest of his life. Maybe it was going to be lonely nights,

244

takeaways and boiled eggs on his own, in an empty house.

'The thing is . . . I need to know. How long I've got. So I can plan things, make sure the children are okay, make sure that Stephen will be all right.'

'Children?' Another shock.

'Well, they're pretty grown-up now. Nineteen and twenty-two. But I want to make sure they're set up, try and sort out the college debts, you know.' She must have realised that I didn't, because she laughed nervously. 'Well, perhaps you don't, but I'll feel happier if there aren't any loose ends. Happi*er* . . . not happy . . .' She trailed off.

'I can't tell you. It wouldn't be right.'

'You do know, though.'

I chewed my lip.

'You do know,' she repeated. 'I shouldn't feel so scared, should I? *In the true and certain knowledge of eternal life* . . .' There were tears in the corner of her eyes now, threatening to burst out and trickle down her face. 'Why isn't that a comfort?'

I was the last person to ask about that. She sat, lost in her own thoughts for a bit. Suddenly, I thought of Britney, how her family had come to terms with her brother's illness.

'I think you should tell him,' I said.

'Stephen?'

I nodded.

'I know. I've put it off. For a start, while it's still a secret, it doesn't seem so real. Sometimes I can pretend it's not happening, for an hour or so – well, for a few minutes. And then, the other thing is – it will break his heart.' Her voice quavered. 'I know he's a bit pompous, severe even, but we've been so strong together – a good team. How on earth will he cope without me?' The tears were coming for real now, and she leaned forward and held her hanky tight against her eyes, like she was trying to force the tears to stay inside.

I waited until she stopped, and was sitting up again.

'I'm sorry I can't help,' I said. And I was, I really was. I felt completely useless.

'Oh, but you have, Jem, you have. Just telling you has made it easier to face. It's given me the courage.' She grabbed my hands, and I fought the urge to snatch them away. I couldn't say anything. I just wanted her to let go, to take her pain away from me. After a while, she did. She stood up, smoothed down her skirt and shook her head, like she was shaking away the despair. She went to open the door. 'Thank you, Jem. God bless you.'

As far as I could see, I hadn't done anything. When she'd started crying, it had been dead embarrassing, but it had also been difficult not to join in. Her tears at the thought of dying mirrored my creeping horror of being left alone. Two sides of the same coin.

Suddenly, the walls of the vestry started to close in on me. I needed a bit of breathing space. I wandered out into the abbey. There were quite a few people around, and I had a feeling that several of them had clocked me as I walked over the memorial stones, trying not to tread on people's names.

After a few minutes, a woman wearing a headscarf came up to me. I was in the chapel, the place where I'd sat to get warm the morning Simon had let me in.

'Excuse me,' she said, uncertainly. 'Are you Jem, the girl they're all talking about?'

'I dunno,' I said, 'I am Jem, but I don't know about anything else.'

'You've been on the news, the hunt for you, and there are all sorts of stories on the internet.' She was standing in front of me, but her legs were starting to sag. 'Do you mind if I sit down? I'm a bit . . . tired.'

To be honest, I did mind. I'd got an idea where this conversation was heading, and I didn't want to get into all that. I just wanted to be left alone. I said nothing but she sat down anyway, right up close to me on the cushioned stone bench.

'The thing is,' she carried on, 'they're saying that you can see the future. People's futures. That's why you ran away from the Eye.'

She stopped and looked at me, and I met her gaze and I did see her future, or at least her end. Two and a half years away. And I thought, *You stupid, stupid girl, Jem*. I should never, never have told anyone – it should have been my secret right to the end.

'It's just rumours,' I muttered. 'You know what people are like.'

'But there's something, isn't there? There's something different about you.' She was searching my face, like she'd find some sort of answer there. 'Can you?' she said. 'Can you see into the future?'

I was squirming in my seat now. I tried not to look at her, kept my eyes down at my hands and my feet, kept my mouth shut. It didn't put her off. In fact, she reached up and picked at the end of her scarf, and then unwound it, revealing her scalp, nearly bald, with a few tufts here and there. It made her look shockingly naked.

She reached out to touch my hand. I wanted to push her away, tell her to back off. I can't explain to you how odd it was to have a stranger sitting up close to me, wanting to touch me. I'd spent a lifetime making sure there was space between me and everyone else, putting up walls. Physical contact with anyone made me pull a face, show my revulsion, move away. Except with Spider, of course.

Everything had been different with him.

The strength of this woman's longing stopped me, though – perhaps somewhere deep inside me I was a decent person after all. I put my hand on top of hers and gently moved it away. Her fingers closed on mine, she felt the scar on my hand and turned it over, gasping when she saw the red, angry tear from the barbed wire.

'What?'

'The mark of the cross on your hand.'

This was too much now.

'You're joking!' I said. 'I put it on some barbed wire, that's all. That's all.'

She carried on cradling my hand in hers.

'Please tell me what you know. I can take it.'

I shook my head. 'I can't tell you anything. I'm sorry.' I felt trapped, useless. I stood up. 'I'm sorry, I've got to . . . I need to . . .'

She took the hint, and stood up too, gathering her bag and her scarf. She started to wind it round her head again.

'I'm sorry I can't help you,' I said, and I meant it. She pressed her lips together into a line and nodded, her emotions too near the surface now for her to speak.

I left her there, fiddling with her scarf, and blundered out into the main church. Simon was standing with his back to me, talking to an old man, halfway down the main aisle. When he saw me, the man broke off in mid-sentence, pushed past Simon and headed straight for me.

He was so thin his skeleton was showing through his skin and his eyes were almost glassy. I tried to avoid looking at him, but I'd seen his number as he came staggering up towards me. He had four weeks.

I knew from the look on his face, it was obvious what he wanted from me. A date, the truth. And I knew I couldn't give it to him, so before he could say anything I turned quickly away and walked back into the vestry. As I reached the door I heard a voice.

'Let us help you, sir. Come and sit over here. Would you like a drink of water?' Simon and one of the ushers had swooped in, gently coaxing the old man to sit in a pew.

Relieved, I slammed the door behind me.

Chapter 35

I think the ushers, maybe the police, kept everyone else away that day. And people brought me food and tried to talk to me. I allowed them to take my trainers off, put a blanket over me, but I stayed curled up all afternoon, locked in a silent circle, and eventually, long after it had grown dark, they left me. All except Anne, who volunteered to stay with me for the night.

Just after the abbey bells had chimed eight, I heard her pottering about. I turned over on my makeshift mattress.

'I brought some soup in a flask. Do you want some?'

I felt queasy, disorientated. I sat up slowly.

'I don't know.'

'I'll pour some out anyway – see if you fancy it in a bit.'

She sat at the table, with her bowl in front of her. I got up slowly and joined her. I wasn't really hungry, but I tried just a little of the soup. It was delicious, home-made. I steadily worked my way through it.

'Nice to see you eat,' she said, when I'd finished. 'You're

carrying a great burden, aren't you? It must be dreadful for you.'

I nodded. 'I wish it didn't happen. I wish I didn't see the numbers.'

'It's hard, isn't it? But perhaps you should view it as a gift.'

I snorted. 'You mean someone has given me this. I must have done something bloody awful to deserve it.'

'God may have given it to you. Maybe it's not so much a gift to you, but a gift to all of us.' She'd lost me now.

'I don't get it.'

'You're a witness, Jem. You bear witness to the fact that we're all mortal. That our days here are numbered, that there's so little time.'

'But everyone knows that anyway.'

'We know, but choose to forget – it's too difficult to deal with. That's what you made me realise yesterday. We choose to forget.'

'Yeah, you're telling me. I can't go anywhere, look at anyone, do anything, without being reminded. It's doing my head in. I can't deal with it any more.'

'God loves you, Jem. He'll give you the strength.'

This was too much – I might have mellowed over the past few weeks, but the old Jem wasn't far beneath the surface.

'What are you on about? If God loves me so much, why did he let my mum die of an overdose, why did he give me to a string of people who didn't care about me, why did he make me twist my ankle, or put my hand on some bird shit, or give me a big zit on my chin?'

'He gave you the gift of life.'

There was no answer to that one.

I managed to stop myself saying that actually that was my mum and one of any number of punters, giving her twenty quid to feed her habit. I was the result of a quick shag in a dingy flat, a business transaction. It wasn't what Anne wanted to hear, and I didn't want to upset her. So I just grunted and shut up.

We had another bowl of soup each and then tucked into bed. I kept going back to the two people in the abbey, to Anne herself. If I had the chance to find out when I was going to die, would I take it? The answer had to be no, didn't it? Why would you want to carry that around with you? And surely knowing about it would change the whole thing anyway. What if that knowledge, knowing your own death date, drove you to despair, and you killed yourself before then. Could that happen? Could you cheat the numbers, by choosing to go early? Perhaps Spider was right, maybe they could change.

Whichever way I thought about it, it would never be right to tell someone their number. I'd known that instinctively all along, and now, with my secret out, it seemed even more important. Surely, I thought, as I drifted off, there weren't that many people who would want to know anyway.

The next morning, there was a queue of fifty.

Simon came to tell me, while Anne and I were having breakfast. Well, Anne was – I only managed to sip some tea.

'There are a lot of people there today, Jem.'

It was just what I didn't want to hear. I was tired, I felt really ropey, and besides, I only wanted to know about one visitor – today they had to bring Spider back to me.

'What do they expect me to do? I'm a kid.'

He shrugged. 'We can keep them away from you. Our team here can counsel them.'

Anne agreed. 'That's right. We're used to dealing with people in crisis. When I've cleared up in here, I'll come out and help.'

She looked so ordinary, standing there; polo-neck jumper, cord skirt and boots, short, horrible permed hair. But she wasn't ordinary. She was prepared to sit all day and hear other people's terror as she struggled with her own. Even I couldn't scoff at that. Respect. It was more than I would be able to manage.

'Whatever. I can't see them. I don't want to. I've got nothing to say to them.'

'That's fine. We'll deal with it.' Simon disappeared to make the arrangements. Anne pottered about, washing up the cups and her breakfast things.

'You know,' she said, 'you need to think about what happens next. Where you want to go. This isn't the ideal place to stay.'

'I know what I want to happen – I want some time with my friend. And then . . . and then, I dunno . . .' The truth was I'd stopped even thinking about life after the fifteenth. After today.

'Karen will be here soon – I think the consensus is that you should go back home with her. She can help you through all the legal stuff, if they decide to bring charges. She knows you, Jem. She really cares.'

'I'm not going back to Karen's.'

'You're fifteen, Jem. You're not old enough to be out there on your own. Not yet.'

'Please, can we leave it? I don't know what I'm doing until Spider gets here.'

I suddenly realised I hadn't had a proper wash since my shower at Britney's. I wanted to look nice for him. I took myself off into the little cloakroom, stripped down and washed as best I could with soap and water from the sink. At least I could be clean, even if I was still stuck in Britney's slightly-too-large clothes. It woke me up, too, that wash – I got rid of that sickly, hung-over feeling. I couldn't wait to see him now – I'd never looked forward to anything so much in my life.

Back in the vestry, Karen had reappeared. As I emerged from the cloakroom with bare feet and a towel round my head, she came over to hug me. 'Jem, how are you? You're looking a bit better than last time.'

She held me away from her, but kept both hands on my shoulders. 'People out there are desperate to see you. It's all gone crazy, but I think you should think carefully before doing anything because—'

She didn't get a chance to finish because at that moment the door from the abbey burst open and a flash, middle-aged bloke breezed in, making a beeline straight for me.

'Hi Jem, good to meet you. Vic Lovell.' He strode across the room, with his hand thrust out, practically shouldered Karen out of the way, grabbed my hand and shook it vigorously. Instantly, the room was full of him – his presence, his energy. He wasn't after my help. He was after something else.

He started talking even before he took his coat off. 'Now, Jem, I'm here to talk to you about your future, which is looking very bright indeed. I've had some amazing offers coming in for you and if we play this carefully, you can be set up for life. Literally. We've got press, radio and TV interviews. I'm certain we can get a major magazine deal. This will cover the next couple of months, and then we need to get a book out, and there are already publishers desperate to talk to you. Don't worry, I wouldn't expect you to sit and write it, there's people who can help – you just need to talk to them and they do the rest. But the important thing is that I need you to sign up with me, so that I can manage all this for you. If it's not carefully managed, you could get over-exposed, or miss a key offer – but done the right way, as I said, you're made for life.' Finally, he stopped. He gave me a broad smile and nodded encouragingly at me.

'What?' I said.

'What do you think? Are we going to be partners?'

Still reeling from his verbal attack, I just shrugged, and said, 'I dunno.'

And he was off again.

'I know, it's a lot to take in, isn't it? Perhaps you don't really understand what I mean. I can make you rich, Jem. We're talking hundreds of thousands here. You're young, you've got an amazing story to tell, the whole world is talking about you. This is it, Jem. This is your moment. You can have everything you want – clothes, parties, cars, holidays. You name it, you've got it. The world wants to hear from you now. It's all about you.'

'And what do *you* want?' I looked at his camel-coloured overcoat, the fat gold signet ring on his finger and the Rolex half-hidden by his crisp white shirt cuff.

'I want to help you.'

'And you get . . . ?'

'A percentage, of course.' He fixed his hard, grey eyes on me. I couldn't avoid seeing that, middle-aged as he was, he still had another thirty years of hustling, wheeling and dealing ahead. 'I'm not a charity. We'll be in this together, Jem.'

'No. Fuck off.'

'You what?'

'Fuck off. I don't want any of it – I don't want your *help*,' I spat it out like a swearword. 'I don't want your money. I don't want fame. I don't want to be a poxy celebrity.'

He looked at me like I'd lost my marbles.

'You have no idea what you're saying. You can't walk away from this. You'd be mad to.'

'I know what I'm doing. I know what I want. And I want you to leave.'

He held his hands up. 'Let's not be hasty. You're under a lot of stress here, I know that. I'm going to leave you to talk it over with your mum here. Give you a bit of space. I'll be right outside.'

Sitting in the corner, Karen had been watching all this. I thought of her little house back in London, with the wallpaper peeling off the damp patch in the kitchen. She'd struggled all her life without money. What would it mean to her, if I went along with all this? I knew she only had a few years to go. Perhaps this guy could make sure that those last ones were the best years of her life.

'What do you think, Karen?'

She shook her head. 'You know what I feel about all this. It's gone too far already. If you start giving interviews and writing books, it'll just get worse.'

'But I could get you things – a bigger house, with more of a garden for the boys.'

Her face softened. 'They'd like that, wouldn't they?' she said. 'But you don't have to get me anything, Jem. 'We're all right where we are. His kind of world – it's a fantasy, it's not real. I know you, Jem – that's not what you really want, is it?'

Perhaps she did know me, after all. I grinned at her.

'No – it's all bullshit.'

Karen opened her mouth to object to the language, then shut it again and came over to give me a hug.

'I don't want any of it,' I said. 'I want it all to go away. I should never have told anyone.'

'It's all right. It'll be all right.' She was still holding me, but

I eased away.

'But it won't, will it? This sort of thing feeds on itself. Now it's out there, there's no stopping it.'

'I think you could stop it yourself.'

'How?'

She looked straight at me, clear-eyed. 'Just tell them – tell them you made it all up. That it's not true.'

Chapter 36

The last time I'd had to stand up and talk to a group of people had been back at school: 'My Best Day Ever'. When was that? A month ago? I couldn't remember. I'd stood up at the front of the classroom that day, and I'd told the truth, at least the truth as I saw it. That hadn't exactly turned out well. Now, I was getting ready to stand up in front of a crowd of strangers – the sick and dying, journalists, people like that agent, God knows who else – and call myself a liar. I was going to deny the truth that had dogged me my whole life.

'Okay, let's do it.'

Karen gave my arm a squeeze. 'Good girl,' she said. I think she honestly felt I was coming clean. She'd never believed me, and she was pleased now that I was owning up.

We walked out of the vestry and into the abbey. Well, there were way more than fifty people there now. It looked like there were hundreds milling around, all keeping near to the vestry door. As soon as I appeared, the noise level rose, and people started moving towards me. Karen steered me through them towards the front of the abbey, where Anne was standing with Stephen, the rector.

'Jem wants to make a statement,' Karen told them. 'Where's the best place?'

'Well— ' Stephen started to say, when the pushy guy from yesterday elbowed his way to the front and butted in.

'I'd totally advise against a general statement. We need careful media handling with a story like this. You're much better with some specifically negotiated one-to-ones. Come on, let's get you back to the vestry.'

He put his hand on my arm. I tried to shrug him off, but his grip was pretty vice-like.

'Get off me!' I yelled. 'I don't belong to you, and I'm not going to do a deal with you.'

He looked genuinely shocked, and puzzled, like he didn't understand what I was saying.

'Weren't you listening to me in there?'

'Yeah, I was listening. But *you* weren't. You never let me get a word in edgeways. I'm not interested. Now get your hand off me, or I'll bite it.'

He removed his hand, but he didn't back off. Instead, he leaned in close to me.

'I can't believe someone would waste such an opportunity. You're either very naïve or very stupid.' His voice was pitched low now, but Karen and the others had heard him.

'She's neither,' said Karen firmly. 'She's her own person, and she's made her own decision. Now I'd like you to leave her alone.'

Vic did move away then, but he didn't leave the abbey, he stayed at the back of the crowd, watching.

'You've got something to say, have you?' Stephen was asking.

'Yes. I think it's time . . . time I stopped wasting everyone else's time.'

Anne glanced worriedly at Karen, but Stephen nodded and looked relieved.

'Good. I'm glad. This farrago has gone on long enough. You can speak from here.' There was a slight step up into the part where the choir sat, but it only brought me to the head height of most of the crowd.

I looked up at the pulpit. 'What about up there? There's a microphone too.'

He went redder in the face.

'That would be completely inappropriate . . .' he started to bluster, then thought better of it. 'Oh, very well, if it gets it over with . . .'

He led me up some steps and suddenly I was there, in the dark wooden pulpit of Bath Abbey. He switched the microphone on, and introduced me, his voice booming out across the pews.

'Ladies and gentlemen, please find a seat. Our young . . . guest . . . here at the abbey has a few words to say to you.' He spread out his arm, inviting me to step forward and speak, and then retreated down the stairs.

A hush fell over the crowd.

I made the mistake of looking up. A sea of faces met me – a sea of numbers. I had nothing prepared; no clever words, no speech, no beginning, middle or end. And one thing to tell them: a barefaced lie.

I took a couple of deep breaths.

'Hello,' I said, 'I'm Jem. But you know that, that's why you're here.' No reaction. I swallowed hard and carried on. 'At least I don't really know why you're here. I'm just a kid, the same kid I was a month ago, a year ago, five years ago, when no-one wanted to know me. I suppose what's different is that I've been saying stuff about knowing when people are going to die. And I suppose you're here, because you think that I might tell you. But I've got to tell you . . . I've got to tell you . . . that it's all a lie. I made it up.'

There was a collective gasp.

'Attention-seeking, that's all. Boy, did that work. I'm sorry. I'm a fake. You've been scammed. You can all go home now – there's nothing to see here.'

I turned to make my way down the stairs. People were starting to call out – it wasn't what they'd wanted to hear. There were angry shouts, but also, rising above the other noise, a scream of genuine anguish – a terrible noise. I turned back and scanned the crowd. The lady screaming was the one in the headscarf, the one who'd touched my hair yesterday. Even though it was unfair of her to look to me for answers, I couldn't help feeling I'd let her down. I went back to the microphone.

'What did you expect from me?' I was looking at her, talking directly to her, but the whole crowd fell quiet again. 'If you want, I can tell you what you came here for.'

I paused, licked my lips.

'You're dying.'

She clapped her hands to her mouth, eyes wide with shock. More gasps rippled through the church.

'And so is the guy next to you. And the one behind. And so am I. We're all dying. Everyone in this church, and everyone outside. You don't need me to tell you that. But there's something else.'

At the back of the church, a door opened. A group of men came in – policemen in uniform.

'You're all alive too. Right now, today, you're alive and

kicking. You've been given another day. We all have.'

The men walked over to the end of the main aisle and started moving towards the front. There was one guy in the middle, way taller than the rest of them, ridiculously tall, in fact, with his head bobbing and nodding to a rhythm all its own. It couldn't be. Could it? My heart stopped beating, I swear it did, but my mouth kept going.

'We know it's all going to come to an end one day, but we shouldn't let that weigh us down. We shouldn't let it stop us living.'

Spider had come to a halt now, about halfway down the church. He was just standing there, looking up at me, with that big, silly grin on his face. I was talking to him now, there was no-one else in the abbey for me, only him.

'Especially if you've found someone who loves you – that's the most important thing of all. If you've got that, then you should appreciate every damn second with them . . .'

He flung his arms up in the air then, and let out a great whoop. Other people started clapping.

I backed away from the microphone and stumbled down the steps. I didn't care who was looking at me, how many lenses or cameras were trained on me. I ran towards him, through the clapping, cheering, confused crowd, my feet nearly slipping on the polished tiles. Spider hadn't moved, he was clapping too and then holding his arms out wide. I launched myself at him and he gathered me in, swinging me up and round before holding me close. I wrapped my legs around him, clinging like a limpet.

'What's going on, man?' he laughed into my hair. 'I only left you for a few days and you've turned into a preacher! Here,' he bent his face down to mine, 'come here, I've never kissed a vicar before.' And he kissed me, so tenderly, in front of everyone. 'I missed you,' he breathed.

'I missed you too,' I said back, and above us, way up in the bell tower, the rods and levers clunked into place and the great abbey bells started to chime the hour.

Chapter 37

'You're okay, are you?' I searched his eyes, for any signs of illness. Nothing, just his number, ever-present, unchanging.

'Yeah, bit tired. Can't sleep in those cells.' He wiped his big hands over his face. 'Kept thinking about you. Wondering where you were. I'd no idea you were holed up in a church.'

'It's mad, isn't it? I kept thinking about you too. It was doing my head in, thinking about you shut up in a cell. But that's it now, you're out. Are they bringing the car here?'

He frowned.

'What you talking about? What car?'

'That was one of my conditions – they had to bring you and a car and some money, and then I'd talk. So we can carry on. Get to Weston. It's less than thirty miles from here.'

'Nah, you've got that wrong. They haven't finished with me – they haven't charged me yet. They just brought me here for a few hours, must be the deal you had, and then they're taking me back again. 'Spect they'll take you an' all.'

'But they agreed – they signed an agreement! It's all legal!'

'What you gonna do? Take them to court?' He shook his head. 'You can't trust anyone, Jem, you should know that. Except me, of course.'

'But they lied. Bastards! What are we gonna do now? How are we gonna get away from here?'

He sighed. 'I don't think we are, Jem. This is it – we've got a few hours, we'll just have to make the most of it. Like you said up there.'

'But that's not right, Spider. We'll never make it now. We'll never make it to Weston. I wanted to walk along the front with you, have fish and chips like you said . . .' I had to stop there, as I was choking over the words. He put his long arm round me.

'Don't get upset. It doesn't all have to be today. We can do it another time. Face it, they're gonna put me away this time, probably you too, but I can wait. I'll wait for you, if you . . . ?'

'Of course I'll wait for you. I waited fifteen years to find you. I could wait another fifteen if I needed to, but . . .' How could I say it? *But time's run out. There is no more after today.*

'But what?'

'Just . . . just . . . I dunno. I just don't think it's going to work out.'

'Course it is. Sometimes things are really simple – I love you and you love me. That's all we need. Whatever happens, we can get through it.'

Why can't things be like that? He loved me and I loved him, but the number in my head was telling me that he was going to die today. And the numbers had never been wrong. Leaning against him, breathing in his muskiness, I suddenly got a sick, sick feeling. There was nothing wrong with Spider. He wasn't lying beaten up in a police cell. He wasn't ill. Tattoo Face had gone, and there was no-one chasing us with a gun or a knife.

The only thing threatening him was me. I'd made it happen – I'd drawn him back to me on the fifteenth of December 2009: 15122009. I saw the number and somehow I knew its message would come true. While I existed, the number existed. I was the number and the number was me. I don't know if anyone else, anywhere in the world, saw them, or if the numbers they saw were the same ones I saw, but once I'd seen one, that was it. They didn't change, they didn't go away. Anne was right: I was a witness, but maybe not just in a general way. I was a witness to the end of particular people on particular days.

There was only one way to deal with it. The only way to cancel that number out was to remove the person who saw it.

I stood up slowly, and looked around. I couldn't expect the keys to be back in the drawer in the vestry, but I knew Simon always had some on him. He was talking to Anne in one of the side aisles, keys glinting in a big bunch at his waist. I ran up to him and lunged at the keys. I had them unhooked from his waistband before he knew what I was doing. Pushing him aside, I raced to the tower door. There were so many keys, so many, but I got the right one second try. I didn't look back, not once, I just wrenched open the door, slipped through, slammed it behind me and locked it, shutting out all the raised voices, even the one I longed to hear. Especially the one I longed to hear. But it was there in my head as I climbed the spiral staircase.

'Jem, what the fuck . . . ? Jem!'

As I stepped out onto the roof, horizontal rain lashed into

me. I locked the door at the top of the staircase and picked my way across, over to the tower. In those few seconds, my clothes were soaked, trousers flapping wetly around my legs. Once in the tower I knew what I had to do. Ignoring the other side doors, I went up until I found the bell-ringing room, then across and up the top staircase. I didn't bother securing the last door – the other three or four would slow them up enough. It would be far too late by the time they got to me. I was breathing fast and hard, my chest hurting with the effort. My legs were wobbly from the climb and the wind buffeted at me, almost knocking me over. I put both hands on the stone parapet to steady myself.

From far below, I heard shouting. I wouldn't let myself look down. I kept my eyes on the rooftops and the hills beyond.

I waited until I'd caught my breath a bit, but not long enough to lose the adrenalin rushing through my veins. Eyes on the horizon, I gave a little jump and using all the strength left in my arms pulled myself up onto the stone wall. I crouched there for a second, getting my balance, and then slowly, with arms outstretched, got to my feet.

The rooftop pool across from me contained a handful of swimmers, defying the storm above them. I knew now for sure that I'd never be one of those people. I would never be anything other than what I was now – a girl who, for fifteen years, had brought death and destruction to those around her. A girl who'd been stupid enough to start to believe in love, and who now knew that there was only one way to save the boy who loved her.

Perhaps, after all, I had seen my own number.
It had been reflected in Spider's eyes all along.
15122009.
The day I said goodbye to it all.

Chapter 38

My toes were curled inside my shoes, as if that would help to grip on to the wet stone. I tried to stand as tall as I could, to face the end with dignity, but the wind and the rain were mocking me. They knew that in the scheme of things, I was tiny, nothing, and by blowing me about, soaking me, they were putting me in my place. It took a surprising amount of strength just to stay up there – the weather was blasting in from the front of me, trying to knock me back onto the flat roof behind. I could lean into it and not fall, except it would suddenly change; the wind would drop and then I was flailing my arms about, reeling on the edge, toes gripping even harder.

I guess my mistake was thinking. I didn't just get up and jump, that would have been the way to do it. But, not me, I had to stand there for a bit with my mind full of stuff. If I jumped would the wind actually blow me backwards? How long would it take to fall? Would I feel it, when I made contact with the ground? Would I actually hit the ground or the pitched roof? Was this really meant to happen? Was this my life, fifteen years and no more? Did I have a future, lying somewhere out there, waiting for me, and was I about to cheat it?

I tried to focus, to bring all these random thoughts back to the important one; if I ended it now, if I found that courage, I could stop the misery for a lot of people. Most of all, there was a chance I could save Spider. If no-one saw his number any longer, perhaps that number would no longer exist.

I needed to do this, and the way to do it was to go in style, like diving into a pool. I raised myself up onto my toes, stretched my arms out wide. I'd count myself out. Numbers would see me through to the end. 'Three . . . two . . .'

'Jem!'

I looked over my shoulder. Oh God, he was there, spilling out of the staircase door in an untidy mess of arms and legs.

'Jem! Please, please, no!' His voice was thick with terror.

'Keep away, Spider. Keep away from me. I need to do this.'

'But why? I don't understand . . . please don't. Oh my God, please don't.' He was inching towards me.

'Keep away!' My words a high-pitched screech, carried away on the wind. He stopped, held his hands up.

'It won't be that bad, Jem. Prison. We can handle it. And then we can wipe the slate clean. Start again. Jem, please, we can do this.'

'It's not that. I can't explain. I'm sorry, I'm so sorry. I have to do it.' I was teetering on the brink now.

'I don't understand, Jem. I don't understand why you'd leave me. Why would you do that?' He was edging forward again. Even in the wind and the rain, I could smell his sweat

– it flooded through me, jolting me back to our first meeting under the bridge, back to our night in the barn. 'Why would you leave me, Jem? I don't understand.'

I owed him that, at least, didn't I? An explanation?

'I've got to stop the numbers, Spider. I'm the only one who sees them. They're inside me. I can't get rid of them.' I dropped my voice, speaking more to myself now, than to him. 'I've got to do this. It's the only way.'

But he didn't get it. He was still hung up on hearts and flowers.

'It doesn't have to end like this, Jem. We can be together now.' His words were so seductive – he was the only person in the world to know what to say to me, what I really wanted to hear.

I started to cry.

'You want that too, don't you Jem? I know you do. You can't tell me that none of it meant anything to you, can you? Please don't tell me that . . .' He was crying too now.

I can't stand men crying. It's wrong, isn't it? Their faces aren't made for it, they kind of crumple, it's painful to watch.

He was close now, so close to me. If he reached one of his long arms out, he'd be able to grab me. I didn't want that – I needed to go through with this. It was the most important thing I would ever do.

Three . . . two . . . and yet, and yet, to feel him again, to feel his arms around me, just for one last time – that sweet thought held me back.

'Wait, please wait a minute.'

'I've got to do it, Spider. You don't understand.' The rain was mixing with tears on my face, with the snot bubbling out of my nose.

'I don't understand. I don't understand, man. We had

something. We can still have something. You and me, Jem.'

'No, it never happens. Happy ever after. It's a lie, Spider. It doesn't happen to people like us.'

He dropped down to the floor, crouched into a ball, clutching at his springy hair. He was sobbing, saying stuff at the same time. I couldn't hear him properly. I should've jumped then, while he wasn't looking, that was the time to do it, but I needed to know what he was saying. I didn't want any loose ends.

'What is it? What is it, Spider?'

He looked up at me. 'I can't go on without you, man. There'll be nothing left.' He got to his feet, held his hand out. 'Give me your hand, Jem. Help me up.'

It's a trick, I thought, *he's tricking me.* I said nothing, did nothing.

'Why won't you help me?' he said. 'I'm coming with you.'

In one easy, fluid movement, he was up on the wall, right next to me. He tried to steady himself against the wind. 'Whoa, this is awesome.' His big grin had broken out again now, he couldn't help himself. 'Look at it, man. You can see for miles. Whoo-hooh!' His whoop was whipped away on the wind.

'You're mental, I always knew you were.' I said.

He grabbed my hand.

'Solid, man, solid. If you really want to do this, I'll do it with you. We'll go together. I love you, Jem. I don't want anyone or anything else.'

Do you know what it's like to hear those words? To hear the person you love telling you they love you too? If you don't now, I hope you do one day.

'I had a blast with you, Jem. These last few weeks, they've been the best time of my life. Don't go without me. I love you.' He was ready to go. We could dive off there together.

His number would be right, after all, and I'd join mine with his.

And then I suddenly thought, *Fuck the numbers, fuck it all.* How many people meet the person they're meant to be with? If we stayed indoors, out of harm's way, maybe we could cheat the numbers after all. What if Karen was right, and it was all in my head – what if the numbers didn't mean anything at all? If I ignored them, eventually they might go away. Spider and I could have our 'happy ever after' ending.

'I love you too, Spider. I can face anything with you. Let's go inside, I'm freezing.'

He smiled at me, let go of my hand and formed a fist. Our knuckles touched. 'Safe,' he said.

'Yeah, safe.'

I bent my knees, put my hands on the tops of the stones and slowly lowered myself back down. When I looked up, Spider was dancing along the top, easy as anything, enjoying the buzz of it, just like he'd danced on the railway sleepers the first day we'd talked, down by the canal.

'Get off there, you silly sod, you'll break your fucking neck.'

He spun round to face me, big daft grin on his face, ready to jump down. Our eyes met, and we held each other's gaze; my warmth and love for him reflected right back to me. It was going to be all right.

And then his foot slipped on the wet stone, and his balance was gone.

He teetered on the edge for a split second, eyes still on me, thrashing his arms wildly . . . and then he was gone, falling backwards, a look of surprise on his face.

It was so quick, so unreal. I didn't scream, although

someone did far down below. I just watched as he tipped over and over in the air, arms thrashing, hands desperately trying to get a grip on something.

He didn't hit the ground. His fall was broken by the roof. His fall and his back. Spread-eagled, lifeless, he lay staring upwards. I looked into his eyes for the last time. They were still wide open, surprised, but he wasn't looking back at me. There was no-one there any more.

His number had gone.

Chapter 39

It had pissed down all the way over there, but by the time we'd parked the car it had stopped. We walked down the pier, the wind whipping off the sea around us. Clouds were racing across the sky like a speeded-up film clip.

Karen kept asking me, 'Are you all right?'

'Yeah, I'm fine.'

Difficult to imagine a time when I'd been less fine, but you know what I meant. I just wanted her to leave me alone.

Halfway down, Val linked her arm through mine. She didn't need to ask me any stupid questions; she knew what I was going through. She'd waited until I was out of hospital to do this. They'd had the cremation without me – obviously they couldn't put that off for ever – but she'd kept the pot with his ashes in until everyone felt I was strong enough to cope.

She'd come to see me in the ward. The first time, I couldn't speak, not to her or anyone. My head was still trying to take it all in. I couldn't look her in the eye either. She'd asked me to look after him, she'd trusted me with him. And I'd let her down. I'd taken him away, knowing he wouldn't be back. She wasn't angry with me, though, Christ knows why not. She was angry with him.

'What was the silly sod doing? He had to show off, didn't he? If I could get my hands on him, I'd wring his neck . . .' Her hands were trembling in her lap, fiddling with the unlit fag she was holding. 'Isn't there a smoking room we could go to, Jem? This is killing me . . .'

She'd come back again, despite me not talking the first time, and despite the company I was keeping these days; the silent, the screamers, the deluded and the sad. I managed to get a word out the second time. I'd spent days forming it in my mind, trying to remember how it started, what your mouth did to form the sound. She was talking, but I couldn't hear what she was saying, I was concentrating so hard on what I needed to get out. She stopped when she saw me lean forward, saw my jaw working as I forced my mouth to work.

'Sss . . . sss . . .'

'What is it, Jem?' She leaned forward too, breathing her stale, smoky breath into my face.

'Sss . . . sso . . . rry.'

'Darlin', it's not your fault. It's not anybody's fault. Well, it's his own silly fault, I suppose. How were you to know? He was always doing daft things, wasn't he?'

I wanted to tell her that I had known. It had all happened just how I thought it would, so fast that you couldn't stop it, and so slow, each minute leading inevitably to the next. So many chances to do something different, to change the path we were set on. I'd played it over in my mind a thousand times. I should have kept him safe. I should've . . . should've . . . should've . . .

'I saw him, you know, in the police station,' she said. 'I sat in when they questioned him. They didn't want me to – I'd been questioned too, see – but I insisted. I was responsible for him. I was all he had. Apart from you.' She picked at the side of her yellow thumbnail with her index finger. The skin was very red, near to bleeding. 'He said you two were heading to Weston. Gave me a start, that did. Didn't know he remembered. I took him there, you see, when he was little. Sort of holiday. I'm glad he remembered . . .'

She trailed off into silence, and we sat there, while in a chair in the corner another patient rocked backwards and forwards, backwards and forwards.

'I've been thinking, Jem. When you're a bit better, we could take him there, to Weston. Say goodbye properly. Only when you're better. No hurry, love.'

I didn't notice anything getting any better. One day was much like the last to me: flat, empty, crushed under a huge weight. After a few weeks, though, everyone round me started saying they were pleased with my progress. I was able to string words together now, when I felt like it, and was managing to eat a few mouthfuls at each mealtime. I'd still wake up in the night, tormented by nightmares, too scared to scream or cry out, and would lie there for hours, unable to close my eyes again. During the day, the nurses encouraged me to draw, to start to let the feelings out. I didn't mind that, sitting at the table with some paper and felt pens – I could do it for hours.

Karen was a regular visitor too. Fair play to her, no matter how often I kicked her, she still came back for more. One day, she said, 'Jem, the doctor says you're ready for a change. Come home, love. Come home with me. Let me look after you for a bit.'

She'd kept my old room free. 'I'll decorate it for you. We can start again. What colour do you want?'

And so I went back to Sherwood Road, and walls painted Crème Caramel, warm and honey-coloured, the colour of Bath stone. I stayed in my room, and listened to music and stared at the walls, until one day, I heard Karen going out to take the twins to school, and I started drawing. The first one was by my bed, an angel watching over me, keeping me safe, and I worked outwards from there until they were everywhere, walls and ceiling; creatures with wings, climbing up and falling down. Some of them had their faces missing, or an arm or a leg. One of them had ridiculously long limbs and springy afro hair – I put him at the top, spreading his wings and flying across the ceiling. I did a little bald one right down by the skirting board, sort of hunched up, wrapping her wings around herself.

When Karen brought my dinner in, she dropped the tray. Spaghetti Bolognese splattered on the walls.

I grabbed a tissue and started wiping it off. 'Look what you've done, you're spoiling my pictures, you silly bitch.'

I was back in the hospital after that, and when I came 'home' again it had all been painted over – Bluebell Haze this time, more calming apparently. Except that you could still see some of my angels faintly under the paint, and I found that comforting. I didn't have so many nightmares, knowing that they were there.

It must have been five or six months later that we found ourselves at the end of Weston Pier.

We stood there awkwardly for a bit, then Val said, 'Well, then.' She unscrewed the lid of the pot. 'Do you want to do it, Jem?'

'Um, I dunno. What do you do?'

'Just tip it out. Hold it at arm's length, over the sea and tip it.'

Tears were pricking the back of my eyes. I'd kept them away for a long time, but they were there now, like little knives. 'I can't. I can't do it. You do it, Val.'

She pressed her lips together tightly, trying to keep herself together, and stepped forward. 'Wait a minute,' she said, 'which way's the wind blowing? We don't want him . . . well, we don't want it going all over us.'

Karen licked her finger and held it up. 'It's coming from over there. Hold it over this side, it'll be okay.'

'Right.' Val took a deep breath. She had her body right up against the railing and held the pot out as far as she could.

'Goodbye, Terry, love. Goodbye, my precious boy.'

Her voice caught on her last words, and she gave a little sob as she tipped the urn over. Grey ash streaked out. Most of it fell onto and into the water, but a rogue gust of wind took some of it and blew it straight back at us. It went in our hair and on our clothes.

'Bloody hell, I've got some in me eye! Can you see it, Karen?' Val stumbled back from the railing, empty pot in one hand, the other rubbing at her left eye.

'Come here, Val. Let's have a look.' While Val blinked and gasped, and Karen peered at her face and dabbed her with a hanky, I watched a film of ash bob slowly away from us. That was all that was left of him.

I looked down at my coat, swelling out over my belly, and ran my hand down the cloth. Inside me I felt that fluttering feeling again. I didn't know for sure, but I had a pretty good idea it was a boy. He was always moving about, always restless. Just like his father.

A little line of grey ash built up on the edge of my fingers as I smoothed my coat down. I scraped it off with the other hand and put it in my palm.

Spider.

How could we have done that? Just thrown him away? I needed him with me, near me.

'Come back!' I shouted to the sea. 'Come back, don't leave me!'

Karen and Val looked round and were instantly by my side.

'It's all right, love,' said Karen. 'You let it out.'

'But you don't understand, I wasn't ready. I'm not ready yet, to say goodbye.'

Val put her arm round me. 'You never will be. There's never a good time for it.'

I was crying properly now, and so were they. We all put our arms around each other, a sad triangle, coats flapping in the breeze. I rested my arm on Val's waist, but my fist was closed. I kept the last remaining particles of Spider safe in my hand.

Safe.

Five Years Later

I don't hang around the places where kids go skiving off any more. I guess you could say I've moved on. These days, you'll find me in playgrounds, on the beach, down the community centre or waiting outside school. It's all part of the normal pattern of things, isn't it? Kids like me turn into parents like me. And our kids will turn into teenagers, and then into parents themselves. And on and on.

I'm not so different any more. That whole time with Spider, it changed me, and not just the obvious – growing up, falling in love, having sex and that. It showed me what I was missing, what I hadn't had for fifteen years: having real friends, someone to have a laugh with, learning to trust people, open up a bit. It changed my whole outlook on life – I'd been so hung up on the numbers that I'd let them paralyse me, I can see that now. The numbers had stopped me living. But Spider, and all those other people – Britney, Karen, Anne, Val – they changed that for me, made me realise I was wasting what time I did have.

I wish I could tell you I'd done something great with my life – become a brain surgeon or a teacher or something – but you wouldn't believe me anyway, would you? I suppose, looking back, I've done two things so far. For a start, I stayed with Karen and looked after her after she had her stroke. I'd known she only had three years to go, so it shouldn't have been a surprise really.

I was trying to sort out getting my own place; in fact, I was over at the flat the council were offering me, when I got a phone call from the hospital. Karen had collapsed in the street. It was a massive stroke, left her partially paralysed down one side. Her speech went too – she still had all her marbles, just couldn't get the words out without a struggle. It was just accepted that I'd look after her. She lost the twins – Social Services found them another home – broke her heart, that did. But everyone assumed that I'd stay with her and care for her.

It was hard, really hard, trying to look after Adam, as well as dress Karen, feed her, take her to the toilet. It was like having two kids. I can't tell you the number of times I nearly walked away. I even packed my bags. But in the end, I couldn't do it. I knew she didn't have long left. Besides, she'd stood by me, through being pregnant and then bringing Adam home. She'd helped so much, showing me how to cope with him, giving me a break when I was fed up. I reckoned I owed her.

Towards the end, we had some very bad days. The thing was, although I couldn't see the numbers any more, I could remember them. They disappeared when I was pregnant – when I was in and out of the psychiatric ward, drugged up, sedated. I can't remember exactly when – just that one day, I realised I couldn't see them. They were gone. I felt sad, to

281

lose something that had been a part of me for so long. But I felt relieved too. It took away something that I'd been dreading – the moment I would have to look in my newborn baby's eyes and see his death date. That day, I realised that I could face the future, whatever it would bring. I could have Spider's child, and we could have a life together.

Anyway, I didn't forget the numbers that I'd already seen. So I knew when Karen was due to check out. She didn't know though, obviously, and her illness, her disability, got to her. The last few weeks, she was really depressed. I mean, desperate. She kept having more strokes. Every time she got a little bit better, another one would come along and wipe out the progress. It was frightening for her, I know it was.

She begged me to help her end it, exhausting herself, forcing the words out. 'Please, Jem. I've had enough.' Pleading with her eyes. I told her not to be so daft. What would we do without her? Adam loved his Nana. Her eyes brimmed over. She loved him too, loved the bones of him, but she'd gone past logic – she was in a dark and lonely place.

I guess the strain of caring for her really got to me. I used to lie awake at night, torturing myself with these awful thoughts. What if that's what was meant to happen? What if I was meant to help her end it?

As the day got nearer, I got more and more edgy. She kept going on – wouldn't talk about anything else. The last time I took her to the toilet, we had a dreadful time getting her sorted out. Finally installed, she just slumped there, crying her eyes out with the humiliation of it all. Perhaps I let it all go on too long. Maybe I should have asked Social Services for help. Looking back now, I can see that it had got too much for both of us.

I got her back to bed. She was still upset. We both were. She tried to twist round, managed to get hold of one of her pillows. 'Just hold it, Jem.' She tried moving it up to her face, but she couldn't manage.

'No, Karen. Stop it.'

'Please, Jem. I'm tired.'

I took the pillow out of her hands. It would be so easy to do it, press it up against her, lean my weight in. It was what she wanted.

Then Adam came into the room.

'Mum, I'm thirsty. I want a drink.'

That snapped me out of it. I helped Karen to lean forward and propped the pillow firmly behind her back.

'I think we all do, darlin',' I said. 'Let's make a cup of tea.'

I put some juice in a beaker for Adam, and some tea in another one for Karen – like I said, it was like having two kids. I sat with her and held the beaker up to her mouth.

'That's it,' I said, 'everything seems better with a nice cup of tea.' She managed half a smile with the bit of her face that still moved.

'Do you want some biscuit?' She nodded, and I dipped a biscuit into my tea, so it was nice and soggy, and fed her. And then it happened. She started choking. I put everything down and slapped her on the back. She was gasping, fighting for breath. I couldn't do nothing to help. I ran into the hall and grabbed the phone. The ambulance was there within ten minutes, but it was too late. She'd gone.

Adam had seen it all. I should've kept him out of the way, but I was so busy trying to help Karen.

'What's wrong with Nana?' he asked. I took him into the lounge, and sat him on my lap.

'She's gone, darlin'. She's died.'

'Like Daddy?' I was always telling Adam about his dad. I wanted him to know about him, how special he was.

'Yes, just like Daddy.'

That is the other thing I've been doing, you see. I've brought Adam up, been a mum *and* a dad to him. I know I'm not unique doing this. There's thousands, millions of single parents, but when it's you, and your own childhood wasn't exactly rosy, it feels like a big deal to look at your five-year-old son and know that he's healthy and happy. If you'd asked me five years ago if I thought I could be someone's mum, and be a good one at that, I'd have laughed in your face, but do you know what, it's something that I can really do. I'm a mum. I'm Adam's mum, and it's something I'm proud of.

I suppose everyone thinks that their child is special. But I know that Adam really is. He's a lot like his dad. Val says he's the spitting image of him when he was little, and I can believe it. He's tall, for a start, all arms and legs, even when he was a baby. And he's always busy. You can't keep your eyes off him for a minute – he's into everything. That's why I take him out so much. He'd drive me mad, cooped up inside all day. He's the kind of boy that needs to burn off some energy on the swings or running round the park. That's one of the reasons we moved out here to Weston after Karen died. Spider was right: there's so much space here. We can spend an afternoon on the beach, and by the end of it we've walked for miles and miles, and Adam's tired and ready for bed like a good boy.

He finds it difficult to sit still, not got much concentration. The teachers at school have said that too. He'd rather be climbing something or kicking a ball than sitting looking at a book. He's a bit behind with all that stuff, not that that bothers me – I know he'll get there in the end. He's not stupid.

They've been doing the alphabet and counting, one to ten, over and over at school. I don't think anyone thought he was taking it all in. But just last week, we had a bit of a breakthrough. He came out of school and said his teacher wanted to see me. I thought, *Oh, no, what's he done now?* but it wasn't bad, at least not the way I was expecting: getting in a fight or being cheeky or whatever.

We went into the classroom and his teacher showed me a drawing he'd done. Beautiful, it was, in bright crayons – the colours of summer. There were two people holding hands, a big one and a little one. They were on a strip of yellow sand, with the sun in the sky above them, and big smiles on their faces.

'We've talked about this, haven't we, Adam, this lovely picture?' she said.

He nodded solemnly.

'It's you and Mummy, isn't it?' she asked him.

'Yes,' he said. 'Me and Mummy at the beach.'

'I think he's got his numbers and letters a bit confused,' she said, 'but I'm very pleased with his pencil control.' For there, above the head of the taller figure, arching over like a rainbow, was some writing. 'I think you meant to write *Mummy*, didn't you, Adam?'

He shook his head and frowned.

'No, Miss,' he said, 'I told you. It's not her name. It's her number. It's Mummy's special number.'

ACKNOWLEDGEMENTS

I would like to thank all friends, family and colleagues who have taken a kindly interest in my writing; Jonathan for his encouragement and comments on the first draft; Dylan and Sparky for getting me up in the morning to write; Charles for showing me round Bath Abbey; all the lovely literary people at the Frome Festival; and, of course, Barry, Imogen and all staff at The Chicken House.